BARBARIAN
MINE

BARBARIAN MINE

RUBY DIXON

BERKLEY ROMANCE
New York

BERKLEY ROMANCE
Published by Berkley
An imprint of Penguin Random House LLC
penguinrandomhouse.com

Library of Congress Cataloging-in-Publication Data

Names: Dixon, Ruby, 1976– author.
Title: Barbarian mine / Ruby Dixon.
Description: First Berkley Romance edition. |
New York: Berkley Romance, 2022. | Series: Ice planet barbarians; [4]
Identifiers: LCCN 2022014853 | ISBN 9780593548974 (trade paperback)
Subjects: LCGFT: Science fiction.
Classification: LCC PS3604.I965 B376 2022 |
DDC 813/.6—dc23/eng/20220404
LC record available at https://lccn.loc.gov/2022014853

Barbarian Mine was originally self-published in 2015.

"Ice Planet Honeymoon: Rukh & Harlow" was originally
self-published in 2021.

First Berkley Romance Edition: September 2022

Printed in the United States of America
4th Printing

Book design by Kristin del Rosario

BARBARIAN MINE

What Has Gone Before

Aliens are real, and they're aware of Earth. Fifteen human women have been abducted by aliens referred to as "Little Green Men." Some are kept in stasis tubes, and some are kept in a pen inside a spaceship, all waiting for sale on the extraterrestrial black market. While the captive humans staged a breakout, the aliens had ship trouble and dumped their living cargo on the nearest inhabitable planet. It is a wintry, desolate place, dubbed Not-Hoth by the surviving humans.

On Not-Hoth, the human women discover that they are not the only species to be abandoned. The sa-khui, a tribe of massive, horned blue aliens, live in the icy caves. They hunt and forage and live as barbarians, descendants of a long-ago people who have learned to adapt to the harsh world. The most crucial of adaptations? That of the *khui*, a symbiotic life-form that lives inside the host and ensures its well-being. Every creature of Not-Hoth has a khui, and those without will die within a week, sickened by the air itself. Rescued by the sa-khui, the human women take on a khui symbiont, forever leaving behind any hopes of returning to Earth. They join the sa-khui tribe.

The khui has an unusual side effect on its host: if a compatible pairing is found, the khui will begin to vibrate a song in each host's chest. This is called resonance, and is greatly prized by the sa-khui. Only with resonance are the sa-khui able to propagate their species. The sa-khui, whose numbers are dwindling due to a lack of females in their tribe, are overjoyed when several males begin to resonate to human females, thus ensuring the bonding of both peoples and the life of the newly integrated tribe. A male sa-khui is fiercely devoted to his mate, and several humans are now claimed by the males, and pregnant.

Recently, a small party ventured to the "elders' cave"—the broken ship of the original sa-khui people—in search of answers. While they were there, the original Little Green Men returned, stole one human woman, injured the two sa-khui accompanying them, and left the other human woman to get help.

This is where our story picks up.

PART ONE

Harlow

I need two poles for a travois. Two. No problem. There's got to be trees in the distance, and I'm strong and whole.

Okay. I can do this. I can.

Aehako's instructions ring through my mind, over and over. *We need to make a travois and take Haeden back to the healer.* My heart races wildly in my chest as I sprint through the snow, looking for the thin, pink, wispy trees of this planet. Kira's gone, and both aliens are wounded. They need my help, and I can't let them down. I don't know why they don't go back to the alien ship and get healed. They don't trust it, and I guess I understand that. I'm used to technology, and it still freaks me out to think of the cold, emotionless voice of the computer.

Also, I know what it's like to fear the doctor.

My feet sink into the snow with each step, and my leather boots quickly become sodden. There's no time to fix them or reinforce the insides with warm dvisti fur. Time is of the essence. I trudge forward over a drift-covered hill, and when I see the pink, wispy eyelashes of trees in the distance, I pick up the pace.

Almost there.

I have Haeden's knife, since he's too wounded to use it. The bone handle is smooth in my hand, though it's a little too big for my human-sized palm to grip comfortably. Everything here on Not-Hoth is sa-khui sized. I'm a decent height for a girl, but the average person on this planet seems to be seven feet tall, and the snows are deep, the caves huge. Really, everything feels just a wee bit too big. It's like I've been transported to a Goldilocks house, except instead of just right, everything's too large.

It's just one more thing I must adjust to in an endless stream of new and frightening things.

Weeks ago, I went to sleep in my own bed, and the biggest concern on my mind was when I'd start my chemo. Then, a few weird dreams later, I woke up, shivering and weak, pulled from a strange tube. Aliens hovered over me and told me I'd been abducted.

Which would have been hard to believe except that I'd come from Houston, Texas, and my air conditioner had gone out, so I'd spent the evening sweating and praying the repairman would come by soon. When I'd woken up? It had been so cold my bare feet had stuck to the metal floors, and strange blue aliens occasionally entered to chat with the humans.

It's hard to call someone a liar when they're seven feet tall, blue, and horned. After seeing that, I had to believe. And even though sometimes I want to pinch myself until I wake up, I have to accept the fact that I'm now living on a snow planet with no chance of getting home, and I'm infected with an alien parasite that allows me to endure the harsh conditions of Not-Hoth. Not exactly how I'd visualized my future at all.

But . . . at least I have a future.

According to the ship's medical computers, I'm cancer-free

now. I don't know if it's wrong, or if it's Not-Hoth's atmosphere or the new "cootie" (as some of the girls call it) living in my chest.

All I know is that the inoperable brain tumor isn't showing up in scans. And for the first time in the last year, I have hope.

But first . . . a travois.

When I get to the trees, I move to the closest one and touch the bark with my fingertips. It feels spongy and damp despite the chill in the air, and not sturdy enough to support a massive, muscled alien. I have no idea if this will work, but I'll give it a shot. I owe the sa-khui my life, and so I'm going to do my best to help Haeden and Aehako.

Kneeling down, I begin to hack at the base of the first tree. The knife sinks in with a squishing noise, and sap squirts out onto the snow. Ugh. I wrinkle my nose and keep cutting, determined. Kira's gone, and they're wounded, so I'm the only one that can help.

The snow crunches nearby.

I stand upright, surprised. It almost sounded like a footstep. "Hello?" I turn around and look. "Aehako?"

No one's there. The snowy landscape is barren, nothing but rolling drifts as far as the eye can see.

I must be imagining things. I'm not alone out here in the wild. There're creatures everywhere, or so the hunters tell me. It could be one of the porcupine-looking things. Or maybe it's a rabbit. Or . . . whatever the rabbit equivalent on this planet is.

I can't be a silly chicken and freak out at every little sound, though. I turn back to the tree and continue hacking at it.

I hear the crunch of snow again, and a moment later, a heavy thudding. My blood feels like it's surging in my ears, and I press a hand to my head, wincing.

No, wait. That's not thudding or drumming. My heart is calm. Is it . . . purring?

Something slams into the back of my head, and I pitch forward into darkness.

Even there, the strange purring follows me.

Rukh

I move through the snow soundlessly, even though I am trembling with excitement. My heart slams in my chest, pulse racing as if I have sped across the land instead of stalking my prey. There is a whirring sound, almost like the clicking noises the great gray beasts in the salt water make, but different.

It is coming from my chest. From me.

I don't know what this means. All I know is that I've smelled the strange creatures surrounded by the bad ones, the ones my father told me to avoid. There are two strange things traveling with the bad ones—they are so furry it is impossible to tell what their bodies look like, but one has a shock of orange-red mane that fascinates me. I've followed them since last night, and now the reddish-maned one is alone.

And I . . . panic. When it starts to turn, I club it over the head.

It collapses to the ground in a heap of multicolored fur. A bone knife, similar to my father's, falls from its hand.

I rub my thrumming chest, confused.

As I look down at the creature at my feet, I see . . . it's female. It's strange and different from the bad ones. There are no ridges on the brows, and the skin is the soft, pale color of a dvisti's underbelly instead of a healthy blue. It's speckled with dirt, but there's no mistaking the feminine tilt of the lips, or the delicate features. Frowning to myself, I put a hand on the thick furs of its chest to feel for teats. To my surprise, the furs part. It's a fur covering of some kind, not part of the creature at all. It's wearing them like I sometimes wear a covering in the coldest weather.

My hand brushes over one of the teats and my fingers graze one pebbled nipple.

The creature moans and the thrumming in its chest grows louder.

My own body responds, my cock immediately hardening and aching with the need for release. I'm surprised—and more than a little appalled at how my body is responding. This thing is ugly and pale. Why am I reacting to it like I do the strange, unsettling dreams I sometimes have? With one hand, I push my thrusting cock aside. I don't have time to deal with this. I gather up the unconscious creature and put its knife in my bag, then I sling the creature over my shoulder and begin to carry it back to my cave.

I'll decide what to do with it there.

The creature remains unconscious. I set it down in one corner of my cave and ponder what to do with it. It's a her, I decide. It's soft and pretty and has teats. My cock still aches with need, and as I pace, I stroke my hand up and down the length of it, because it feels good.

I don't know what to do. This female thing has unsettled me.

It's not food, like my father taught. She was with the bad ones, but she ran away. Does that make her good? I wonder.

I close my eyes and squeeze my hand over the tip of my cock. It feels so good that my entire body shudders, and the strange thrumming in my chest grows louder.

I wish my father were here.

He's been dead for many, many seasons. I was a tiny kit when he died, and I've been alone ever since. Father always had answers, though. He would know why my chest is thrumming and why my cock aches around the female. A surge of loneliness sweeps over me. Sometimes I hate that I have no answers, only questions, and no one to ask.

I continue stroking my cock until it spits forth wetness, and my body finally relaxes. I watch her as I do it, and I tell myself it's because I'm curious. Her chest seems to be thrumming along with mine, so whatever is causing this affects her, too. I wipe my wet hand in the dirt floor of the cave and then crawl toward the unconscious female.

My movements are stealthy, as if any moment she might wake up and attack me. She's small and still, and I wonder if I've hurt her worse than I realized. For some reason, the thought stabs at me, and I lift her head, examining her skull. Underneath the reddish-gold floss of her mane, she has a lump, but otherwise seems to be fine. I press my cheek against her nose and feel the air move. Still alive. Her eyes are closed, her breathing even.

I feel guilty that I've hurt her. I shouldn't have. She's mine. But I panicked. I do have some pain root, though. It's good for making blood clot up and she's got a gash on her head. I set her down gently and head over to my herb bag and find the dried root. I chew it into a mash, then return to the female and daub it onto her head wound. She will be glad for it later.

I gently lay her back onto the ground, and as I do, I can't help but stare at her. Her skin is speckled with a reddish-brown dirt of some kind, and I scratch at it absently. Her skin is different than mine—there's no soft, light covering of fur. She is bare everywhere except her head and that feels . . . strange. It makes my cock hard again, but I ignore it. I can't sit around and touch it all day. I notice that the spots don't go away when I rub. They're on her skin. It's curious. I lick my thumb and rub at another, but it doesn't move.

Strange creature.

I tug at the fur coverings, curious to see if this female is spotted everywhere. They fall open and reveal another lighter covering underneath, made of something similar to my waterskin. I pull it off and reveal more of the strange, pale skin with the spots on it. Her arms are smooth and soft, devoid of the thick plating mine have. I rub my arm, then touch hers. Very different. She is all softness, and it makes me think she is weak.

I've never seen anything like her. I tug at the leathers again and they fall open, revealing her teats. I draw back, surprised at the sight. They're full and round, with pinkish-brown tips that point at the air. I touch one, curious to see if she'll make that throaty sound like she did earlier.

But she's silent, and I'm disappointed. My cock jerks and aches, desperate for another release. I ignore it and press my hand between her teats, where she is thrumming, just like me. Her chest is vibrating at the same speed as my own, which is curious. It's like we are joined, somehow. Like our bodies have decided to sing a song together.

I like that.

I like looking at the female, too. I like her strange, spotted skin and her odd mane. I like her small, pretty teats and even her tiny, ugly face. She has no horns and no tail from what I can tell, but the scent of her is maddeningly delicious. I feel an odd need to lick her and find where the scent is coming from, but my cock throbs at the thought.

I'm not sure I like how out of control my body is in her presence. Frowning to myself, I replace her furs, hiding her teats from view, and move back to the other side of the cave. There are things I must do before I can go to sleep: there is water to be melted, cords to be braided for trap lines, and blades to be sharpened. I must eat, and I must check my pit traps.

There is no one to help, so I cannot sleep until things are done. As I pick up a bit of dried sinew, I crouch and watch the female from afar. I'm not leaving the cave, nor am I leaving her alone.

This female is mine now. I've taken her from the bad ones. She belongs to me, and I'll kill anything that tries to take her.

Harlow

My head aches fiercely, and the first thing I think is that the brain tumor's come back. That the computer in the alien ship was wrong, and I'm not well after all. That I'm dying and these are my last moments.

But then memories trickle in. Memories of frantic hunting for trees, chopping at one, and then something hitting me hard from behind.

And purring, oddly enough.

Relief shoots through me. I'm okay. My khui fixed my brain tumor. I'm not on Earth, and I'm not dying.

The purring is still in my mind, though, like a gigantic cat that won't leave my chest. Except, I realize as I slowly open my eyes, there are no house cats here, and the purring is coming from inside my chest.

Shit. I've been around the others long enough to know what that means. It's resonance. I'm resonating to a man because my khui—or cootie, as we humans like to call it—has decided I'll be the perfect mate for someone. The only men we were traveling with were Aehako and Haeden, though. One of them? I like Aehako, but I know he's in love with Kira. Haeden is all gruff snarls. I'm not sure I like the thought of being his mate.

Not that I'm given a choice. Thanks, cootie. Thanks for nothing.

My eyes focus slowly, and I realize I'm staring at the jagged ceiling of an unfamiliar cave. Why am I in a cave? Did I get hit by something and then Aehako came to rescue me? Is that why I'm resonating? My cootie has a damsel-in-distress complex?

Movement catches the corner of my eye. I turn my head, and then a gasp escapes me.

There's a sa-khui male crouching in the cave next to me, but . . . it's not any sa-khui I know. I sit upright and skitter backward as I realize he's staring at me, a knife in his hand.

Shit. Shit shit shit.

My back presses up against the hard rock wall by the time I move a few inches, and I stare in horror at the stranger.

That can't be. There're no strangers on this planet. Not on Not-Hoth. There are only Vektal's tribe and the humans. I know every alien face on this planet.

But I can't deny that I'm staring into the face of a stranger. A savage one.

He crouches on the dirt floor of the cave like an animal, his shoulders hunched over his body. He's naked, too. There's not a stitch of clothing on his enormous, muscular blue body. His cock dangles between his thighs, erect and straining, and I see the "spur" that everyone's always talking about—the short hornlike protrusion right above the cock that is standard equipment for all sa-khui males. My face heats when I realize I'm checking out his junk.

Seriously, though, it's just hanging between his open legs for anyone to look at.

His face is broad, his cheekbones high. His features are sharp, his brows heavy and ridged. The black hair on his head is a snarled nimbus that looks as if he tried to braid some of it out of the way and gave up long ago. It looks more like a tumbleweed than hair, and it's clear he isn't a big fan of combs.

Or bathing. I'm pretty sure his entire body is covered in a layer of dirt. If he doesn't wear clothes, though, I guess there's no point in bathing?

He watches me, eyes narrowed, and runs a stone along the edge of the knife, sharpening it. His movements are slow, and I can't tell if it's because he wants to seem threatening, or if he's trying not to scare me. Given that he's holding a knife? I'm going for threatening.

"Who are you?" I whisper.

He doesn't answer, and I realize I'm talking in English. Whoops. I learned the old sa-khui tongue—sakh—while on the ship, so I try that instead. He doesn't respond to it, either.

I . . . don't know what to do. Is he deaf? He's watching me, but he's not responding to my attempts to talk to him.

"I'm Harlow," I say. "Where are my friends?"

Again, there's no response.

I press my hands flat on the ground. There's a pebble under one palm, and I pick it up and flick it across the room to see if he reacts.

He follows the pebble and then frowns at me, a fierce snarl of bared teeth that makes me shiver. He's not deaf. Okay, he's just choosing not to talk to me.

Well, what the hell?

"Did Vektal send you?" I try. "Did Aehako and Haeden make it back to the caves? Have I been out for a long time?"

His gaze moves back to the knife and he runs the stone along the edge again, sharpening it.

"You can't understand me at all, can you?" I'm shocked by this. There's not another tribe of sa-khui, is there? But this man is alone, and he doesn't understand the language of his people. I look around the small cave. Back in the tribal caves, each family has done their best to make their caves seem like home. Baskets and blankets fill the corners, and everywhere there are stored food, herbs, and daily implements.

Here, there's not much of anything. There're a few pouches tossed into one corner of the cave, but there are no blankets, no bed, no firepit, no nothing.

"Do you live here?" I whisper.

The stranger stares at me for a long moment, and then he slowly gets to his feet and begins to approach me.

Eep. I push back against the cave wall, trying to shrink away from him. There's nowhere for me to go, and I cringe as he stalks toward me, and close my eyes. There's nothing but the sound of our two cooties singing to each other, and my chest vibrates from the force of mine.

Oh no, no no no.

Not this guy.

But there's no denying that my body responds when he stands near me. I can feel my skin flush with need, and moisture begins to seep between my legs, as if I'm completely and utterly turned on at the moment. I mean, sure he's big and brawny and could probably carry a girl like she's nothing—

Oh God. This is really bad. Like, worse than worst-case-scenario bad.

I absolutely do not know what to do. My pulse speeds with

a mixture of anxiety and response to my khui, and I hate that it starts to pound between my legs. Georgie wasn't lying when she said that resonating was like Spanish Fly on crack. It feels urgent, like I should grab this guy—this filthy stranger—and fling him to the ground and impale myself on his dick.

And then what? Have his baby? No thank you, cootie.

I squeeze my thighs together tightly, willing my body to calm the fuck down.

Fingers touch my hair, and even though he's gentle, my head still throbs. I squeeze one eye open, ready to pull away, and realize I'm pretty much face-to-face with his erect cock. I stare at it for a long moment, my mouth dry. I'm no virgin, and like any girl, I really like the sight of a nice cock. This guy—whoever he is—has a really, *really* nice one, but that just might be the cootie talking. He's not circumcised, of course, but there's no denying that he's just the right length and girth, and my traitorous mind wonders how that would feel.

My cootie thrums harder in my chest. Jesus. I feel like I'm being betrayed on all sides.

He touches my head wound and I jerk away. "Ow!" I slap at his hands, unable to help myself.

The man grunts and pads away on bare feet, seemingly unconcerned with my reaction. I scowl at him and touch my wound myself. It's covered in some sort of gloppy paste, probably a native remedy of some kind.

"Lucky me," I mutter.

He grunts again and returns to his crouch across the cave. He doesn't pick up the knife again, but just watches me, his hands on his knees.

I look over at the mouth of the cave. It's open to the world, and I can see snow gleaming outside in the thin sunlight. Most sa-khui have decorative hides stretched on bone frames that they push in front of the cave opening to give the semblance of privacy or to keep out the harsh weather. Not this guy. "You a hardcore survivalist or something?" He doesn't respond, and I sigh. "Of course you're quiet. I don't suppose you can tell me what happened to Aehako and Haeden? The two wounded guys?"

He narrows his eyes but doesn't move.

I pantomime horns. "Two big men? With me? Look like you?"

Nothing but a stare.

I worry my lip, thinking. I can't stay here if they're wounded and waiting for me to return. What if they die? I don't think they trust the computer's technology enough to go back into the ship and ask it to fix their wounds.

I'm going to have to escape, somehow.

"Listen," I say. "You're a nice guy and all, and this cootie thing is inconvenient, but I really need to go." I ignore the insistent thrumming in my chest and start to get to my feet.

He snarls at me, baring his teeth again.

I squeak and drop back down to the ground. Okay, so he's not a talker, but he's really good with nonverbal communication. I know "sit down and shut up" when I hear it.

He can't stay here and stare at me forever, though, right? So I just need to wait for him to get bored. I should pretend to sleep. I lean back against the wall and close my eyes, making it seem as if I'm going to take a nap. I'm able to keep my eyes open a hair, just enough that I can see out through my lashes. It takes forever, but he eventually stops staring at me and begins to work on something again, his back to me.

Should I try and escape now?

It's almost like fate hears my silent pleas. In the next moment, the alien gets up and stalks to the front of the cave. He heads out into the daylight and I can hear the crunch of foot-steps in the snow as he heads off to the left.

Surely it's not going to be that easy, is it?

I snatch the bone knife off the floor then jump to my feet. Every muscle in my body aches and feels cramped, and my head throbs at the sudden movement. Too bad. I creep to the front of the cave and see him standing a short span away, looking off at the distant mountains, his hand shielding his eyes. His horns jut ominously from his brow, and his tail flicks as if irritated.

"Time to go, Harlow," I breathe and race out into the snow, heading in the opposite direction. I don't know where I'm going, but I don't really care. *Away* seems like the best answer at the moment.

I can't really race in the snow, though. Human feet aren't made for handling the snowdrifts of Not-Hoth and I sink down with each step. It's like trying to run through mud, and I move slowly. I'm heaving and panting with exertion, my muscles straining, but I can't stop.

An angry, wordless cry echoes behind me from somewhere, and I know I've been spotted. "Shit!" I try to move faster, but my legs feel heavy and weak, and my head feels like it's going to explode with every beat of my pulse.

As I run, I can hear his pounding footsteps getting closer, and wild panic sets into me. I clutch the knife, ready to attack if he grabs me. Let one of those arms try and wrap around my waist and I'll stab the fuck out of him.

A moment later, I'm slammed to the ground on my stomach, a heavy weight resting on top of me.

I scream in rage and fear, and I thrash against him, slashing wildly behind me with the knife. I'm desperate to hit anything. I don't care what as long as he lets go of me.

One big hand closes around my wrist and pins it to the snow over my head. Fingers tighten around my wrist bones until I whimper and release the knife, and he bats it away from my grip.

I kick at him, and then a moment later, I'm somehow on my back and his big body is on top of me. My breasts heave angrily and I glare at him. He's pissed that I ran. It's evident from his face. "Good," I snarl at him. "My cootie may be into Stockholm syndrome but I am not!"

He lets me struggle against him for what feels like forever, and he's not tiring at all. Frustrated, I give one last hard full-body heave to try and fling him off, but I'm unsuccessful. He probably weighs twice as much as I do.

In the process, though, my clothes have somehow come open, and the next thing I know, my tits are bare, my tunic lacings having come completely undone in the struggle. I gasp in shock at the cold air—and at being bared to the waist.

My captor's noticed this, too. His hands grip my wrists. Not hard, not painful anymore, but just holding me down. He's not looking anywhere but at my breasts, though, and the expression on his face reminds me that he's had a boner the entire time he's held me captive. Shit. My khui begins to sing even louder, the vibration so fierce it makes my breasts tremble. Double shit. I can feel his khui's response to mine, can feel the thrumming moving through his body, too. His cock presses against one of my thighs, hard and insistent, and I'm half worried about—and half anticipating—what's going to come next.

The barbarian gazes down at my breasts for a long, long moment. Then, he leans in and inhales deeply, as if filling his nose with my scent.

For some reason, this strikes me as incredibly erotic, and I moan.

My moan is echoed in his throat. The groan that escapes him sounds utterly sexual, and he inhales deeply again, his nose rubbing against my skin. My nipples harden at the touch of his skin to mine. Those traitors want more touching. It doesn't matter that he's filthy, or a stranger, or that he's kidnapped me. My nipples want attention and they want it now.

As I watch, he rubs his nose against my skin, in the valley between my breasts. It's the place where the khui resonance is the most insistent, and a whimper escapes me at the sensation. His tongue flicks out, and I feel him lick my skin, tasting me.

I can't handle it. It's too much. Another whimper escapes me, and even though I want him to rip my clothing off and take me here in the snow, the word that tears from my throat is, "No."

He lifts his head and stares at me.

"No?" he echoes.

Rukh

I know this word.

I'm so excited at the familiarity of it that I forget all about how delicious my female is, how she's thrumming under me and it makes my cock so hard I can barely think straight.

I know this "no" word.

"No," I repeat again, excited.

"No," she agrees, and jerks at one of the wrists I'm holding pinned.

I release it, because I'm curious what she's going to do. I know that "no" means "do not" and so I stop. As I watch, she closes her furs over her skin, hiding her teats from my gaze.

She doesn't want me to touch her or lick her skin.

For some reason, this causes a strange ache in my heart, and the lonely feeling returns. She is mine, this female. Why doesn't she like me? Am I not strong? As strong as the bad ones? But she's gazing at me with fear and worry in her eyes, and she repeats the word again. "No."

I nod slowly, because I remember this, too. Hazy memories of my father slip through my brain, and I point back at my cave.

"Dunwannagohbak," she says, clutching her furs tight across her chest. "Lemmegoh."

She's babbling again. I'm disappointed, because I don't know these words. "No," I tell her. I want to communicate. I want her to know she's mine, and that I haven't figured her out, but I'm going to take care of her. "No!"

Her brows go down, and she smacks my chest. "Dontellmenoh!"

I bare my teeth, frustrated. I don't have a way to communicate with her that she is mine, and she will stay with me. My father had many words, but he's been dead for a long time, and I've forgotten most of them. I use the only one I have. "No."

As I watch, her nostrils flare, and she looks as if she's ready to spit another round of sounds at me. But then her eyes go wide, and she stares at something over my head. I turn to look.

Something large and black is slowly moving through the sky. It's like a giant disk, except it's made of nothing I recognize. There are strange lights flashing on it, and it gleams in the watery sunlight. It's big, bigger than the largest cave I know of. It tilts in midair, then continues on its course, speeding up. It's heading right for the mountains in the distance.

"Theyvegotkira!" the strange woman cries. "No!"

But the thing keeps moving in slow motion, and as I stare, it crashes into the side of the mountain, crumpling. A fiery explosion lights the air, and smoke billows forth. I've never seen anything like it. I get to my feet, awed and a bit frightened at the same time.

I hear the woman get to her feet, as well. But instead of standing next to me, she darts away. Still she thinks to escape?

With an angry growl of frustration, I snag my knife and then go after her.

She cries out when I catch her all too easily and sling her back over my shoulder. My chest immediately begins to thrum in response to touching her, and I want to explore this more. But if she won't stay . . .

I'll just have to make her.

I return to my cave. There are a few soft leather straps left from my father's precious bag, but this female is equally precious to me. I consider for a moment, and then set her down in the corner of the cave, using my body to block the entrance. She curls up in a corner and shivers, holding her furs close to her body and watching me.

I cut straps, enough to bind her, and tie her hands and feet even as she tries to slap me away. Once she learns she is mine, this will not be necessary. I take no pleasure in her unhappy cries or her struggles. It must be done.

I can't lose her. I won't.

Harlow

The asshole makes me sleep with my wrists and feet tied all night and doesn't even have the decency to make a fire. By the time I wake up, my hands and toes are prickling, and I'm so cold my teeth are chattering. My khui helps my body adapt, but humans still have a hard time with the weather on Not-Hoth, and right now I'd give my pinky for a warm blanket or a cup of hot cocoa.

I squirm in my bonds, my bladder full and my entire body uncomfortable. This can't continue. I won't survive if it continues. I have to communicate with my captor somehow and let him know what I need. I'm pretty sure he doesn't want me dead, especially not with my khui vibrating in my chest when he gets near.

As if he can hear my thoughts, the alien stirs from where he is curled up on the other side of the cave, in the dirt. No blankets for him, either. Maybe he doesn't know how to make them? He might not need them, but I do. I've learned a little about tanning in the weeks that I've been with the alien tribe, and at the moment? I'm totally eager and ready to make my own bedding if it means warmth. It's another thing on the mental list we'll have to discuss, once we figure out a way to talk.

The alien gets to his feet and pads to the entrance of the cave and disappears into the bitterly cold wind, stark naked. For a moment, I have an utter feeling of fear that he's going to just abandon me, tied up and alone in this desolate cave.

But he returns a moment later and immediately heads for me. He unties my feet and hands and gestures that I should follow him. I do, rubbing my wrists. My feet are slightly warmer than my hands because they're in my boots, but I'm desperate for a fire. He points at the snow in the distance, and makes a squatting motion, and I realize this is a bathroom break.

I can't fuck this up and scare him. I can't escape, either. It's clear I can't outrun him, so I need to make him trust me. I gingerly step out into the deep snow, pick a rocky outcropping that looks as relatively private as I can find, and do my business. My face burns when I catch him watching me a short distance away. I know it's because he doesn't want me to run, but can't a girl have some privacy? I kick snow over my "toilet," then rub more snow on my hands to clean them. As I do, I look up at the sky.

There's a smoky trail cutting through the air, and I look over in the distance. The wreck of the spaceship is still visible, like a stain on the mountain.

The reality of it hits me. Kira's dead. Aehako and Haeden are probably dead. I'm the only one of our small party left alive. Oh God. I don't know the way back to the tribal caves . . . and I'm not sure I want to go back. How would it look with just me limping back after abandoning the two hunters? Would anyone believe me if I told my side?

Probably not.

I'm fucked. A few miserable tears squeeze from my eyes and freeze on my face. I have no place to go anymore . . .

Except back to my captor. I look over at him, all dirty, wild hair and naked body. My khui immediately responds, and I clench my fists to ignore the arousal sweeping through me. Any logical woman would not be aroused by her filthy captor, but the khui ignores logic.

So I'm going to do my best to ignore my khui. Steeling myself, I return to the alien's side.

His hand goes to my elbow and he steers me back into the cave. *All right, then. See how good I'm playing along?*

I move to the far end of the cave the moment we get inside. There's too much of a breeze at the entrance, and the small cave isn't big enough to provide a ton of protection from the elements, which is unfortunate. I squeeze down against the rock wall, huddling.

He picks up the bonds again and reapproaches me.

"No, please," I tell him, putting a hand up.

He crouches next to me, but he doesn't try to tie me. Instead, he cocks his head, as if waiting for me to speak again. I have to assume that he doesn't understand his people's language, or else he'd have tried to speak it already. He's like Mowgli or Tarzan—completely wild.

I need to start with the basics.

I tap my chest, over my thick clothing. "Harlow." I tap it again and repeat my name, and then reach out to tap him.

He pushes my hand aside, his brows drawn.

I try again. "Harlow." I point to myself. "Haaaaaarlow." Then I gesture at him.

The light goes on in his head. "Arrr-loh." He taps my breast.

My khui immediately responds to his touch, and a hot blush covers my face. I hope he doesn't notice how hard my nipples are. I don't want him to touch me. I really don't. Not when he's that filthy and I expect him to tie me up at any moment.

But there's no denying that my cootie and my brain aren't on the same page. I just hope he doesn't pick up the scent of the moisture seeping between my thighs. Because then he might not be willing to play the name game and instead tackle me to the floor of the cave.

And I hate that my body really, really likes the thought of that.

"Harlow," I repeat. I smile at him, and then gesture at him again. Surely he has a name?

"Ar-loh." He puts a hand to his own chest. "Rukh."

The word is guttural, almost swallowed in his throat. I try to repeat it. "Rooookh."

He snorts and taps his chest again. "Rukh."

"Oh, are you going to correct me, then?" My mouth curls up in a half smile. "Then let's start with my name. It's Harlow. Not Ar-loh. Ha-r-low. Ha in front. Like ha ha ha ha." I repeat the sound.

"Ha ha ha," he echoes. "Ha ha ha-ar-loh."

I giggle. "You're terrible at this."

His hand goes to my face, feeling my mouth. His eyes are wide. I freeze, but he only taps my lips with his fingers and then tries to make a sound. Oh. He likes my laughter. I laugh again, forcing it a bit to see how he reacts.

A smile breaks out on his face. His teeth are big and white and sharp, and they look wild in his dirty face. I smile back at him. We're getting somewhere.

For the next few minutes, we practice saying each other's names. I can get him to make the H-sound in Harlow when he makes a biting motion, but the name still sounds a bit mangled. I'm about the same with his name—he's only pleased when I make a swallowing sort of sound with the R that doesn't feel natural with a human throat.

But we're getting somewhere. I smile at him again and decide to try for the next bit of communication. I put my hands out as if warming them. "Fire?" I try the word in his language, since English would be useless for him. "Harlow needs fire?"

He frowns and gives a small shake of his head. He doesn't understand.

"Makes sense," I say to myself, drumming my fingers on my lips as I think. There're so many things I need to ask for if I'm staying here for a while—blankets, a warmer shelter, fire, food, water, bathing, weapons . . . the list overwhelms me. I feel helpless and more alone than when I first woke up out of my tube. A tear of self-pity slides down my cheek and I angrily scrub it away. "Shit."

"Shit?" he repeats, and touches my cheek. "Harlow shit?"

A laugh escapes me, chasing my sadness away. "Not quite, Rukh. But I'm sucking at this language thing. Maybe I need to try something else." I glance around at the cave but there's nothing that could even be remotely used for fire. So I get to my feet and offer him my hand. "Come with me. Let's go gathering."

I'm still woefully lacking in a lot of survival skills, but one of the first things that the tribe insisted I learn was how to find fuel and how to make a fire. We go walking, with Rukh watching me curiously the entire time. I think he half expects me to run off on him, but that's not part of the plan.

I don't have anywhere to go.

Instead, I look for signs of dvisti, the shaggy, pony-like herd animals of this planet. They eat the wispy, ice-coated fauna of this place, and their dung is the staple of most firepits since wood seems to be rare. I gather an armful and then bring it back to the cave with me, trying to teach words to Rukh as we walk. It's a losing battle, but I try anyhow. Most of his attention seems to be fixed on figuring out what it is I'm doing.

Once we return to the cave, I clear out the center of the floor and make a pit, then line the edges with rocks. I pull out the cord I keep around my neck that I made for myself when I was first learning many of the basic skills for survival on this planet. Fire was number one, so I and a few of the other girls made necklaces with a bit of steel on them. It seemed someone had salvaged a few bits from the elders' ship, thinking they were interesting. We humans quickly cannibalized them, and I kept one circuit-looking square tied to a thong on my neck. Now I just need a striking rock, which this planet has a lot of, and some tinder.

A bit of fluff from the inside of my boot and a dry, torn-up bit of dung provide the tinder, and I try to make a spark. It takes me a few bangs of the rock, but a few minutes later, I have a smoky coal. I blow on it and then feed the flaming tinder to my pile of dung chips, adding more fluff to make it burn.

The lick of warmth is immediately gratifying. I sigh with relief when the flames catch and begin to burn strongly, and I put my hands out over it. "Fire," I tell Rukh.

"Fire," he echoes, and I realize he is speaking in his language. I spoke in English unthinkingly.

"You remember fire?" I point at it.

He nods. "Fire."

I smile at him. "Harlow needs fire." I mock-shiver. "Too cold otherwise."

His brows draw together, and then he nods slowly. "Harlow fire." His warm hand touches mine. Oh God, he's really, really warm. I pull away, even though the only thing I want to do is keep touching him.

My traitorous cootie? It purrs loudly.

Rukh

Har-loh fascinates me. She feeds animal scat to the licking flames—the fire—and holds her hand over it. I realize what she was trying to communicate to me.

She's cold. Her strange, five-fingered hands are small and don't hold heat. She shivers even in the furs she wears. Her body isn't like mine, impervious to the weather. She's affected by it, and as the suns go down and the air grows colder, she moves closer and closer to the fire.

I realize how inadequate my small cave is to make her comfortable. I chose this one simply because it was near to where she and the bad ones were staying. It's not home—I have no home. I simply stay in a place for a time, and then move on. There are better caves, though. Some are warmer, with pockets of hot melted snow in them. She would like that, I think, as she drinks from my waterskin and shivers at the chill of the snow-water.

She is fragile, my Har-loh. I must make sure I take good care of her. The thrumming in my chest demands it.

I feel strange around her. Possessive. I've seen the bad ones and have never felt about them the way I do about this strange, flat-faced female. There's something about her that gnaws at me, that makes me want to spend every moment with her in the cave, watching her. To feed her from my hand and to go out and collect all the dung I can find so she can have the fire she so desperately needs.

I killed a creature for her earlier and brought the meat back to her. She ate it, but it was clear she was not pleased. I need to find what pleases her.

She yawns, and the motion is delicate and feminine, her small hand going to her mouth. "Tmrrohweneedhabigkilltewskinfr-blankits." She rambles sounds when she needs to communicate, and I watch her small mouth work around the noises. I want desperately to know what she is saying, but I am ignorant.

It frustrates me.

Har-loh gives me a sleepy smile. "Wishewhaddapilloh."

Even though her face is flat and her brow is not ridged in the slightest, she is utterly beautiful in that moment. I feel the urge to touch her, and I reach out and take her hand in mine. She has one more finger than I do, and they're cold against mine. I can feel her startle but a moment later she relaxes and grips my hand back.

"Har-loh," I say in a low voice. Her skin is so soft. I want to explore all of it, to see what lies underneath the heavy furs she insists on wearing. Her scent emanates in the cave and it makes my cock stir.

A shiver moves through her and she bites her lip. For a moment I think she's cold, but then her chest vibrates hard, singing like mine is, and I realize she is feeling the same things I am.

Encouraged, my hand goes to my cock.

"No!" she says quickly. She looks embarrassed and gives a small shake of her head. "Dondoodat."

I frown. Being around her—smelling her incredible scent, touching her skin, hearing her song—all of it makes me want to touch my cock. But she has used the "no" word and I want to please her. Aching with need, I force myself to let go of her hand and I back away.

She settles in the corner of the cave, pulling her clothes tight around her, and goes to sleep.

Night. It's dark, and the inside of the cave is bitter with cool air. Something is clattering and has awoken me. I immediately reach for my weapons, then realize that the sound is coming from Har-loh.

Her small, blunt teeth are chattering together with cold.

I go to the fire but it is out, the scent of smoke replaced by nothing but ashes. There is no way for me to make her warm. I growl in frustration.

"R-R-Rukh?" she says between chattering teeth. "That-y-y-yew?"

"Har-loh. Fire?"

"Toodarkh," she says between clacks of her jaw. When she doesn't get up to fix it, I realize she is telling me she can't, for whatever reason. I am hit with a sense of worry—what if I can't take care of her? I brought her to this place; what if it kills her?

I move to her side and touch her face.

She leans into my caress. "Sowarhm." She reaches out to me with her shaking arms. "Cmere."

I don't understand her words but it's clear she wants me to

move closer, and I'll take any opportunity to touch her. I slide my body down next to hers, curious. To my surprise, she immediately pulls her clothing off her body and piles it on top of me. Then, she flings herself against me and clings to my chest like a baby metlak.

I'm stunned at this. She's baring her flesh and pressing it against me?

Her ice-cold fingers grip my sides, and she moans. Her cold feet press against my legs, and she burrows down against me. Ah. I understand now. She is seeking my heat, my warmth. It's almost too warm for me under the pile of thick leather clothing she has thrown on top of us, but she seems pleased, so I do not move. Instead, I wrap my arms around Har-loh, pulling her closer.

The sound of pleasure she makes sends a jolt through me. My hands slide over her skin. She's so incredibly soft. I can't stop touching her. I don't want to stop touching her. I touch her arm, her back, her soft buttocks. There's no tail, which is bizarre, but my cock responds just the same. I can feel the hardness of it pressing against her belly as I hold her. It's leaking from the tip, and I have to fight against the urge to rub up and down against her stomach.

Har-loh inhales softly and wraps her arms around me. She's not pushing me away, even though my cock is stabbing her in the stomach and leaking fluid onto her. She nestles her head under my chin and rubs her nose against my skin.

The breath hisses out from between my teeth. This is too much. I can't help myself; slowly, I rub my cock against her. The feel of her smooth skin against mine is like nothing I've felt before, and my cock aches so badly I could scream.

Instead of pushing me away like I expect, she moans. Her

fingernails dig into my shoulders, and she hooks one leg around my thigh, dragging it between hers.

"Har-loh," I groan. I can feel the vibrations in her chest. I know they mean something, that we are connected somehow, but the only thing going through my mind is the need to claim her. To make her mine. I grip her against me and drag my aching cock over her belly. I'm leaving wet trails on her skin, but I don't care. If she's not going to push me away, I'll seek release.

To my surprise, she nuzzles against my neck and gently bites down on my skin.

I explode; I can't help it. My sac tightens to the point of pain and then my cock unleashes a sticky torrent on her body. I seem to spurt forever, unable to get the image of Har-loh's little teeth biting down on my neck out of my mind. It's the most erotic thing I can possibly think of.

But now I've gotten her all wet with my spend. Vaguely ashamed, I ignore the singing vibration of my chest and her clinging arms. I reach between us and find a sticky pool on her skin.

"Sokay," she breathes. "Happens."

I don't know her words but her voice is gentle. She reaches between us with a corner of her clothing and cleans her stomach and my hand, and then flings it aside. She burrows down against me again and my chest thrums with pleasure. I don't understand what just happened between us . . . but I liked it. I liked it too much.

And . . . Har-loh didn't seem to hate it, either.

Her small hand—no longer ice-cold—touches mine. She tugs on my fingers, and I let her guide me. When she pushes my hand between her thighs, I suck in a breath. She is hot and wet here. She's wet like I am when I am aroused. Is she aroused? Does she like it when I touch her? Tentatively, I brush my fingers over her body, exploring her. There is a patch of hair here, which strikes me as unusual. Her scent washes over me, though, and my cock stirs again. This is the scent of her arousal. I recognize it, and I want more of it. My fingers feel big and clumsy as I continue to touch her, learning her body. Underneath the tangle of curls, her soft skin parts, and she has wet, slick folds. Har-loh likes for these to be touched, I think, because she rubs up against me and moans. I want more of her moans, so I keep touching and exploring. She's so very wet; her scent is everywhere, permeating my skin. There is nothing that has ever smelled finer to me. I want to pull my hand to my mouth and lick it clean of her, to taste her.

But she takes my hand and guides it again, to a little bump between her folds. And she uses my finger to gently circle around it, then stops.

Is she . . . showing me what she likes? I mimic the motion. Immediately, her nails dig into my shoulders, and she cries out. "Rukh!"

I growl, because the sound of her is making me wild all over again. My cock throbs and fills with blood, hardening again. I touch her bump again, but it doesn't get the same reaction. I try a few different touches before I realize that she likes it when I circle it gently. I do that, and she jerks against me, crying out.

I want more of those responses from her. So I keep touching and stroking her just the way she likes, and a few moments later, she shudders against me, her leg locking around my thigh, and I feel a surge of wetness coat my hand. She has had her release, too. I'm fascinated. I was too young when my father died for him to tell me of men and their mates, but I have vague memories of his stories, and how things should be.

Her scent coats my hand and I raise it to my nose and inhale deeply. It's sweet and musky at the same time, and it makes my mouth water. I lick my fingers—

She pushes my hand aside. "Dundoodat."

I growl at her. Why is she depriving me of this? Of her sweetness?

But she only pats my chest. "Tmorrohwetakeabaf."

PART TWO

Harlow

In the morning, I can't even be mad at my cootie. Oh sure, I just spent the night curled around the world's dirtiest alien barbarian, but I was warm and slept better than the night before.

Plus, you know, I taught him about petting. It's weird that I feel proud of that, but I'm starting to figure out a few things about Rukh. He doesn't really grasp what clothes are. He doesn't grasp a lot of his own language, and he sure doesn't know what I am. I'm not even sure he understands what it means that we are both resonating to each other. He might not even know about sex.

It's clear to me that he's been alone for a long, long time. And because of that, I'm starting to understand him a bit more, and why he reacts the way he does. He carried me off and tied me up because he doesn't want me to leave. Whether that's the cootie and the resonance or if it's simple loneliness, it doesn't matter.

I can't change things. I can't make my khui stop vibrating when he's around. I can't turn back time and bring Kira, Ae-hako, and Haeden back to life. I'm here with Rukh, and I'm going to make the best of things.

And that means some changes. It means I start making the cave into a home. It means teaching him more language so we can talk. It means bedding and more clothing and figuring out how to store food and so many things that my head spins. A tiny part of me wants to go back to the elders' cave and get Rukh lasered so we can talk, but I think about Aehako's and Haeden's dead bodies just outside. I can't go back. We'll just do things the hard way.

But first . . . I have to figure out how to slow down my cootie. It's been a few days since I started to resonate to Rukh. I'm not unattracted to him—well, provided that under the layers of grime and the tumbleweed of hair, there's a normal alien guy under there. But I'm not sure I'm ready to jump right into making a family. The cootie, of course, has other ideas; the longer we spend fighting our urges, the more powerful it makes them. Already this morning I feel a bit more aroused and sensitive than before. Last night's heavy petting felt good. Really good. We'll have to continue that, I decide.

Of course, while Rukh is out finding something to eat for breakfast, I make a fire and masturbate quietly. I give myself a quick bath with some melted snow, I have the fire roaring, and I've even cleaned off the dried cum on the corner of my skirt from last night.

Rukh returns, carrying an entire dvisti over his shoulders. He throws it down near the fire and then looks at me for approval.

I clap my hands, excited. "That is awesome! Thank you, Rukh!" Dvisti are furry and shaggy and will make a small but warm blanket.

He bares his teeth at me, imitating my grin. Then he moves to the creature to start carving it up.

I stop him, because if it's anything like yesterday's butcher-fest, there's not going to be a skin left to treat. "No! Wait!"

"No?" Rukh frowns and looks up at me.

Through gesturing and a lot of demonstrating of my clothing, I get him to understand that I want the hide. I sit down next to him, and over the next hour, we figure out how to skin the creature. We're both bloody and smelly by the time we eat, but I'm pleased because I have a big, mostly whole skin to work on. I don't know what I'm going to stretch it over yet, but I'll figure something out.

Instead of tossing the extra meat, I spit it over the fire on a few of the longer bones and smoke it. Rukh watches me, and then offers his waterskin.

I smile at him and take a sip. I'm tired and I feel like the day's just begun. There's so much to do, I'm overwhelmed with it.

"Fire," Rukh says, pointing at my fire. Then he points at me. "Har-loh." Then he points at the skin.

"Water," I tell him. I pour a little onto my hand and wash my fingertips. "Water."

"Water," he repeats.

It's progress, and I smile broadly at him. We can do this. We just have to learn what the other wants.

A WEEK LATER

I sniff my armpit and wince. "That is a not-so-fresh scent."

"Repeat?" Rukh says from across the cave as he scrapes a fresh hide.

I wave him off. "Just talking to myself." I've taught him the word "repeat" so he can ask me to restate things, but I'm not going to go into explicit detail about how smelly I am. Not when he's not exactly a fragrant blossom himself.

It's been a long week. I make another chalk notch on the wall, just because I like counting the days. Seven sunrises and sunsets of backbreaking work. Seven days of skinning, smoking meat, weaving baskets, and whatever other chores I can possibly think of. Seven days of curing hides with their own brains, seven days of sweaty, bloody, gross work and not a single bathtub in sight. I enviously think of the big heated pool in the center of the tribal cave. I'll never see that again, and right now, something like that sounds pretty damn nice.

Rukh doesn't seem to mind my smell, but, well, he's Rukh. I don't know if he's ever had a bath, so of course he doesn't mind if I stink. The sad thing is? I'm getting used to his smell, thanks to the close quarters. At night, he comes and lies down beside me and I happily cling to him, dirty skin and all, because he's as warm as a furnace.

We also dry hump and pet each other to orgasm every night. I'm pretty sure it's not normal—we haven't even kissed—but Rukh seems pleased, and it seems to be keeping my cootie from totally flipping out on me. The urge to mate is harder to avoid every day, and now when Rukh goes hunting, I have to masturbate several times in quick succession just to ease the ache.

I am freaking exhausted.

With a sigh, I give the dvisti hide in front of me another hard scrape with a bone knife. My plan for blankets is coming along well. In another week or so, I'll have a luxurious bed full of crudely tanned furs, but it'll be warm at least.

And then I will just sleep for days.

"Har-loh?" Rukh squats beside me and offers his waterskin.

I smile at him gratefully and take it. It's not his fault I'm needy and require so much more crap than he does. "I'm just tired."

"Tired?" he repeats, not understanding.

I mime a yawn and feign sleep. "Tired. And dirty. I want a bath." I think for a minute, then glance up at him. It's still early in the day and rather sunny out for Not-Hoth. "Is there a stream near here? Water? For washing?" I mime and say the words slowly until he grasps what I want.

Rukh nods and goes to get his snowshoes, then gets my pair. We're going out.

He straps them to my feet, then his own. It's kind of funny to think of a naked barbarian running around in nothing but shoes, but lately, the snows have been getting higher and higher. I worry that winter is going to suck hard, since everyone keeps telling me this is the milder season.

And if we're stuck in a tiny cave together and a blizzard hits? It won't matter how dirty or smelly we are—I'm going to end up tackling the man. I've learned that when I'm in the heat of the moment? The cootie doesn't care about a bit of dirt.

Baths are definitely imperative. I admit, I'm a little curious to see what Rukh looks like without all the caked-on grime.

We head out, and I bring a bag of smoked, dried meat, the waterskin, and a knife. The snowshoes take some getting used to—Rukh's are nothing more than three large prongs that leave a chicken-like mark in the snow. Mine are made from a dozen ribs or so and leave little star patterns as I walk. They help, and it's easier to walk when I'm not sinking two feet with every step.

Rukh leads me into the next valley. It's clear he could walk faster, but he hovers around me to make sure that I'm all right. Through our stilted conversations, I've indicated to him that I'm not leaving, so I think he trusts me a bit more now. We're no longer captor and captive but more . . . friends. At least, I like to hope so.

I smell the sulfurous scent of rotten eggs before I see the water itself. Not-Hoth is riddled with hot springs, which makes me think the core of the planet is pretty seismically active. Which would be scary . . . if I had a choice about living here. I don't, so I just don't think about it. The hot springs are nice, though.

Rukh leads me down toward it, and we pass by a bush covered with bright red berries. I recognize these and stop to pluck a handful. The barbarians use them as soap, and to drive away the inhabitants of local streams.

"No," Rukh says when he sees me gathering the fruit. He touches his tongue and makes a face. "Har-loh, no."

"They're not for eating," I tell him. "They're for washing. You'll see." I put them in my bag and follow him.

We approach the stream, and I see long, bamboo-like reeds sticking out near the banks. Georgie and Liz both have warned me about the fish they call "face eaters." They pretend to be plants, and when you step close enough, piranha time. As we get closer, Rukh puts a hand on my shoulder and squats, rubbing his chin as he stares at the stream. It's obvious he knows it's dangerous, and he's not quite sure what to do. He wants to please me, but he also doesn't want me to get eaten.

No wonder the man's so dirty. I feel a twinge of pity for my poor barbarian.

"Watch," I tell him. I grab a handful of snow and smash several berries into the snowball, then lob it upstream. It takes a few minutes, but then, one by one, the reeds move farther and farther downstream, until they're out of sight. The face eaters don't like the fruit, and this little trick works like a charm every time.

Rukh grunts, impressed.

"Come on," I tell him. "Let's go clean up."

He insists on checking the water before I get in anyhow, and I wait patiently on the shore, stripping my furs off. I'm anxious to get cleaned up. I wish I could clean my fur clothing, too, but I'm not exactly sure how one launders fur, and I don't have anything to change into. They'll just have to stay dirty for now.

When he gives the go-ahead, I tiptoe into the water. It's like heaven. I sink in all the way and give a moan of pure pleasure. "This is the *stuff*." I immediately grab my pouch from the shore and squeeze a few berries, scrubbing at my skin and hair.

Rukh watches me for a moment, and then steps into the water after me. He's hesitant, and it's clear he feels a bit out of his element. It's also clear he doesn't know what to do with all my naked skin, because he keeps reaching out to touch me. The only time we normally get naked together is bedtime, because it's easier to share heat, so I understand his confusion.

"Wash," I tell him, and show him how to crush the berries and form a bit of lather. I reach out and rub some on his arm. "It's good for you, I promise."

He stares down at the dirty rivulets coursing over his skin. Then, he looks at me and rubs at my skin. It's a little grimy, but nothing like his. Realization dawns and he begins to scrub at his skin. "Wash."

"That's right," I say enthusiastically, and scrub with him. I move to his back and begin to scrub it, taking extra care to get into all the nooks and crannies of the plates along his spine and arms. He shudders when I rub his skin, and I know he's getting aroused. My own cootie is going wild in my chest, vibrating at high speed. I can hear his doing the same.

I didn't intend for this to turn sexy, but how can it not? We're both naked, and I'm running my hands over every inch of him. As I rub at his backside, his tail flicks in the water. It feels strange to clean another person, especially one with a tail, but I want him to be clean. I bit down on him the other day in the heat of the moment, and I try not to think about what I might have inadvertently licked off his skin. "This bath is really for me, you know," I tell him as I run my hands down one incredibly muscular arm. "It's because sooner or later, I'm going to give in to this resonance, and I might as well get a clean guy out of things, right?"

"Repeat," he says in a thick voice. He doesn't understand what I'm saying.

"It's okay," I tell him, soothing. I smooth my soapy hands over his big shoulders. Goodness, he's big. I mean, sure, the guy is seven feet tall if he's an inch, and he's not got an ounce of fat on him, but somehow looking and touching are two different things, and I can't get over how big and how strong my alien is.

And then I realize I just thought of him as "my" alien. Hoo boy. That's a loaded line of thought. Still, I'm not hating on the idea. "I just need a bit of time to get used to everything that comes with the package," I murmur to myself. Then, to him, I say, "I'm going to wash your hair."

He stiffens when I put my hands on his head.

"Bend down," I tell him, and pat the surface of the water. It's at waist height, so it's not dangerous.

He turns and looks at me, his eyes narrowed with mistrust.

"I promise, it's fine." I pat the water again and give him an encouraging smile. "You want to make me happy, don't you?"

He growls, though I know he can't understand my words. And then he sinks lower into the water, until his chin is touching the surface and the rest of him is submerged.

"Thank you," I say, keeping my voice sweet. I dig my hands into the tangled mass and begin to lather it. I massage as I do, and his breath hisses between his teeth. I can't tell if he likes it or not, but I'm determined to give my barbarian a makeover, so he's just going to have to suck it up to please me. I work around his horns, rubbing as I go, and his hair's so thick that it takes an extra handful of berries to get a good lather going.

I'm so focused on cleaning his hair that I don't notice that my breasts are practically in his face until his hands touch my hips. "Har-loh," he murmurs, and the husky sound makes my nipples tighten, and I immediately think of our late-night furtive dry-humping.

Blushing, I flatten my hand on top of his head. "Dunk."

He goes under the water a few times, and by the time his hair is no longer sudsy, I've recovered a bit. I smile brightly at him as he wipes water from his eyes. "You look so much better."

It's true, actually. His face is no longer smeared with the dirt of years, and his skin is this deliciously smoky blue. He looks younger, and with his thick, wild hair flattened around his face, I get an image of how he'll look with it combed and cleaned up. A weird feeling of déjà vu hits me. Is it that Rukh's scowling face reminds me of someone? Or am I just crazy?

I shake the thought off, a moment before a handful of mashed berries land on top of my head.

"Har-loh wash," Rukh instructs, and begins to massage my own hair. All right, fair enough. I get low in the water and close my eyes so he can give me the same treatment.

His hands caress my scalp, rubbing gently, and then he traces my ears. I shiver as he works his fingers through my wet hair. I don't think I've ever been treated so very gently as I am at this moment. He touches a sore spot on my head, and I remember the guy clubbed me a few days ago. Hm. I push his hands away.

He makes an unhappy sound and insists on touching the sore spot. Oh. He's checking it. I purse my lips and remain silent so he can finish checking. After a moment, he's satisfied, and then he pushes me under the water.

I emerge a moment later, coughing and spluttering. "You have to warn me when you do that!"

"Har-loh wash?"

"Oh, I'm definitely washed now," I say in a peevish voice. I rub my eyes.

Rukh frowns and touches my arm, then tries to rub one of my freckles away. "Wash?"

"Those are part of my skin, big guy." I scratch at one and then shake my head. "They don't come off. See? And they're all over me. They're 'freckles' in my language."

"Fruh-kuhl?" He touches one.

"Close enough." I smile at him and point at several on my arm.

He taps a finger on top of a freckle on my arm, and then one on my shoulder. Then, he taps one on my collarbone and I suck in a breath. Do I want him to keep going?

I . . . kind of do.

So I remain utterly still while his fingers trace over my skin, exploring my freckles. I'm not one of those lucky girls that only gets a few cute freckles here and there. If there's a bit of sun to touch my skin, I freckle madly. My cheeks are covered, as well as the bridge of my nose and my forehead. My arms and upper chest are, too, and they fade out to a few moles here and there on my breasts and belly.

It's clear he's not all that interested in the freckles on my face, though. His fingers drag slowly between my breasts, and my khui begins to thrum in response to the touch. My nipples perk, and I ache for him to touch them.

Rukh looks up at me, and his fingers brush over my skin, petting the same spot over and over again, and my entire body feels charged. He studies me, then asks, "No?"

Oh. He wants to know if he can touch me.

I show him. I take his hand in mine and press it to my breast. "Yes, Rukh."

His touch is gentle, almost reverent as he circles my breast, stopping to touch each freckle. Then, his fingers move over my nipple, and it hardens in response. I moan softly and my arms go around his neck, leaning in closer. I want him to kiss me, but I'm pretty sure he doesn't know how. The man's a blank slate. I suppose that can be a good thing, but right now, I wish he'd lean in and press his mouth to mine.

Rukh knows how to do other things, though. His hand slides down my belly and moves to my pussy. His fingers dip between my folds and he finds my clit and immediately starts to circle it with the pad of his finger in just the way I like.

I moan and cling to him, my knees weak at his touch. He pulls away, startled, and tries to help me stand.

"No, it's good, I promise," I tell him. And so it won't happen again, I nestle up against him, my back pressing to his stomach. His cock pushes at the small of my back, hard and insistent. I move his hand back to my breast, and he cups it from behind me. "Like that," I tell him. Now, if my knees get weak, I'll just sag against him.

A low groan rises in his throat and he strokes my breast while his other hand goes to my pussy. He seeks out my clit and begins the soft, slow touches that I like so much. I shudder against him, pressing back against his body. He holds me close, and his face presses against my throat. I feel small against him, cherished and adored at his careful caresses. My cootie purrs heavily, and I feel his vibrating against my back. His touch feels so good, and it doesn't take long before I'm writhing against him, desperate to orgasm. I need to show him so much more—

But then I come, and the world explodes behind my eyes, and I cry out.

He groans and holds me tight against him. I feel his cock rub against my back, and he grips me against him, rubbing hard. A moment later, hot warmth spreads over my back, and I realize he's come, too.

At some point, we really should take the next step. I sigh blissfully and sink back into the hot water, boneless and numb. He keeps touching me, stroking and petting my skin, wiping his come off of my back, and then just touching me as if to reassure himself that I truly am here.

My fingers are wrinkling up, though, and I wring out my wet hair, then gesture at my clothing on the bank. "Let's get dressed and then we'll go back to the cave and talk about . . . things."

His brows draw together. "Repeat?"

I chew on my lip, thinking of the best way to explain. I decide to just show him. Leaning forward, I take his face in my hands and pull his mouth down to mine for a quick kiss. "Harlow wants to show you things." And then I reach down and caress his still-hard cock under the water.

Recognition dawns on his face, and he strokes his hands over my shoulders. "Har-loh . . . things."

"Yes, all kinds of things." Maybe it's time we take this resonance thing head-on. I smile up at him and wipe wet hair from his brow. "Harlow and Rukh things."

He bares his teeth in a grin and presses his mouth to mine. It's not quite a kiss—more like a mashing of faces—but the sentiment is there, and I chuckle. The man gets points for effort.

I get out of the water and climb onto the bank. Immediately I feel the chill—the air is frigid and emerging from the hot water into the icy breeze is brutal. I need to find a better way of bathing. Shivering, I drag my clothing on as quickly as I can, but I feel like an icicle by the time I'm dressed. I swathe my thick fur cloak over my hair, making sure to keep it covered so it doesn't freeze over in the wind. "I'll probably regret this later," I tell myself, but I'm willing to put up with some sniffles to be clean. I bend over to put a boot on—

—and am tackled into the snow.

The breath escapes my lungs and I cough, only to have one big hand cover my mouth a moment later. "Hsst," Rukh whispers, and his big body covers mine.

What the hell? I try to drag his hand away from my mouth. He shakes his head, staring off into the distance. I follow his gaze . . . and gasp in surprise.

There's an alien in the distance. One of the tribe. I can't tell who it is from here, but the horns and swishing tail are a dead giveaway, even in silhouette. I gasp in shock. Someone's here. Someone might have seen us.

And Rukh is freaking out. His hand tightens over my mouth, and he hunches low in the snowbanks. His body covers mine, as if he's trying to shield me from sight. I can't see his face, but I can hear his breathing, heavy and angry.

"Rukh," I whisper, but he tenses and makes another shushing noise. He doesn't want them to see me. As I watch, he draws his knife out, and a new kind of worry overtakes me. This is more than concern over seeing a stranger—is he going to kill the hunter if he approaches us? I don't want to be responsible for anyone else's death. I put my hand on his. "Rukh, no."

He only holds me tighter, a warning growl low in his throat.

I'm terrified of what might happen. I wait, scarcely daring to breathe, as the hunter crouches low in the distance, as if taking a break. He leans on his spear, scans the horizon, and then moves out of view again.

I exhale with relief.

Rukh jumps to his feet, knife in hand, and starts to go after him.

"No! Wait!" I lunge for Rukh, but he's moving too fast. "Rukh, no!" I make my voice louder, because I know that will get his attention.

I'm right; he immediately comes storming back and puts a hand over my mouth. "Har-loh, shhh." His nostrils flare; he's visibly upset.

"Rukh, stay here with me," I say, putting my hands on his chest.

"Har-loh Rukh," he growls. "*Rukh!*"

I know what he's saying. I'm his, and another male is encroaching on his territory. How to explain that the man probably isn't looking for me at all? That he wouldn't resonate to me because only Rukh can? I hate that we don't have enough words between us. "I know," I say in a soothing voice. "Harlow is Rukh's, okay? But please stay with me. Please don't go kill someone just for me." My voice trembles and cracks. "I need you with me."

He cups my face with one hand, then looks off to the horizon, clearly torn. His big shoulders heave with tension, and I feel as if he's moments away from totally snapping. I know other resonating males get possessive of their mates, but like this? Like he wants to carve the stranger's face up simply because he got within a hundred yards of me? Is it because we haven't fulfilled our resonance? Is it because he doesn't trust anyone but me?

Is he worried he's going to lose me?

"Harlow belongs to Rukh," I say again in a soft voice, but he keeps staring off at the horizon. I don't trust him not to gallop off and go after the hunter. I need a distraction.

Of course, the moment I think "distraction," my mind goes to dirty places. I think of dropping to my knees in the snow in front of Rukh and showing him what a blow job is. That'd be a good distraction, all right.

Then again . . . why not? My own breathing quickens at the thought, and imagining his reaction to my touch is enough to make my pussy damp. He definitely wouldn't leave my side after that, would he?

Maybe it's my cootie that's making me so forward, but I can't get the idea out of my head. I get on my knees and put my hands on Rukh's hips.

His entire body twitches at my touch, and as I watch, his cock visibly elongates. This has his attention, all right. His growl is questioning, though. He isn't entirely sure what I'm up to.

"Allow me to show you just what I have in mind," I murmur, gazing up at him. I slide a hand up one big thigh. He's soft like suede to the touch, and his skin is clean and a lovely blue now. Just looking at him makes my mouth water with anticipation. "Rukh belongs to Harlow."

And I wrap one hand around his cock, and then look up to see his reaction.

He's utterly frozen in place, my big barbarian. Not a single muscle twitches as he stares down at me.

My mouth curls into a smile at the sight of him. "Bet you never imagined this, did you?" I slide my hand over his cock, feeling his length and girth. He's really big, but that's not surprising. A seven-foot-tall alien with shoulders like a linebacker is going to have a big cock, and Rukh definitely fulfills that promise. The length—and girth—of it reminds me of my forearm, and it's a delicious dusky blue. Veins trace over the shaft, and I slide my hand up and down the thick length in a stroking motion before leaning in and dragging my tongue over the tip.

Rukh makes a choking sound.

I glance up at him, my mouth still hovering oh-so-close to the head of his cock. "You okay?"

"Repeat," he says in a ragged voice.

I chuckle, because my clever alien is using the few words he knows very well, isn't he? I give him what he wants, licking the head of his cock in a leisurely fashion. The head is beaded with pre-cum, and I lap it up. My khui is resonating hard, and my thighs are clenched tight together, because touching him like this is arousing me to no end.

Funny how that works—giving him pleasure is giving me pleasure. I don't even know if I can blame my cootie for that. I just like touching him and seeing his reaction. He looks like his mind just exploded. I lean in and give him another playful lick, enjoying myself very much.

This time, a small groan escapes him, and his hips jerk, his cock pushing against my hands.

"Ah," I murmur. "You like that, do you?" I brush the tip of his cock over my lips, letting the head drag over my mouth. He's big, and there won't be any deep-throating of this man, but enthusiasm goes a long way. I decide to explore him with my mouth, nibbling down the length of his shaft and licking skin all the way to his sac. He's warm and weighty, and I love the feel of his suede-like skin against me. I have to resist the urge to rub my body up and down his, and settle for simply running my cheek and mouth all over his scaldingly hot flesh.

His sac is heavy and tight, and I brush my fingers over it, curious to see his reaction. Is he sensitive here? Rukh jerks at my teasing touches, telling me the answer to my question. His hand goes to my hair and then pulls away again, as if not sure what to do with himself while I minister to him. I give a throaty chuckle and flick the tip of my tongue against his skin. My mouth moves over the hard ridges on top of his cock. This is a difference from humans, I note. Like his arms and his chest, he has hard plating protecting sensitive spots, and the ridged plating seems to cover the top of his cock, leaving the underside velvety soft.

I can't help but wonder what that will feel like inside a girl. Does that make me a little pervy? Maybe.

I continue exploring him, and my fingers come upon the much-gossiped-about spur that the human women lose their shit over. It looks like nothing more than a blunted horn a few inches above his cock. I'm not really sure what the purpose of it is, but it's there for me to play with, and so I do. I run my fingers over it, treating it like I would his cock, playing with the tip, teasing the underside, and seeing what gets a reaction from him. There's a spot underneath, just where his spur joins with his skin, that is especially sensitive. When my finger grazes over it, his entire body jerks and his breath hisses from his throat.

"You want to learn some language?" I purr at him, my cootie throbbing mercilessly in my breast. It's making me into a total wanton, and I don't even care. "Here's something for you to learn. Repeat after me. Lick." I lean in and lick the head of his cock. "Taste." I drag my tongue down over one thick vein. "Suck."

I put my mouth over the end of his cock and take the head of it in my mouth, sucking lightly.

His entire body quakes, and a moment later, my mouth is filled with wet, salty heat. Rukh's feral growl as he comes sends an illicit thrill through my body. A moment later, before I can truly appreciate his reaction, he staggers backward, staring.

I wipe the corners of my mouth delicately. "Guess that blew your mind. Pun intended."

He pants, a sheen of sweat on his ridged brow. And he can't stop staring at me, as if I'm some magical dick-sucking unicorn come to life. A giggle escapes me. Well, I wanted to distract the man. I definitely got what I wanted. "Feel better?"

"Har-loh . . ." Poor Rukh sounds utterly breathless.

"Yes?"

He presses a hand to his chest, then gestures outward, a frown on his face. I recognize that frustration. He wants to tell me something but doesn't have the words. I get to my feet and take his hand in mine and squeeze it.

"I know, big guy. I know."

Rukh

Har-loh has shattered me from the inside out yet again. Just when I think I have learned all the pleasure to be had, she shows me something new. I move toward her smiling, speckled face, and press my mouth to hers in the gesture she showed me earlier.

She looks startled, and then pleased. I will have to remember more of her gestures. I want to make her happy.

She shivers and tugs her furs closer to her body, reminding me that we are not here at the water's edge for simple pleasures. One of the bad ones was nearby. Panic flares through my body again. He could have seen Har-loh taking me in her mouth and . . . doing things to me.

He could have taken her from me.

My chest squeezes tight at the thought. No one will ever, *ever* take Har-loh from me. I will rip them open with their own tusks if they should try. My hands clench, and it takes everything I have not to drag Har-loh against me.

I've never had a companion. I've never even thought of having one, and my memories of my father are long distant. But now that Har-loh is here? I cannot bear the thought of her leaving me. My hands clench in her furs. If the bad one that is nearby tries to take her—

"Rukh?" Her small hand pats my arm, trying to get my attention. "Cawmdownbigguyh. Aymheer." She smiles up at me. "Sokay. Allsokay."

At the sight of her smile, my frantic anger dissipates a little. I'll take care of the interloper and return to my sweet female. I pull my father's knife out.

Her expression is troubled. "No, Rukh. No kill." She pushes the knife down.

She doesn't want me to go after them, to defend my territory. Does she know they are bad? I stare off toward the horizon, where the hunter disappeared. I can go after him and track him down and kill him . . . but it will leave my Har-loh here, vulnerable. I can't take her with me, because he cannot know I have her.

And I cannot abandon my Har-loh. My chest vibrates and purrs in that strange way it has been since I found her. I look over at her troubled face, and my heart aches. I don't want to leave her.

I can't leave her.

I sheathe my knife and grab her hand. Instead of heading back to our old cave, I will take her somewhere new, somewhere more remote. There are places even the bad ones don't like to go. I will take her there, and she will be safe with me.

"Rukh?" she asks as I tug her along after me. "Wayrrwegoin?" When I don't answer her, she plants her feet on the ground. "Rukh? Ansormee!"

I look over at her. Why is she not walking? A look down at her small feet shows she is not wearing the snowshoes I made for her. I release her hand, retrieve the shoes, and bend down to strap them to her feet.

She taps my shoulder. "Rukh? Wayrwegoin?"

Har-loh lets me put the shoes on her feet, but when I gesture that she should follow me, she doesn't. Instead, she crosses her arms and gives me a frustrated look. I scrub my face with my hand and force myself to be patient. I will carry Har-loh if I must, but I need to get her away from here. Already the bad one might have found our footprints or discovered the cave full of Har-loh's creations. All of my important things—my knives, my waterskin—I have with me. Everything else can be abandoned, and will be abandoned, for Har-loh's safety.

There are more caves, and better ones. I take her hand and gesture that we will walk. Not in the direction we came from, but a new direction.

Her brows wrinkle together in the funny, flat-faced way she has. "Notgobak?"

I point ahead.

She points behind me and repeats herself. "Notgobak?"

"No." I point ahead.

"Butmytings!" She tries to pull her hand out of mine. "Mifursenmiskins. Eyeneedem."

"No," I say flatly. I will not go back, no matter how upset it makes her. I cannot take the chance that the bad ones will take her from me. The fear gnaws at my mind, and vague flashes of memory come to the surface: My father's tired face. Another man—no, a boy—at home with us. Then, gone and the sense of enormous loss.

I squeeze Har-loh's hand tight and pull her along. She will see I am right in this, given time.

We walk until both suns have disappeared and the little moons are rising in the sky. There's no shelter to be found, not out here.

If it were just me, I would walk through the night and into the morning. I know where the next cave is, and were I alone, I would already be there.

But Har-loh has small feet and takes even smaller steps. She tires easily. She cannot keep up with me, and so I must slow down and wait for her.

She hasn't complained, but I can tell she is exhausted. Her strangely colored face is pale, and her small fingers feel like icicles in my hand. Her steps are slower than usual, and her teeth sometimes clack with the cold.

My female needs to rest. The drumming in my breast says so, and I am filled with more fierce possessiveness. I find a hollow in a cliffside, out of the wind, and take her there. "Sleep." It is one of the words I have learned from her. "Har-loh Rukh sleep." I point at the snowy ground.

She rubs her exhausted face. "Heer?"

I don't know this word, but I am guessing she is asking where her cave is. I gesture at the ground. This is our place for tonight.

Her face crumples a little and she sniffs. Then she nods.

She looks so sad. I am filled with despair at the sight of it, and I touch her cheek. "Har-loh . . . fire?"

"Firenao? ButIdonhafdetings . . ." She gazes around at the snowy embankment, and another sniff escapes her.

I am filled with shame, and I press her small face to mine. I am not caring for her properly.

"Sokay," she tells me with a small pat to my cheek. "Iyam-justired." She takes off her snowshoes with slow movements and kicks them aside, then moves closer to the rocky wall. There's a bit of a nip in the air, but I don't feel the need for skins like she does. My initial thought of crouching low on the ridge above and watching for intruders disappears, and I know what I must do.

I take her cloak from her shoulders and then sit on the ground. I pull my Har-loh into my lap and pull her clothing open so her bare skin can press to mine, and then I wrap my body with her cloak. I will make her a warm cocoon of my skin, so she will not have to touch anything cold.

Her shivering stops and she gives a small sigh of pleasure and curls up against my chest. "Tankyew, behbeh."

I feel like I've done something right. I hold her close to me and watch the horizon, my knife close at hand. I'll stay up all night and guard her.

The next morning, the air has the bite of snow in it. Not just any snow, but the thick, blanketing snows that last for months and do not let up.

And again, my plans must change. There is a cave nearby, but it will not be warm enough for Har-loh in the deepest of snows. I will take her farther, more days' walk to the cave by the salty waters that never completely ice over. I go there when the storms are too brutal for even me. It will be a good place to take my Har-loh, if she can withstand the journey.

I hunt small game to feed us as we walk, and by the time both suns are high in the sky, my next cave is in sight. I scout it out to ensure that no metlaks have made it their home while I have been gone, then bring in my female.

Har-loh gives the cave a dubious look. "Eezsmohl," she says. "Smohlerdandalastwun."

I take her hands in mine and kneel before her. She looks tired, but how do I explain to her that I must ask her to keep going? I think, frustrated, and then try to string a few of my meager words together. "Har-loh Rukh . . . no." I point at the cave. "Sleep yes. Fire yes. Har-loh Rukh no."

She tilts her head, digesting my attempts at communication. "Westayeerendenwegoh?" She makes a walking gesture with her fingers. "Harlow Rukh go?"

Relieved, I nod.

A bright smile crosses her face. "Lookitchew, behbeh. Yewll-bespeekin innotime." She leans in and gives me a smacking of her lips against mine. "Sohprowd."

Harlow

I'm kind of glad this cave is temporary, because it's worse than the last one.

I mean, granted, the last one wasn't amazing, but this one barely has enough room to turn around. We can probably build a tiny fire on one side, cram our bodies on the other, and that's about it. But it's out of the wind and so I'm not complaining, especially when Rukh heads out for a few minutes and returns with some dung chips for me to make a fire. He knows I'm cold and tired, and I suspect that if he was alone, he wouldn't have stopped here.

He prepares the fire for me and I hand him my striker, since he wants to learn how to do it on his own. "So where are we going tomorrow?" I ask him. "Where Harlow Rukh walk?"

Rukh concentrates on the fire, and when he has a tiny coal, he begins to feed a bit of tinder to it and considers my words. "Wa-ter," he says after a moment. Then he gestures at the horizon and all around us. "Water."

"Lots of water? Like a lake?" I draw in the dirt, hoping it looks like a pond. "Small water?"

He shakes his head and drags his finger across the dirt, indicating a long stretch. "Water." He gestures at the horizon again. "Water." Then he touches his tongue as if tasting it and makes a face.

It's not . . . drinkable water? Realization dawns. "Are we going to the ocean?" I mime a crashing wave and it rolling forward. I probably look like an idiot making whooshing noises, but he nods eagerly.

Oh, holy crap. I'd love to see the ocean. I'm excited. I clap my hands. "I'm excited."

He grins back at me, looking relieved for the first time since we've seen the other hunter. He wants to make me happy. Poor guy. He's trying really hard, and even though I don't understand everything he's doing, it's clear that I'm his foremost concern.

So I gesture at the fire. "Go get more fuel?"

We make the cave cozy for the evening. I take a nap while Rukh hunts, and when he returns, I've got the fire roaring again, a store of more chips nearby in case the weather takes a dip in the night, and he's brought home a kill. I'm going to have to eat it raw, but I'm too tired to be picky.

My body's humming and aroused, reminding me that we still haven't given in to the whole "resonance" thing. I'm doing my best to ignore it, even though it feels a little like drinking a sugary soda before bedtime. I can relax, but I can't quite *relax*. Something's always setting me off-key just a little, and I'm twitchy and ill at ease.

To occupy myself, I decide to make Rukh into a project.

I eye his tangled, dry hair. It's flatter than the nest it was before, but it's long and in his face. There were tiny, cleaned-white rib bones at the back of the cave from an old kill, and I've been playing with them all afternoon. I eventually bind them together with a bit of sinew Rukh had in his carryall, and use another bone crosswise to make a handle for my rinky-dink comb. It fits in my hand just right, and I use it to comb through my own tangled hair and am pleased with the results. Once we've eaten, I smile sweetly at Rukh and pat the ground next to me. "Come here, baby."

I find myself calling him baby more and more. Even though we aren't officially "mated," it feels like we're in the "going steady" stage. I'm almost ready to take it to the next level. Almost.

My entire body twitches at the thought, reminding me that it's more ready than my mind is.

Rukh drops to the ground next to me, curious. I glance between his legs. (I mean, the man is always naked. Of course the eye is drawn there.) And he's got a stiff one working. That, of course, sets my cootie off, which sets his cootie off, which means it's going to be one dry-humping-filled night. I'm too tired to think about sex, though, so my body will have to wait.

"I'm going to comb your hair," I tell Rukh. I drag the comb through my own tangle-free hair and show him what I mean, and then I gesture at his hair.

He gives me a wary look, then reaches for the comb.

"I'll do it," I tell him. Truth is, I want to do it. I like the thought of brushing his hair into a silky waterfall. I want to be the one responsible for taking care of him, weird as it sounds. So

I fold my cloak into a lap pillow of sorts and indicate he should set his head down there.

His eyes gleam with interest, and he goes eagerly. Instead of lying on his back, though, he moves onto his stomach and pushes my legs apart, seeking out my pussy with his fingers.

I squeal in protest, clamping my thighs together. "Time out! Time out!" My cootie is zinging, and I can hear our joined resonance reverberating between us like a swarm of locusts. "Hair brushing tonight, okay?"

Rukh sits up, scowling, as if I've deprived him of some great pleasure.

"You can go down on me tomorrow or something, when I'm less tired." Great, now I'm passing up oral sex in exchange for brushing a man's hair? I must be tired. Or insane. Something.

Eventually I get him to put his head down and he gets comfortable in my lap, gazing up at me. The horns are a bit of an issue to work around, but I manage. His hair's so tangled that I take small portions at a time and comb through them, starting from the ends and working backward. It's one big tangle closer to his scalp, and I'm as delicate as possible, but it takes a lot of time. Rukh doesn't seem to mind, though. He lounges in my lap and though his eyes are mere slits, I still get the impression he's watching me move as I carefully undo knot after endless knot.

After what seems like hours, I have a long, shining section of his hair untangled. It's soft, a rich black, and rather beautiful to look at. I'm filled with hair envy—my own wispy reddish-orange hair is nothing like this. "You're going to be quite the handsome devil when you're done, aren't you?"

Rukh gives me a sated smile. He takes my hand in his, and instead of squeezing it like he normally does, he pulls it to his mouth and nips the fleshy mound under my thumb. It sends skitters of desire racing through me.

"Flirt," I tease him breathlessly.

Tomorrow, this man is going to learn how to kiss . . . among other things. I think of the blow job I gave him yesterday. Maybe I'm moving way too fast for my own personal Tarzan. The man might not even know what resonance is, and I'm falling to my knees at the drop of a hat and fishing for his dick. "Jesus, Harlow. Way to show some self-control."

"Har-loh Rukh," he says in a sexy way. Yeah, I can guess what he's thinking. He nips at my palm again.

I slide my hand out of his grip. "I'm going to finish detangling you first, you shameless hussy of a man."

Except I don't. I fall asleep somewhere halfway through my long, involved task, and only have vague memories of Rukh pulling the comb from my hand and bundling furs around me.

When I wake up in the morning, though, I'm greeted by a surprise. There's fresh meat spitted over a new fire, and the man tending to both is utterly flipping gorgeous.

I stare in shock at Rukh, who looks like a changed man. While I slept, he finished his own hair with the comb. No longer wild and bushy around his head, it falls in a smooth waterfall down his back, making the twin crests of his horns that much more outrageous as they arch from his brow. He looks very much like one of Vektal's tribe, and I'm struck by another sense of déjà vu. But Rukh doesn't really look like anyone I remember. He's still got a wild air to him as he squats near the fire, completely naked.

I lick my lips at the sight. Not a bad thing for a girl to wake up to. I stretch in the covers, feeling rather good. Rather . . . excited about what the future holds.

Because if it's me and this man in the future? Just the two of us alone against the world?

I'm . . . kind of down with that. Really, really down with that.

Rukh

Traveling with Har-loh at my side is very different than traveling on my own. I'm slower, of course. I can't go off and hunt whenever I want. I have to be mindful of the landscape and things that will attack, or places that are dangerous for her fragile ankles.

But . . . I enjoy it. Every moment awake is a joy. Every night, I pull her against me and let her cuddle her soft body against my bigger one. Every day is full of excitement, and there is someone to share it with.

I cannot imagine going back to my old life without her. Not now. She is everything to me. Little by little, I find myself adjusting to please her. If she shows a preference in meat, I seek it out. I down my kills carefully, knowing she will want to salvage furs, or the bladders for cooking. I carry my bag at all times and make sure that we have enough fuel for a nightly fire.

I always, always make sure she is warm and safe.

After a full day of walking, we eat dinner near our fire and she drags the thing she calls a "comb" through my hair. She likes to brush it and makes soft humming noises in her throat as she touches me. Me? I just crave her presence. Her small face is the last thing I see before I go to sleep, and the first thing I search for when I awaken.

Sometimes it still feels like a dream that she is here with me, and I clutch her to me harder, afraid to wake up. Afraid that I'll rouse and be utterly alone once more.

The world changes as we travel. It grows flatter, the snow less deep. I begin to smell the salt of the big water in the air, though I do not know if Har-loh notices these things yet. The trees change, spiky and taller, and the herds of dvisti that are so thick in the mountains thin down to a few stragglers. It is warmer here, and even Har-loh seems to shiver less. I like that.

I push hard but we don't make it to my cave that night. Har-loh's steps slow and she sags in exhaustion when we pause for a rest, and so I decide to camp for the evening. We can make it there in the morning. We crawl into the furs and I immediately reach for her folds, expecting to find her wet and willing.

Instead, she pushes my hand away. "No. Donfeelgud."

I frown. Is she tired? Her face looks drawn, but normally she welcomes my touches no matter how exhausted she is. Instead, she moves away from me, just enough that our skin isn't touching, and curls up in her furs, trying to sleep.

I feel . . . odd. I don't know the words. All I know is that this feels . . . not right, and it makes me miserable. I move to the fire and sit there, tending it for hours and watching her as she dozes fitfully. She seems as restless as I am. My chest throbs and hums, so loud that it feels as if it's shaking my insides like a ground-quake.

Something's wrong. But what?

I'm nodding off, watching the fire, when Har-loh cries out.

It's a sound of pain and loss, and I immediately bolt to my feet, terrified for her. Was I not watching? Did something bite her? Is she wounded?

But when I pull her against me, her eyes flutter as if lost in a dream, and her chest drums wildly, in the same frantic beat of my own.

"No," she cries in a weak voice. She's not looking at me. Instead, she shakes her head, as if arguing with an unseen person. "Yusehdtwasgawn!"

"Har-loh." I tap her cheek, then brush my fingers over it. What is happening?

Harlow

It's back.

I know the tumor's back, because all the symptoms are there. I sit up and look around the campsite, but everything's blurred and double. Two fires, two Rukhs, two trees when there should only be one. There's no color; the world is black-and-white. That's another symptom. My head pounds and my entire body pulses.

This is just like before.

It's not gone. The ship's computer lied to me. The brain tumor isn't eradicated by my khui. It's been lying dormant, waiting for my guard to go down. I raise one of my hands in front of my face. It's shaking. I'm seizing—another symptom of the tumor pushing on my brain.

"No," I cry out, squeezing my hand into a fist in an effort to make it stop shaking. "You said it was gone! You said the tumor was destroyed! That it wasn't there!"

"Harlow," the computer chides me. "There are rules and

you're not following them. You ask a lot of your khui and you give it nothing in return. What did you expect?"

"What does it want?"

"Harlow."

"What?"

"Harlow." The computer's voice is all around me. It's in my head, resting on the tumor that's determined to kill me. "Harlow. *Harlow.*"

I jerk awake with a gasp, like water has been splashed on my face. My eyes focus in on the face—the single, crisp face—inches from mine. There's no blurring. No vision doubling. I tap the roof of my mouth with my tongue. No stroke. The shaking I feel? It's my cootie, reminding me that I'm joined to Rukh. It's vibrating so hard that my chest feels like there's a motorboat trapped inside it.

My stomach heaves, and I fling myself out of Rukh's arms a moment before I throw up.

It was just a nightmare, I tell myself as I cough dinner up into the nearby snow. My brain's just being overactive. The intense vibration of my cootie scared my sleeping brain into thinking it was a seizure.

I'm just scaring myself.

I rock back on my heels and wipe my sweating brow. Throwing up didn't make me feel much better. I only feel worse, really. I don't feel like it was just a bad dream. Maybe it was a warning. I've been putting off resonance with Rukh because I don't want to get pregnant. Is this my subconscious letting me know that I need to take action and do what my khui asks? I don't know what happens if I keep ignoring things, other than get more miserable. Already my skin is so sensitized that it feels almost . . . unpleasant to touch Rukh. It's like it's too much to bear.

And my poor Tarzan. He doesn't understand. I look over at him and feel a stab of guilt. What we need is to get good and drunk somewhere so we—so I—can lose my inhibitions.

He moves to my side and strokes my hair off my face. "Har-loh?"

"I'm okay," I tell him with a faint smile. "Really."

Rukh reaches into his bag and pulls out a sprig of curled leaves. I picked them from a bush as we walked, recognizing the plant as one that grew near the caves. It makes a good tea and soothes the stomach. Apparently Rukh knows this as well. I take it from him and chew on the leaves, thinking.

Maybe I can find something alcoholic when we get to our destination. Or maybe I should just suck it up and tackle the man. It's not like there's anything physically wrong with him. He's gorgeous, he's clean, and his hair is no longer a tangled mess around his head. He's utterly devoted to me and it's clear that I can do no wrong in his eyes.

I'm just . . . really scared at the thought of being a mother. A wilderness mom, no less, with no one around me but Rukh. Yeah, that's the part that scares me.

As I chew the bitter leaves, Rukh grabs my cloak and tucks it around my shoulders, fussing over me. He leads me back to the spot I've claimed as my bed and doesn't relax until I lay my head down and feign sleep.

I may not want to be a mother, but do I have any other choice?

Rukh

We're here.

I grab my tired female's hand and lead her forward, excited. I want her to love the new place I've taken her to live. It's safe here. The bad ones rarely come to the salty waters because they're so far away, which makes it perfect for us. There are several large caves nearby, and I know the perfect one for my fragile woman.

I touch her cheek and she smiles at me, though her face is still troubled. Whatever happened in her sleep last night has taken some of the spark out of her today. She is quiet, less talkative than usual. Normally I listen to her babble and try to pick out words, but today she is silent, and I find that I miss our game. I miss the cheery sound of her voice.

I want things to go back to how they were, but I don't know how to ask. It's endlessly frustrating.

I point at the distant cliffs. There is a valley that cuts through the hills. On one side, there are many caves, shielded from the worst of the winds by the high walls. A short walk away, there are the endless salty waters that roll and ripple all day long. Here, there are many things to eat. Much of the water cannot be drunk, but there are streams that taste good and are pure. The caves here are bigger.

The caves here are safe.

I want her to be pleased. So I gesture at the cliffs and then search my small collection of words to find the right one for "home." "Here," I decide on. I know that one.

Her flat brow wrinkles. "Here? Weerhere?" She puts a hand to her forehead and tries to peer into the distance. "Where?"

She seems excited, so I take her hand in mine and lead her forward. I want her to see the caves, and to be impressed by them. I want to please my . . . my mate. Memory bursts in my mind. I remember the word "mate" and what it means. It means she belongs to me and I belong to her. Har-loh is my mate. Together we will be a family. And I know—I *remember*—that the song humming in my chest along with hers? It declares that we are mates.

I turn to her and press her hand to my breastbone. I have ridges in this spot to cover and protect my vulnerable parts, but she is only softness. I press my hand to my chest, and then my other hand to hers. "Mate. Yes?"

Har-loh's eyes widen. "Righteer?" She points at the ground and says again. "Here?"

Now I am confused. "Har-loh Rukh mate. Har-loh mate. Rukh mate Har-loh."

Recognition dawns in her eyes. "Ohhh. Younodeword 'mate'?"

"Mate," I tell her happily. I am singing with joy inside. A mate is a wonderful thing. It means I will never be alone again.

"Mate," she agrees, her expression shy. "Still rappinmahbrain round datwun." But her smile is bright. "Show me here."

I lead her forward. It's a short walk into the valley, and here the snows are so light that we no longer need the snowshoes. I toss them over my shoulder and carry both mine and hers, so she can be free to explore. I want her to be pleased here. I want her to delight in this new place I've taken her. There are so many things to show her—where we will drink, where we will sleep, the game that crawls along the beach, the shells just inside the water full of tasty things to eat, and the icy islands that float past in the salty waters. It is a new world here, very different from the snowy mountains we just left. It has been a while since I have been here, but I want to show her everything. To share my world with her.

And I want to show her my father's resting spot.

Harlow

There's a distant gentle roar that takes me a few minutes to realize is the beach. Rukh's brought me to the ocean. A sense of wonder takes over. I've never lived near the ocean. It's warmer here, the winds less biting, and the snow isn't as deep, which makes moving around easier.

Rukh holds my hand tight in his as we walk, and it's clear that he's anxious about something. Does he want me to be pleased with this place? Right now, I'm just pleased that we're no longer traveling. I'm ready to put down roots. I don't know why Rukh felt the need to leave at the sight of the other hunter, but I'm with him. My cootie vibrates in my chest, agreeing with me. It fills me with a weird ache, as if reminding me what I need to do soon.

Yeah, I know, stupid cootie. It's not like I can forget with the thing going off like an alarm clock every time I turn around. I rub my chest as Rukh leads me forward.

The rolling hills curve into a steep valley, and I notice a cave mouth set off into the rock.

"Here," Rukh says again, and gives my hand a squeeze.

I have to admit, the cave looks promising. The entrance is nice and big, taller than myself and Rukh combined. It looks like there's a bit of a twist once you walk in, which is also good— that means the wind won't whistle through the cave all night and chill my sorry human butt. Rukh motions for me to wait outside while he goes in, knife in hand, to ensure nothing's living inside. I hear a scuffle a few moments later, and then Rukh appears with a pair of fat quill beasts hanging from his hand. He's got a few quills sticking out of his arm but seems pleased.

"I guess we're stealing their home, huh?" I smile at him. The animal lover in me should be upset that we're raiding their cave and taking it over, but living on Not-Hoth has taught me that it's very much kill-or-be-killed around here.

Plus, the quilled beasts make a tasty lunch.

I follow Rukh into the cave, cautious. There's not a lot of natural light to see by, but the ceiling of the cave is tall, so at least we can keep a fire going and not choke on the smoke. There's a nice big interior room in the cave and a few nooks that we can use for storage. There's a perfect spot for a firepit, and an alcove that will make a good sleeping spot. It's the nicest cave I've seen so far, and it makes me happy. "I like it," I tell Rukh excitedly, not that he can understand me. He'll grasp the tone of my voice.

He smiles at me and gestures at the floor, indicating sleep.

"Yes, this will be home," I agree. The place needs a good sweep and some prepping, but the potential is awesome. I can't stop smiling. Home, after so long. I love it. Eager, I follow behind him as he shows me the stream of fresh water nearby that comes from deep within the rock and trickles down the cliffs. He leads me to the beach, and I make mental comparisons. The waves are larger than the gentle surf I remember at home, and each one crashes hard against the sand. The sand itself is a dark, glittery green, and the water has a greenish tinge instead of Caribbean blue. But it's the beach, and it's familiar to me. It makes this feel like an Earth vacation instead of being totally stranded.

That is, until I see the sand-scorpions.

They crawl along the beach, a weird, Geiger-esque cross between a spider and a scorpion. Many legs scuttle along the sand, all leading back to a thorny-looking carapace covered with spikes. As a wave rolls in, the legs dig into the sand and it hunches down. When the wave rolls back again, it unhooks itself from the beach and scuttles along its way, a feeler (or stinger) bobbing overhead.

It's easily the most disgusting thing I've seen so far. I make a face of horror and point it out to Rukh. "Look! So gross!"

He gives me a surprised smile and then trots forward in the sand. When he drives his knife through the center of one, I squirm and gag quietly. Damn language barrier. He must have seen it and thought I wanted lunch. Eeeew. Guess I'm having crab legs for dinner. As Rukh holds it up and legs twitch wildly, I amend that thought.

Rukh is having crab legs. No way am I letting that thing near my mouth, cooked or not.

The salty breeze picks up, and I gaze down the beach. Actually, now that I look at things, there's not a lot like Earth here on this beach other than the water and sand. The waves are rough, and out in the distance, I see greenish icebergs floating in the water. Dark shapes move on the distant ice, and on the shore there's an ostrichlike something bobbing for things in the waves a short ways away. As I peer at the water, undulating humps flash and then disappear again.

Oh well. I didn't want to swim anyhow. I just want a nice home, and this will do. I smile encouragingly at Rukh as he returns to my side. "I like this place, big guy."

"Eat?" he asks, holding the leggy sand-scorpion out to me.

I shake my head, swallowing hard. "Later." Much, much later. I wish I had a piece of paper to write on, because I feel like I need to make a list of everything we need to make this place a home. Blankets, spears, a stack of dung-firewood, maybe some of those pink potato-like plant trees that grew near the old tribal caves if we can find them . . . I stare off into the distance, mentally cataloging things. Just thinking about everything that needs to be done is exhausting, because the only people here to work are myself and Rukh.

At my side, Rukh puts his kill into his bag, sheathes his knife, and then takes my hand in his. The smile dies from his face and he reaches out to touch my cheek.

Uh-oh. "What's wrong?"

His throat works, and then he stares off at the ocean. Worry shoots through me, and I reach out and touch his arm, squeezing it. Or I would if he didn't have those strange plates running along his skin. But he gets the idea, and he reaches out to touch my cheek, a faint smile on his face again. "Vaashan home."

I tilt my head and my brain scrolls through the alien language, looking for a match. "I don't recognize that word."

"Here." He gestures at the sand, then at the distant cliffs. When I give a small shake to indicate my confusion, he pulls my hand to his cheek and rubs my knuckles against his skin. Then he sighs sadly and begins to tug me forward.

I follow, though I admit I'm wary. What now? I can't possibly imagine what he's going to show me. We head down the beach, and Rukh seems to know exactly where he's going. He already showed me the cave we were going to stay in . . . is someone else—or something else—nearby?

I'm not prepared for what he shows me, though. We find another cave, and Rukh holds my hand tightly as we stoop and enter. This cave is some distance away from the other one, and very small. But I figure out what it is the moment I see the mound of rocks piled into an oval, and the beaded necklace hanging above on a rocky outcropping.

This is a grave.

Rukh drops to his knees by it, and he holds my hand tight, as if terrified of letting go. After a moment, he looks over at me. "Vaashan home."

"Vaashan is your father?" I ask. That has to be who this is. I've gotten a few hints from him over the time that I've known him that he was with his father, but then his father was gone. And of course, a wild boy has to come from somewhere.

I stare down at the grave. I don't even mind the crushing grip that Rukh has on my hand. He needs the comfort, and if there's any small amount I can give him, I will. I try to imagine how heartbreaking this must have been for him: to be alone except for one other person, and then to lose that person? And then to have to bury them, alone? I stare at the mound of hand-sized rocks. These could not have come from the beach. How long had it taken him to gather them to bury his father?

How long has Rukh been alone?

I rub his arm, utterly full of sympathy for my poor barbarian. "Were you very young when your father died?"

The sad look he gives me has no comprehension, and I don't press. It's not something that needs to be told at the moment. I can guess from his wild appearance and his utter bafflement about certain things that he was rather young, indeed.

My poor Rukh. No wonder he freaked out when we saw the other hunter. No wonder he clubbed me over the head and carried me off. He must have felt the resonance and acted on the possessive surge of feeling. He doesn't know how to cope with needing another person.

Hell, the fact that he cares for me probably scares the shit out of him. I know how that feels, but not to the depths he does. I've been ripped from everything I knew at home, but my family there was dead, and here, I've had the company of other humans.

He's had no one for so long.

My chest resonates, and his picks up the song.

I stroke his arm and lean my cheek against his shoulder. My poor mate. After all, we are mates, aren't we? I've been fighting this so hard because I've been afraid, and seeing this has totally changed my perspective. How long has Rukh had to suffer alone? And now that he has someone—me—I've been pushing him away. I've been ignoring resonance because I've felt like I'm not ready.

I wonder if anyone is truly ready, though.

In that moment, I want to give Rukh everything I possibly can. I want to give him a mate, a family, teach him about sex, and share everything every day together. I want him to know he's not alone.

I want him to know someone else loves him. Someone else is there for him.

My heart aches, and under the thick purring in my chest, I feel that this is good and right.

Now's the time for us to become one.

PART THREE

Rukh

Har-loh's quiet as we leave my father's grave. Seeing it always makes me sad, but today there's only an ache of loss that she never got to meet him. I'm not beside myself with sorrow, not today. Today there's too much to show my Har-loh. I need to make her a fire and set up the bed in the cave before it gets too dark.

I can't dwell on my past any longer. I say a small internal goodbye to my father and take Har-loh back to the portion of beach we will claim as ours. She says nothing, but I can tell she is thinking hard. I recognize the look on her face that tells me she wants to say many things to me, and we will have a language lesson later, perhaps.

I touch her speckled hand. Is she hungry? She pointed out the crawler earlier, so I assumed she wanted to eat.

She gives me an absent smile and squeezes my hand. "Snothing. Justhinkin."

Again, she gets the distant look on her face and I worry. Is something wrong? I'm pensive as we return to our new cave and we get to work. I make a firepit and build a fire while she finds a dried branch on the beach and sweeps the floor of the cave. By the time I spit the crawler over the fire to cook, she's taken off her outer layer of furs and has set them up as a bed. I feel a twinge of guilt that I made her leave the others behind. It's warmer here, but will she still be cold? Am I making her suffer?

I don't want her to die like my father did. My heart clenches in my chest, and I can't breathe at the thought. What will I do if Har-loh gets sick like my father did? I move to her side and swiftly pull her against me, holding her close. Touching her helps, but . . . it doesn't feel like enough. What are we missing? A helpless growl of frustration sounds in my throat.

As if she can sense my unease, Har-loh wraps her small arms around me. "Ino." She cuddles with me for a moment, and then inhales. "Issat food? Smellsdelishis." She gestures at the fire. When I pull the many-legged crawler off the fire and offer it to her, she wrinkles her nose. "Gahdtitsugly."

I rip off one of the legs and succulent pale meat shows from inside the hard shell. I've never eaten one of these cooked, but it looks and smells much better than it did raw. But because Har-loh is the most important thing to me, I won't eat until she's full.

She makes a face as she takes the bite from me and gingerly puts it to her mouth. Her tongue flicks out to taste it, and my cock stirs in response at the sight. A moment later, her eyes light up and she looks at me in surprise. "Isgud!"

She likes it? I tear another leg off and offer it to her.

"Yeweet." Har-loh gestures at me and picks at her leg, removing the hard carapace before prying out the flesh. I do the same, and the food is indeed tasty like this. My Har-loh knows so many things. She's incredible. My chest thrums and hers picks up the song. She looks over at me and smiles, then takes another bite.

And I relax and eat, too.

By the time we've picked all the meat off the bones, Har-loh is full and washes her hands and mouth with some of the water from the skin. I do the same, since cleanliness seems important to her. Instead of sitting back down next to the fire with me, though, she moves to her bed.

Har-loh pats the furs next to her. "Come here, Rukh."

I move to her side and crouch, curious. Is she tired and wishes to sleep early? Or does she want me to hold her close and touch her folds? My cock throbs at the thought and I resist the urge to stroke it. I like it better when she touches it, anyhow.

Her hands move to my hair and she smooths it off my chest and pushes it behind my shoulders. "Rukh eez Har-loh's mate, yes?" She touches her breast, which is thrumming with song. "Mate." Then she taps my chest. "Rukh mate. This purr-purr-purr? This means 'mate.' No purr-purr, no mate."

I don't catch all of her words, but what she is saying makes sense. My chest did not start thrumming—purring, as she calls it—until she appeared. If it means she belongs to me, I will gladly let it purr all the time.

"Purr-purr is 'resonance.' Doyew nodatword?" She looks at me with wide blue eyes. When I don't respond, she sighs and repeats her words. *Purr-purr is resonance.* I repeat them, too. Then it dawns on me. Ah. That is what this thrumming is called. "Resonance," I say, and tap her chest, then mine.

She nods. "Resonance . . . mates. Mates . . ." She screws up her face and then makes a gesture with her fingers. "Mates mayk bebbies. Kits."

"Kits?" For some reason, I recognize this word. It reminds

me of what my father used to call me when I was young. Kits . . . are young ones, aren't they? What does this have to do with *resonance*? My cock aches and I long to rub it against her belly. If she lies down on the furs, I'll take that as my signal that she wants to, but for now she's sitting up, a look of concentration on her face. What she's saying is important and I shouldn't be focused on my aching cock or how much I want to touch her and rub her until she makes that throaty little scream.

Her gaze softens and the look she gives me is heated. "Resonance makes kits."

I grasp what she is saying, but I'm baffled as to how. My frown must show that, because she reaches out and strokes my cock.

It immediately spurts, intense relief rocking through me, and I come all over her hand.

Har-loh looks startled, and then she gives me a wry look. "Sortalikedat." She gestures at the wetness I've sprayed on her hand and that now covers my cock. "Yewmake kit witdis."

It takes several minutes of explaining and her gesturing at her body before I grasp what she's saying. When I . . . release, it needs to get inside her? She takes my hand and guides it to her folds, and I feel an opening—hot and wet—and she gives a little shiver when I touch her there.

I watch her face and I want to do this right. So I stroke my hand over my messy cock, and then take two of my slick fingers and push them at her entrance. She's so wet here, her body sucks at my fingers. I bite back a groan at the sensation, then look up at her.

She bites her lip and looks . . . unhappy. Then, she gives a small shake of her head. She takes a bit of fur that she keeps with her and wipes my hand and both of our bodies clean of my coming. "I'll just show yew," she whispers, and then tosses the cloth aside. Then, she touches my jaw and pulls me forward.

Her lips brush over mine.

I remain stiff, uncertain as to what is happening. Is this part of resonance?

"Kiss," she says softly. Then she moves her mouth over mine again. "Kiss."

"Kiss," I repeat, and put my lips on hers.

She nods, pleased. She seems to like kisses, so I do another, repeating the word. It feels ticklish, to graze my mouth against hers. And just when I'm getting used to the feeling, her tongue flicks out and darts against the seam of my mouth.

I gasp and pull back, shocked. Scorching, recent memories of her tongue on my cock flood through my mind, and my cock returns to life, growing hard again. My chest begins to purr—to resonate—and Har-loh's smile widens.

"Kiss," she says in her sweet voice, and then licks her lips.

I'm fascinated by that small tongue. I want to feel it again. I lean forward, inviting her to return, and she presses her mouth to mine again. This time, her arms twine around my neck and she presses her body against me. Eager, I follow her lead and put my arms around her, too. I hold her close, and when her tongue brushes against my lips again, I part mine to see what she will do.

Her tongue snakes into my mouth and flicks against mine, and my cock instantly reacts. It's like she's licking me in all the places I'm most sensitive, and I tug her closer. I slide my tongue against hers cautiously, and when she makes a small sound of pleasure, I grow bolder. Is this how her people show affection?

If so, I like it. Soon, I lose all worry that I don't know how to act and just concentrate on tonguing her sweet mouth. My hands roam over her body, touching her back, her arms, everywhere I can.

By the time she pulls her mouth from mine, we're both panting. There's a dazed look of pleasure in her eyes that I recognize. It's like when I touch her late at night. Does this affect her similarly? I want to reach between her legs and see if she's wet, but I wait to see what she will show me next. My body throbs with need, and my chest rumbles with the resonance. She's going to show me how to make a kit with her. I think of the animals I've seen in the wild. Normally the male climbs atop the female and there is much screaming. Is this what we are about to do? Realization dawns. Of course I would not move my spend to her body with my hand. I have to get it inside her somehow. I look down at my cock, aching and erect.

"Sokay," Har-loh murmurs to me quietly. Her fingers dance over my skin, touching me. Then, she pulls her clothing off of her body, revealing herself to me. I've seen her nude before, but there's something different about it as she sits in front of me. Maybe it's the arch of her back that pushes her teats out. Or maybe it's the look of anticipation in her face. I want to touch her all over.

She lays aside her clothing and then scoots back on the bed, then reclines. Her teats thrust into the air, the little tips taut. The area between her thighs is shadowed but I can smell her arousal, and it makes my mouth water. My cock jerks and I have to fight hard not to touch it myself.

I . . . want her to touch it. I want her to show me this thing. I want to learn all of it for her.

Har-loh reaches for me, and I lean forward, unsure. She tugs at me, indicating I should join her, but instead of lying next to her, she pulls me until I'm practically on top of her. I support my weight with my arms braced on either side of her, not wanting to crush her smaller form with my bigger one.

She smooths a hand over my chest, caressing me. "Rlax." Her touch glides up my arms. It feels so good that my entire body quakes at those small caresses, and I fight the urge to press myself against her until I come.

As if she can read my thoughts, Har-loh raises one leg up, and then locks it around my hips. Her ankle digs into my buttock, and she pushes me down. I resist for a moment, and then rest my hips between hers. My cock throbs as I make contact with her skin, and I have to fight the insane urge to . . . push against her? That's not right.

Har-loh moans, her body moving under mine. I'm fascinated by the sight of her, especially when her hands move to caress the tips of her teats. Then, she points at one. "Kiss."

Put my mouth there? Or my tongue? Either way, I'm fascinated. I lean down and brush my lips against her skin here. She's so soft, her scent warmer here, in the valley between her teats. I nuzzle her and then flick my tongue out to touch her pale skin.

She moans and her hands go to my hair, then the base of my horns. She strokes them and it sends an answering surge through my cock. Her touch makes me wild with need. I lick and nip at the soft globe of her teat, but I'm drawn toward those pink tips. I brush my mouth over one and a hiss of breath escapes her. They're sensitive? Then I want to play with them more. I tease them the way she taught me to kiss—strokes of my tongue, nibbles of my lips—and watch for her reactions. I learn which kisses get soft sighs, and which ones make her squirm wildly underneath me.

Then I remember what she did to me, down by the stream. She took me in her mouth and played with me. I wonder if I can do that with her? I move down her soft belly, trailing my lips, and then I brush my fingers over the curls of her folds. "Kiss?" I ask.

Her mouth parts, and a small moan escapes. There's excitement in her flushed face, and she nods. Her hands squeeze the bases of my horns, and it almost feels as if she's squeezing my cock with those hands. I stifle my own groan.

"Rukh," she pants, but she doesn't seem like she wants to stop me. That's good, because I'm dying to explore her with my tongue and hands. I slide down her body and bury my nose in her curls. Her scent is strong and musky here, and it sends cravings through my body. My chest rumbles hard, and my cock twitches in response. It wants more of everything.

Gently, I touch her with my hand. After the last several days of our late-night rubbing, I know what touches she likes, but putting my hand here and putting my face here are two different things. I want to please her like she pleased me, so I push her folds apart and tongue her, seeking the small nub that she likes rubbed just so.

She nearly comes off the furs. Her cry is loud and fierce, but her hands clench my horns so tightly that she keeps me locked into place.

Not that I want to leave—I want to stay here forever. Here, her taste is strong, and here I can pleasure her. I run my tongue over her bump, then stroke up and down her silky folds. I find the small hole she has tucked away, the hole that is hot and wet, and I remember pushing my fingers here.

I explore the spot with my tongue, and it seems she is juiciest here. Her flavor saturates my mouth, and I love it. I push my tongue into the spot, and she squeals, her legs jerking. I look up, surprised.

"Wasgood," she pants, and tugs on my horns, indicating I should return. "Kiss. Kiss!" Her hips rock against me, as if she could persuade me to return with her movements.

I don't need persuading, though. I love touching her. I return to kissing her, tonguing and licking and nibbling everywhere I can. Her movements become more frantic, her voice more demanding, and I recognize this from our late nights in the furs. She's about to clench up in her own release. My cock aches, reminding me that I want release, too, but her pleasure is far more important than mine. I love to see my Har-loh lose herself. Her hips arch higher and higher, pushing against my face, and her little cries grow more frequent. Her thighs tremble, and I lick her harder, waiting for her to lose control.

To my surprise, though, she pushes my head away. "Wait," she pants. "Wait."

I lift my head. "Kiss?"

"Bettah," she says. I frown, because I don't know this word. I want to return to her folds and keep licking her. But she tugs on my horns, indicating that I should stop.

I growl at her.

She reaches to my hips and tugs me forward even as she lifts her legs to wrap them around me. My cock is pressed against her slick folds again, and she rubs up and down against me.

I groan, my eyes closing, because the feel of her like this is incredible. I want to spray her body with my spend, but I'm torn. I want her to show me how to make a kit with her.

Har-loh slides a hand between us and she grips my cock in

her fingers. My breath hisses out, but she's not stroking me. Instead, she seems to be . . . aiming me. I feel the head of my cock press against her warm, wet opening a moment later and I realize what I've been missing.

Ah. I put my spend inside her, and it will make a kit. This is what she's been trying to tell me.

Cautious, I push forward a little. Her heat seems to suck me inward, and it takes everything I have not to thrust my way forward. I watch her for a reaction instead. As I push into her, she moans again and wraps her arms around my neck.

"Likedat," she breathes. "Juslikedat."

"Good?" My voice sounds like a growl, but I can't help it. It's taking all of my control not to come right now.

"Good," she says in a voice that makes my sac draw up tight with anticipation.

My body jerks, and I'm unable to help myself. I thrust forward, and she sucks in a breath.

Her nails dig into my back. "*Yes.*"

I barely hear her. I'm too busy struggling with my own control. This is what I've been missing. This is what my frantic thrusting against her belly at night should have been about. I should have been claiming my mate by pushing my cock into her and filling her belly with my spend. This is what feels right. And her body clasping mine so tightly? Her walls squeezing my cock so tight? It feels better than anything I could ever imagine.

I could stay here forever, buried deep inside her.

I move slowly, and notice that my spur nudges against her little pleasure-nub between her legs. She gurgles when it does, but presses up against it a moment later, so I know it's good. It's like I'm perfectly made for her, and she for me. I thrust harder.

Under me, Har-loh moans, and I feel the ripple of her body. She tightens around my cock, impossibly. "Gahdi'mcomin."

I thrust into her again, wanting to feel her tighten and quiver around me. "Good?" It's a question, but it comes out more like a demand. My voice shakes as I struggle to keep control. It's taking everything I have not to lose myself and let pleasure take over.

But I want Har-loh to have her pleasure first.

"Good," she pants. When I stroke in again, she arches. "Good!" she cries again. I thrust into her harder, pushing at her, and her cries become a babble of words I don't understand. Her body clenches around mine, and her legs lock at my hips.

I feel it when she comes, her entire body quivering. Her chest purrs so loud I think it might shake her heart loose. Her mouth opens and closes, but no words come out. She just gasps, and her walls clutch me so hard it feels like a fist around my cock.

I lose my control then; I explode, gritting her name as my spend flies from my cock. I feel as if I'm coming forever, my balls drawn up tight. When there's nothing left to milk from my body, I fall, breathless, onto my elbows over her. I'm careful not to crush her, but I want to touch her right now, to bury my face in her teats and just surround myself with her scent.

As if sensing my need, she wraps her arms around me and tugs me down against her. "S'good," she murmurs, stroking my hair back from my face. "My Rukh."

"Har-loh," I say, voice thick. She's my mate now. I've put my cock inside her and given her my spend. We will make a kit together. I put a hand to her stomach, wondering how she will look when she has my child inside her. The dvisti grow fat and shaggy, their sides sticking out. I cannot imagine that happening to my delicate Har-loh.

She chuckles and puts her hand over mine. "S'earleeyet. Tahkes tyme."

"Mine," I tell her softly. "Mate mine. Har-loh mine." I stroke her soft skin and revel in the feel of her under me. This feels right. This is what I have been missing for so long.

She gives a small, contented sigh. "Har-loh mate Rukh."

In this small moment, I've never been happier.

PART FOUR

Harlow

I tug a boot off one of my swollen feet, then kick it onto the rocky shore. Off goes the other boot, and the cold air bites into my skin. I get to my feet—not an easy task given the size of my middle, and then gingerly step into the rushing tide. It's ice-cold, and a shiver moves through me. I don't go in far, though. Just far enough to cover my toes.

And then I wiggle them and wait.

It doesn't take long. Never does. A long, white tendril snakes forward, toward my feet. I force myself to stand totally still as it touches one wiggling toe, then another. In the water, I see the thick body of the creature surge forward, toward my foot. I quietly flip my spear over in my hand, point down, and then jam it right into the eye as it opens to look at me.

The creature flails and thrashes in the water, and I lean on the spear to hold it steady. A moment later, the water stills and the tendrils go limp.

Dinner caught.

I shiver and bound out of the water, dragging my freshly killed "spaghetti monster" with me. I don't know what the critter's called, but it's got a lot of snaky arms and a meatball-looking body, so I went with that. It's also Rukh's favorite seafood item, so I can't wait to see the look on his face when he comes home and sees it cooking on the fire. He does love himself a good spaghetti dinner, I think, and then giggle at my own joke.

My back twinges as it has been lately, and I groan, rubbing the base of my spine. The baby seems to be resting on something in my upper right-hand abdomen, as that part of my body constantly aches lately. I go back and forth from rubbing the side of my belly to rubbing my lower back. My shoes suddenly seem like a lot of effort to put on, especially pregnant, so I pick them up and shove them in my shoulder bag. In the other bag goes my kill, and I use my spear as a walking stick as I pick my way across the sand and head back home.

Funny how this weird beach is "home" now, but it is. I hum a nursery rhyme to myself as I hang up my bag on one of the rocky outcroppings that serves as a coat hook. I want to rub my aching, swollen feet, but I can barely reach them these days, so I shuffle toward the fire and stoke it instead.

After the fire is good and roaring, I chop up, skin, and spit the spaghetti monster on the fire. By the time I've done that and washed my hands, I'm pooped. I rub my aching lower back and head toward my furs to lie down. Being pregnant is taking a lot out of me, and it seems like an eternal pregnancy with no end in sight.

I ease my body onto the thick pile of furs and relax, closing my eyes. My swollen feet are propped up on a pillow stuffed with feathers from one of the raptor-looking birds that hunt the shoreline. There's another one behind my head, and the pelts under my body are soft and supple and warm, even if they're not all that pretty to look at. I'm not the best at tanning, but I get better every day.

I glance over at my "calendar." It's the first of December.

Okay, so it's not really the first. Nor is it December, like it says. We don't have paper or much wood, so I took several rib bones from different creatures and carved the months of the year into each one, then strung them up like a xylophone. It's a modified calendar in that I have hash marks for days and I only put thirty days in each month regardless of how long it truly was. It's just a general way for me to count time, since the seasons are all out of whack here on Not-Hoth, and Rukh pays zero attention to them.

I rub my belly and muse at the time that's passed. I created that calendar in "January." It was an arbitrary date, but I got tired of time passing and me not knowing when it was. With a baby on the way, I wanted to track somehow. I'm pretty sure it's been a year since Rukh and I mated for the first time and made the baby.

I'm pretty sure I'm gonna be pregnant forever. I run a hand along my belly, frowning. It's big, but nothing's dropped like I hear in pregnancy stories. I've already been pregnant for about two months longer than a human woman. The fourth trimester, I like to joke, not that Rukh gets my jokes.

The baby kicks and then flips in my belly, and I rub a hand over it soothingly. "You get them, though, don't you?"

A flutter in my stomach makes me think of laughter. Baby laughter. I fall asleep in the furs, wondering what it's going to be like when the baby gets here. Rukh's going to be such a good daddy.

Rukh

I snarl in irritation at the family of plumed "raptors" that squawk along the beach. All day, I've been out looking for small ones, because their feathers are softer than the adults and Harloh wants them for our kit's bedding. I've ranged far and wide today, searching for the perfect ones, and managed to find one when I was at the end of my temper. Now I come home and see three of the things frolicking in the waves. Irritating. They'll live another day, because I already have what I came for.

I hoist my kill over my shoulder for the final time, tired and ready to relax with my mate after a long day. The heavy snows have all but disappeared, the thick ice breaking up over the salty waters, and the weather is warming enough that my fragile Harloh will not need her heaviest cloaks. She will be happy. She did not like that the coldest season was over ten of her "months" long. I picture her small face beaming with excitement at my finding a raptor kit with downy feathers, and my pace picks up.

When I make it home to the cave, though, I'm not greeted by a smiling mate. There's food on the fire, but the coals have gone down to a licking flame, and the smell in the air tells me that the meat is charred and inedible. My eyes narrow, my nostrils flaring at the awful scent. "Har-loh?" I move toward the bed.

My mate is there, curled up in the furs, her big belly protruding from her clothing. She has a hand under one cheek and sleeps so peacefully. My khui rumbles and purrs at the sight of her, and I feel a fierce sense of satisfaction. She's mine, and she carries my kit inside her. A burned meal doesn't matter.

I remove the offensive food from the fire and take it down to the shore, where scavengers can partake of it safely away from our cave. Har-loh is still asleep when I return, so I'm quiet as I carefully pluck the raptor kit clean of its feathers and put them aside for my mate. I eat a few bites of meat while it's raw, and then smoke the rest, because with my kit inside her, Har-loh does not like the taste of raw meat anymore.

Thinking about Har-loh pulls me toward her. I can't resist my mate any longer. I kneel down next to the bed and stroke her cheek. Her eyes flutter open and she gives me a sleepy smile.

"Hey, baby."

"Tired?" I ask. There are hollows under her eyes that I don't like, but she promises me she is fine. She nods and starts to sit up, but I gently push her back into the furs. "You tired. You rest."

Her nose wrinkles and she tries to peek around me to the fire. "Oh no, did I burn your dinner? I got you spahgetteemawnster."

She calls it a weird word in her language, but I recognize the creature from its shape, and know of her thoughtfulness. "Is not important."

Har-loh looks upset. "I'm sorry. I was just tired." She yawns as if to emphasize this. "I'm so tired all the time now."

My hand goes to her rounded belly. She's so big, like one of the dvisti females before she's about to drop her kit. Of course,

I don't point this out. The last time I did, she cried and then blamed it on something called hawr-moans. "You carrying kit. Is tired-making."

"Tiring? Yeah, it is." She shifts on the bed and rubs her back again.

I know what will make her feel better. I move to the foot of our nest, where her feet are propped up on one of the strange puffy things she insists she wants under her head. I take one cold foot in my hand and begin to massage it. She likes her feet rubbed, my Har-loh.

She moans and falls back in the furs. "God, you're a good man."

Her praise is pleasing and I do more, working her small foot over before switching to the other. As I continue to rub, her moans grow louder, and my cock responds in kind. The next time she groans, mine matches it.

A soft giggle escapes her throat, and she pulls her foot from my grip to rub it against my cock. I'm wearing a breechcloth like she prefers, and for the moment, I hate it because I can't feel her skin against mine. "Seems like someone missed me today."

"Always miss you," I tell her. Of course I do. She is my mate. The best days are the days we spend all day together. Now that she is carrying our kit, she has to stay closer to the cave. It's hard not to resent my child at times because he already takes up so much of her time. But then I think of the family waiting for me, and my resentment fades. I have gone from being alone to having a wonderful mate and we will soon have a kit.

I would change *nothing*. Not a tail flick of it.

I crawl into bed behind Har-loh and nuzzle her neck. Because her belly is so big, we cannot mate from the front as usual. For the past moon, we have been creative with our mating, and I pull her against me, gauging her mood.

She sighs and reaches back for my hair. "I love you, Rukh."

"I love you, my mate," I tell her and nip at her soft ear. My hands slide to the front of her tunic, to her sensitive, swollen teats. Breasts, she calls them. I touch one and she moans, tugging at her clothing. That tells me she wants my touch as much as I want her. I help her undo the laces at the front of her tunic until it falls open, and her ripe breasts are free for my hands. I gently brush over the nipples, because I know they're too tender for much more.

She pushes back against me, whimpering, and her hand knots in my mane. I push her skirt down her thighs and she kicks it off even as I rip my breechcloth off my body. Then we are pressed against each other, flesh to flesh, body to body. Her khui hums loudly in her chest, and mine answers.

I murmur her name as I push her thighs apart and enter her from behind. She gives a soft little cry and holds tight to my hands as I begin to thrust into her, my spur prodding against the tiny bud of her backside with each pump.

We are perfection like this, me and my Har-loh.

The next morning, Har-loh wakes up and moves the small arrowhead from the first notch in her kahl-un-dur to the second one. "Dee-sem-burr second," she announces. She rubs her side and winces. "This baby has to be coming soon, right?"

"I do not know." I wish I had answers for her. She has so many questions and I do, too. The hollows under her eyes seem to be worse today, despite the fact that she slept heavily through the night. But there is no one to ask, and I do not know if this is normal. My memories of my father are so faint and growing dimmer with every day. Instead of his face in my dreams, I see

Har-loh's smile, her freckled skin, her soft body. "Come eat," I tell my mate and gesture at her stool by the fire. I've even put one of her fluffy puffs on it to ease her bottom.

She sits down and gives me a grateful smile. "The baby's active today."

I put a hand on her belly and feel the flutters there, the gentle movement. I grin up at her, and then jerk my hand away as the kit kicks hard.

Har-loh winces. "Pissy today, too."

"He is hungry. He need eat. You eat, too." I get a chunk of dried, smoked meat and offer it to her.

She wrinkles her nose at the sight and looks unhappy. "Is that all we have?"

"No." I pull out one of the baskets she's woven and take out additional chunks of meat she has salted and smoked. "This one is raptor, and this one is spagayteemawnster, and this one is . . ." I hold it to my nose, sniffing. Burned dvisti. "Dvisti."

"Maybe just water," she says, and rubs her belly again.

"Eat," I tell her, and ignore the gnawing worry that creeps up. I give her a bit of smoked dvisti since it is the tenderest, and she takes it from my hand and gamely nibbles on it. I notice she drinks more water than anything and eats slowly.

My worry threatens to consume me, and so I stay by the cave with her that morning. I tell her I have hides to cure, but we have more hides than two people can use. She stuffs feathers into one of her leather puffs for the baby, and then sews the edge shut. When I take a break, she pulls out her boots and smiles brightly at me. "Can we go get clams? I'm hungry for those."

Our cave is bursting with dried meats, and it seems wasteful to hunt more. But I will do anything for my Har-loh. I nod and help her put her boots on, lacing them for her while she comments about being unable to see her feet. I tell her they are swollen and fluffy like one of her puffs.

She snorts.

Then we are off to the beach, and the weather is nice. I can see Har-loh improving as we walk. Her face has the pink color in it that tells me she is healthy, and she smiles when the two suns come out from behind the clouds.

I am worrying over nothing, I tell myself. I give her belly a small pat as we get to the edge of the water. "Clams?" I have my spear to use as a digging stick.

"Yes, please." She clasps her hands in front of her and looks excited. "The big dark ones, hopefully."

She has told me before that her home place has something very similar to the clams, but they are smaller. I watch the surf, looking for a small spout of water to surface from the sand once the tide rolls out.

I spot one and jam the end of my spear into the sand, then push the end up, trying to dig it out. I catch a glimpse of dark shell before it burrows deeper into the sand. Growling in frustration, I forget all about the spear and dig my hands through the sand, determined to get this for my mate and to make her smile. Harlow laughs as I try to shovel faster than the creature can dig, and sand flies everywhere.

At last, success. I grip the thing in my hand and hold it aloft. "For you!"

"Yay!" She claps her hands. "That's one! Let's get more and then we'll go home and boil them."

I nod at her belly, as if speaking to it. "Your mother is hungry today."

"She's starving," Har-loh answers warmly, and rubs her stomach.

"Then your father feed you," I declare to her belly, and get to my feet.

There is sand all over my arms and chest, and my legs. It's even in the tangle of woven braids that Har-loh has made out of my mane. She steps forward and dusts me off with her small fingers.

And then she stops. Her fingers twitch on my arm, and then her nails dig into my skin.

I look up into her face. She is pale, her freckles dark against her cheeks.

"What is it?"

Her mouth thins into a line, and she nods over my shoulder. She casts me a worried look and then squeezes my arm. "Don't freekowt."

She sometimes slips into her language when she is worried, and when I don't recognize the word, my senses tingle with alarm. I turn, determined not to "freek," and look.

Our beach is surrounded by rocky, high cliffs. High up a distant one, there are things moving. At first I think they are metlak, the lanky, hairy creatures of the mountains. But this is not their territory, and as I watch them move, my heart fills with dread. One is carrying a spear, and I can see horns on another. There are many of them.

The bad ones.

They've found us.

Harlow

The sight of the people on the ridge fills me with more annoyance than worry. Why do they have to show up now? I don't want company. I'm pregnant, cranky, swollen, and the last thing I want is the careful nest we've been building for so long interrupted by unexpected visitors.

Rukh, however, reacts very differently than I do.

The breath hisses out of his throat and he grabs my hand. He hauls me forward, dropping spear and clam on the sand, forgotten, and races toward our cave. I put a hand to my belly and try to follow after him, but running with a baby belly? Not that easy. I take a few steps and then pull my hand from his, wheezing. My lower back feels like it's on fire and that horrible cramp on the right side of my abdomen is returning. "Rukh, wait," I gasp. "I can't run—"

Instead of calming down, he grabs me and lifts me into his arms, and continues to race toward the cave as if the beach were on fire.

I cling to his neck, worried he's going to drop me. I want to reason with him, but I've seen this wild look in his eyes once before. When he sees the other aliens, there is no reasoning with him. He loses control.

Thank goodness we make it back to the cave in one piece. I release the breath I'm holding as he gently sets me down on the floor onto my feet. Rukh touches my cheek. "Stay here, Har-loh. If the bad ones come, hide."

The "bad ones" is his name for the tribe. I have no idea why they're bad in his eyes. He has memories of his father telling him to avoid them, to hide from them, because they were "bad," and that is the only knowledge he has of them. Other than me, and worrying they're going to take me away. My own experience with them was good, but then I remember Aehako, Haeden, and Kira, all dead. They won't like to see me alive after all this time and with their tribemates dead. It worries me.

But I don't want Rukh going after them, either. There's more of them than us. I hold on to his arm to try and stop him. "Wait. Where are you going?"

"I go try lead away from you. Will trick. Hide path to cave." He pulls his bone knife from the sheath on the wall and looks around for his spear, except it's still on the beach. I move forward and give him mine, because the thought of him leaving with little to defend himself scares me more than being here without a weapon.

They're not our enemies, I remind myself. But a year has passed, and a lot can happen in a year. My belly and Rukh's language skills are a testament to that.

He gazes down at me, and there's such softness and love in his eyes that my lower lip trembles.

Everything's going to change after this moment. We've been so happy . . . I'm afraid it's going to be ruined.

"Don't cry, *beebee*," he says, breaking into English in an imitation of my words.

"Please be careful." I want to grab handfuls of his hair and hold him back, but I can't. The tribe is here, and they must be here for a reason. "Just . . . whatever you do, stay calm, okay? Listen to what they say and don't attack first. Promise me."

He nods and gives me a quick, fierce kiss. "I will be as the shadows. They will not see me."

"Mmm." I'm not sure I believe that, but I trust him, and I feel better when he moves to one of the storage baskets I have neatly lining our cave and pulls out his white fur cloak. It will hide him amongst the snow like camouflage.

Then he's gone, heading out the cave entrance, and I fight the urge to panic. Instead, I stay busy. I put out the fire (lest the tendrils of smoke bring curious wanderers), straighten the cave, sharpen my small knife, eat a bit of meat, rub my belly, and wait.

The waiting seems endless.

After what feels like forever, I head to the front of the cave, peeking out. I scan the snow-capped hills in the distance for a flash of blue skin or dark hair, but I don't see him. That's both good and bad. I pace at the mouth of the cave, worried.

What if they find him and he attacks them? What if something bad happens?

What if my Rukh doesn't come back?

Hot terror clenches through me and my hands grip my belly. The baby kicks, hard, as if sensing my worry.

They won't kill him. They're not murderers. Vektal and his people are kind.

But Rukh is an unknown warrior, and he wants to defend me. I worry my lower lip with my teeth, my mind spiraling through all the things that can go wrong. I'm so focused on my thoughts that I'm not paying as much attention as I should be. I'm staring at the ground, and when a shadow moves, it catches my attention. I look up, but the ridge nearby is empty.

Goose bumps prickle my skin. I rub my arms and head deeper into my cave, remembering Rukh's words. I need to hide if someone comes. I stare helplessly at our comfortable cave. There's clearly a firepit, and a nest of furs. My handwoven baskets made from dried sea-reeds are neatly placed along the walls. It's going to be obvious that someone lives here.

But I don't want to be found. I don't want to be found and blamed for the deaths of three others.

More than anything, I don't want to be taken from my mate. I love Rukh and I'm happy with him. I don't care that I have to brush my teeth with a hard twig or my panties are made from leather instead of silk. I love my man and I don't want to leave him. So I head back, deeper into the cave than I normally go. There's a hiding spot back here that Rukh and I have commented on before, a sliver of jutting rock that's big enough to conceal someone through optical illusion, as long as the viewer stays a few feet away. I slide into the spot, wincing as the jagged rocks tear at my skin.

And then I sigh and give up, because my belly is sticking out a lot farther than the wall can conceal. This nook would have been useful about eight months and twenty pounds ago. Grimacing, I pull myself back out, and then rub my back again. It hurts worse than usual today. Stress, likely.

"Hello?" a voice—high and female and human—calls out.

It's coming from the front of the cave. "Harlow? Are you in here?"

I straighten in surprise, my hand protectively going to my stomach. That sounds like Liz. I recognize her Oklahoma twang. How did she find me? Then I think of the shadow on the ridge. Of course. I'm so stupid. She must have seen me come in.

No sense in hiding now, is there? I cautiously move forward into the main room of the cave.

It's Liz, all right, and she looks incredible. Beautiful. Not-Hoth obviously agrees with her. Her cheeks are ruddy and pink, her face rounded and full. Her blonde hair cascades over her shoulders, pulled back from her face by a few decorative braids. She wears a long dress made of ornately dyed leather that makes my own patchwork tunic look downright shameful. A furry hood is pushed off her face and frames her shoulders. She looks like a Viking princess, right down to the bow slung over her shoulder. And she's peering around my cave with surprise.

I say nothing, waiting for her to notice me. It takes a moment, as she's assessing my cave, and then she turns and her gaze lands on me.

Instead of the mistrust I expect, her eyes light up and she flings her arms wide, rushing forward to hug me. "Oh my God! It *is* you! Harlow! Holy shitballs, girl. We thought you were dead!"

I hug her back, and for some reason, I start to cry. It's part nerves, part relief, part loneliness. I didn't realize until now how good it is to see another human. I love and adore Rukh, but seeing another woman takes away some of the anxiety of being out here alone.

She squeals and hops up and down as she hugs me, and then

pulls back when she realizes my belly's poking into her. "Ohmi-god! Look at you!" Her gaze flicks from my belly to my face with shock. "You're fucking pregnant!"

"I am," I say, wiping away some of my tears. "What are you doing here?"

"Me?" she sputters. "Girl, what are *you* doing here, you bitch? We thought you were dead!"

I laugh. Liz is so crass but she's open and loving. I've missed her. I squeeze her hand. "It's a long story."

"I'll say," she agrees, and pats my distended belly. "You look ready to pop. I'm not carrying quite the same."

I digest her confusing words for a moment, and then realize that Liz's belly is gently rounded under her flowing, colorful leather tunic. Of course she's pregnant, too. She and Raahosh were mated for only a short time before Rukh stole me from the ship. It's like I've forgotten everything.

I bet there are a lot of pregnant girls back at the tribal caves now. I bite my lip, hating the wistful envy that rises in me. I love Rukh and I want to stay here, but . . . the thought of having girlfriends again? Girlfriends who are going through the same scary, unknown pregnancy I am? It fills me with longing. "Pregnancy is hard," I say with a smile and rub my lower back again.

Her brows go down, as if she wants to disagree with me. Then, she takes me by the elbow and steers me toward one of the plump leather pillows I've made. "Here. Why don't you sit down? You look like hell, girl."

"Gee, thanks," I say dryly. Good ol' Liz. But I do want to sit, so I let her steer me toward one of the stuffed pillows. She grabs another and pulls it close, then flops down. Her eyes light up. "Oh wow. Why haven't I thought about freaking pillows in the last year? This thing is awesome!" She wiggles her butt on it.

"Raahosh tried to make me a hammock but I fell out of it and that was the end of that."

I smile at her. "So you and Raahosh are well?"

"If by 'well,' you mean 'shagging like bunnies' and me arguing when he tries to mansplain at me about how to hunt, and then me proving to him I'm just as capable as he is without a pair of balls? And then make-up sex and cuddling? Yup, we're great." She looks cheerful at the thought. "We're supposed to be in at least a two-year exile, but everyone's pregnancies are moving along a lot faster than Maylak thought, so I imagine we'll have to stay home this winter. Last one was cold as the tits on a snowman." She mock shivers and then looks around my cave again. "This place is real nice, though. Weather's a lot milder."

I nod. "There're these scorpion things on the beach that look ugly as hell but they taste like lobster."

She gasps and pretends to wipe her chin. "My mouth is watering, seriously. We totally have to get some of those."

I grin and brace my hands on my aching lower back. "Yeah, I like to tell—" I pause, not sure I want to say Rukh's name to Liz. "Um."

She tilts her head, waiting for me to continue.

I hesitate. I don't know what to do. Confess what happened? It feels disloyal to Rukh. Sure, he clubbed me over the head and stole me away when I was sent out to get help, thus ensuring the deaths of three others, but . . . he didn't know what to do. He's grown up wild. I don't hold that against him, and I worry others will.

So I give Liz a thin smile. "I look like hell, huh?"

She gives me an uneasy look and clasps her hands in her lap. "You just look really tired. And really pregnant. Like, more than me." She gazes down at my belly and her hand goes to her own stomach. "I'm glad I found you," she says. "You can come home and get checked out by the healer when we get back."

I hesitate again.

"Oh, come on," Liz says with a groan. "I know you didn't get yourself pregnant. A guy's obviously here with you. And judging from the lack of a plasma TV and sofa, I'm guessing that he's an alien, right? Who is it?" She leans forward. "One of the hunters, right? I can't believe some bastard squirreled you away and hasn't said a thing to anyone. That is seriously not right, keeping you here."

I pull back, a bit alarmed by the venom in her voice. "It's not one of the tribe."

She sits up and frowns. "It's not? Is he not *sa-khui*?"

Oh jeez, now I'm really painting myself into a corner. "I didn't say that."

She scoots forward again. "Harlow, I'm not the enemy here. What's going on? Why are you being so weird?"

I lick my dry lips, worried. My side chooses that moment to send a sharp pain across my belly and I bite back a wince. "It's been a year, Liz. I just need some time to adjust to things."

Her eyes widen. "This is Stockholm syndrome, isn't it? I don't want you to worry, okay? I'll keep you safe from him."

"Wait, what? No, that's not how things are at all." She reaches for my hands, but I pull away from her and get to my feet. My side is aching painfully and I rub it as I pace. "I'm happy here. I love . . . my guy. I don't want to go back to the tribal caves, okay?"

"I guess I don't understand," Liz says slowly. "Did you run away? Is that what happened when you abandoned Aehako and Haeden and Kira?"

Abandoned. God, I guess I did, didn't I? Because I was so

dazed and caught up with my own mess that I never went back to even bury the bodies. "They were dead, Liz. There was nothing I could do."

Silence. Then, "Whatchoo talkin' bout, Willis?"

I snort-giggle at the saying. It reminds me of home and another wave of longing spirals through me, followed by another ache in my belly. I rub it, trying to massage away the hurt. "It's not funny, Liz. I didn't leave them of my own volition, but I didn't abandon them." I swallow hard. "I hate that I cost them their lives. I think about it all the time."

"Uh, I hate to break up your martyr-trip and all, but no one's dead." Her dry voice cuts through me like a knife.

I turn so fast I get dizzy. "What?"

Liz's brows are drawn together, her expressive face confused. "Yeah, I don't know where you got the idea that everyone was dead? But Aehako and Haeden are fine. I mean, Aehako's great, and Haeden's his usual pissy self, so I guess that qualifies as 'fine.'"

I don't know what to think. I want to laugh with relief, but I have too many questions. "Kira—the spaceship—"

"Oh, yeah." Liz gets to her feet, ungainly for once, and as she moves, I see the swell of her belly through her clothing. "Kira went all badass on them. Crashed the damn thing into the side of a mountain and got out in an escape pod. Who knew that Eeyore had it in her, eh?" She looks proud.

"I don't understand."

Liz, always happy to have an opening to talk, takes the opportunity to chatter my ear off, telling me all about what happened after I was kidnapped by Rukh. Apparently somber Kira's dashing rescue is a popular story around fires, and she embellishes the tale, going on about how Kira saved the day and took down the bad guys by her lonesome. I'm impressed, but more than anything, I'm relieved.

I'm not the cause of three deaths. No one in the tribe hates me.

I . . . can go back if I need to. For some reason that fills me with relief. I've hated the thought of being on the run, hiding from the world as if everyone will kill me if they see me. Knowing I still have friends out there? It's a wonderful feeling.

I pace slowly as she finishes the story. I can't get over it. Not dead. None of them. Aehako and Kira are apparently expecting a child, too. They must have resonated after I was gone.

"Now," Liz says, moving to my side. She steers me toward the cushions again. "Why don't you fill me in on you? What happened to you? From what Aehako said, he sent you out to get poles for a travois and you never came back. They thought a wild animal got you or something. I mean, clearly something got you." She pats my belly. "But there are some major holes in this story that need filling in, and I'm not leaving until I get answers."

"Isn't someone going to come looking for you?" I ask.

"Oh, I told Raahosh I had to pee. Pregnant ladies always have to pee." She waves a hand in the air. "He'll think I got lost and lecture me about following tracks and blah, blah." A fond smile curves her mouth. "I'll let him talk for a bit just to make him feel better, of course. Now tell me about you."

"Me?" All this news must be getting to me. I feel weak and dizzy, and it's difficult to concentrate.

"Yeah, how'd you end up on the beach? We're a long way from the mountains, if you hadn't noticed."

"Why are you guys here?" I can't help but ask.

"People are bored after the long winter and wanted a big hunt. Plus, salt stores are low, so someone suggested heading to the ocean, and we got together a party of hunters. It's a salt hunt," she teases. "I told Raahosh if I don't have salt on my morning root-potatoes, heads are gonna roll."

I try to chuckle, but nothing comes out. I'm still overwhelmed.

"Did you come here for the salt?" she leads gently. "You and your mate?" She frowns at me and her movement turns into a blur out of the corner of my eye. "Harlow? You okay, girl? You just got really pale."

"Just a little dizzy." Which is weird, considering I'm sitting. But I am dizzy. I'm in a cold sweat, and nausea is creeping up my throat.

"No touch her!" Rukh's snarled voice breaks through my muddied thoughts.

My head jerks up and I stare as my gorgeous, wild mate storms into our cave, holding a spear aimed for Liz.

"You must be the mister," Liz says as he comes in. And then she gasps when he nears. "Holy fucking shit."

What? I want to ask, but I press my fingers to my mouth. I feel . . . awful. Something's wrong. The baby kicks hard, and this time it doesn't make me feel happy. It worries me. Blackness creeps in on the edges of my vision.

"No touch my *mate*," Rukh snarls, and the spear gets closer, edges under Liz's chin. "Har-loh, come to me."

I try to get up, but Liz jerks me back down.

"She's sick, you jerk. Look at her. Does she look well to you?"

"I'm okay," I breathe, but the blackness creeps in heavier, and I'm really, really not okay. My head suddenly feels like it weighs a million pounds and I wobble on the cushion I'm seated on. It's only Liz's supporting arms that keep me from falling backward.

Then Rukh's there, and he touches my face. I feel clammy but sweaty at the same time, and the nausea in the back of my throat won't go away. His face swims into my blurry vision, and he looks so handsome and so worried that it makes me want to cry. I want to comfort him, but I just feel . . . awful.

"I'm fine," I tell him again, but his tormented expression is the last thing I see before the world blacks out.

Rukh

My heart thumps in my chest, frightened like a stalked quilled beast. Har-loh is limp in my arms, unconscious. Her skin is covered with a sheen of sweat, like she is hot, but her hands and her cheeks are cold.

Another human scurries around my cave, a female. I want to snarl at her to leave, to go back to the bad ones, but she's got a bladder of water and she dampens a square of leather and brushes it over Har-loh's face. She looks upset, too. She wants to help.

It's only because of that I let her stay.

My Har-loh is sick. I hold her close, stroking her jaw and neck, waiting for her to wake up. At her side, the female dabs the wet square on her cheek.

"Has she done this before?" the female asks.

I want to snarl at her to go away, but I don't know what to do to help. Maybe she does. So I shake my head in answer.

"Has she had problems with the baby? Spotting? Nausea?"

I don't know some of these words and bare my teeth, holding her closer. "She is fine."

"*Bullshit*." She doesn't stop to explain the word. "Look at her face. Her eyes are like hollows. She looks tired and even I can tell she's hurting. She rubs her side constantly."

"She is carrying a kit," I snarl.

"So am I! And I'm not sick like her. Something is *wrong*." The female all but yells at me. She gestures at her belly and I see a rounded bump there for the first time. She's right—her face doesn't have the same exhausted look that my Har-loh's does.

I cradle Har-loh closer to me, worried. She . . . is pale. And she has difficulty waking some mornings. I've noticed that she struggles, but I don't know how to fix it. It concerns me that this female sees it right away. Have I been turning a blind eye to my mate because I am afraid of what I will see? Of losing her?

I hold her closer, agonizing. I will die if I lose her. She is the only thing worth living for. Now that I have Har-loh, I can't go back to the loneliness of before. I cannot bear the thought of a day without her smile, her touch, her scent. Her small, cold hands on my skin as I wake up.

"What do I do?" The words escape me before I can bite them back.

The female purses her lips, and for a moment she looks so strangely similar to Har-loh that it fills me with longing. I stroke my mate's sweaty face again. "She needs to come back to the tribe."

Leave me? Leave here and go with the bad ones? I bare my teeth at the female for suggesting it. "No!"

"You think it's safe to be out here in the middle of nowhere with her?" The small female smacks my arm as if trying to beat her words into me. "What are you going to do if the baby comes early? What are you going to do if she starts bleeding and doesn't stop? I don't know if you've noticed, but there's not a lot of sa-khui and human interbreeding going on around here, buddy. This shit is all new and we don't know what's going to happen."

I stroke Har-loh's soft cheek. We are different peoples. I didn't think that it could hurt my mate, but now my heart clenches with worry. Survival instinct wars with the need to keep Har-loh safe. All my life, I have been warned never to approach the bad ones. Now this small female that has the same flat features as Har-loh is telling me I need to take her to their den?

I cannot comprehend the thought.

The woman's voice gentles after a moment. "Who are you, anyhow? Where are your people?"

"I have no people."

"You had to come from somewhere." She tilts her head and studies me. "Do you have a brother? Because you look really familiar to me."

I say nothing, because she is asking too many questions. Instead, I snatch the cloth from her hand and press it to Har-loh's face. "Bring your healer here," I tell the female after a moment. I will endure the presence of a healer if it means Har-loh will be taken care of, but no one else.

The female makes an exasperated sound. "The healer isn't here. She's back home with the others because there are several pregnant women and not all of them are having an easy time."

There are others in their tribe that might be suffering like my Har-loh? They would know what to do? I look up at her, torn.

She holds a flat, five-fingered hand in the air. "Okay. I can tell you're not big into trust. Can I bring someone down here? My mate?"

I crouch over Har-loh defensively and reach for my knife. "No one come!" I loathe the thought of even one of the bad ones finding our cave home. Bad enough that this female knows. We will have to leave if she says anything. We must avoid the bad ones—

Except the bad ones have a healer.

I'm torn.

"My mate will be worried over me like you are over Harlow," she says, casting a concerned glance down at my unconscious woman again. "Please. Let me bring him, and I think if you talk to him, you'll feel more comfortable."

"I not trust bad ones," I grit out.

"Bad ones?" She sounds taken aback. "O-kay. That's unexpected. I promise he's not bad, though. He . . . actually reminds me a lot of you." Her expression turns up in a smile. "I will tell him no weapons, all right?"

I hesitate, but Har-loh moans and stirs in my arms at that moment. If these people know how to get Har-loh to a healer, I must do whatever it takes to protect my woman and the kit she carries.

My mind flashes with memories of my father, pointing at distant hunters. *You must always avoid the bad ones, my son. Do not trust. Do not approach them.*

But Har-loh's people live with them. And Har-loh is good and kind. And this human seems to want to help.

"One only," I say, my voice flat with distrust. "No weapon."

She nods and gets to her feet, then slips out of the cave.

I don't trust her, but what choice do I have?

A few moments after the female leaves, Har-loh's eyes flutter open and she focuses on my face, dazed. "Rukh?"

"I am here," I murmur, my voice husky with worry. I gently caress her face. "Are you sick, my Har-loh?"

"No, I'm fine," she says, but her voice sounds shaky. She pushes against my arms, but I refuse to let go of her. "I just got dizzy for a moment."

"The other female says the kit is making you sick."

Her reddish brows furrow together. "Liz?"

I nod. "Do you hurt right now?"

Her hands smooth over her belly, and she licks her dry lips, hesitating. That strikes worry into my heart. Leezh is not wrong. "My back hurts, of course, and my side aches all the time. But these are normal things, aren't they?"

"I not know. She go get mate. Want to talk to me."

"Raahosh?" Again, Har-loh's brow furrows. "About me? I promise I'm fine."

"You are not." I help her sit up and give her a waterskin to drink. I notice her hand trembles as she does, and it's like a spear through my guts. Leezh's accusing words run through my mind, over and over again. *You think it's safe to be out here?*

I moved Har-loh here because I knew no one came here. I knew, and I took her away from the healer that could make her well. Guilt threatens to swallow me.

Her small hands flutter over my arm. "Rukh . . . you won't hurt them, will you? I know you don't like . . . strangers."

"You not wish me harm the bad ones?"

For a moment, Har-loh looks unhappy. Troubled. "I love our life here. You know that. But the others . . . some of them are my friends. I don't want them hurt."

I say nothing.

"Liz is just looking out for me," Har-loh continues in a soft

voice between sips of water. "I thought . . . well, it's not important."

"Say it."

She looks troubled. "One reason why I never went back to
them is because I thought they blamed me for the deaths of three
others. Liz tells me they are alive. No one hates me."

The sick feeling in my gut returns. So she came with me because she felt she had no other choice? It never occurred to me
until now to question why Har-loh did not attempt to run away
again. I foolishly thought it was because we were mates, that she
felt the same way about me as I do her. Maybe I have imagined
this all along.

Maybe Har-loh wants to return to the bad ones. If she does,
what will I do?

"Could you get me something to eat?" Har-loh asks, putting a
hand to her forehead. "Maybe that will help with the dizziness."

My unhappiness is immediately pushed aside. My mate needs
me. It doesn't matter what I want. "Stay here," I tell her, and
move to one of the baskets of dried, salted meat. I choose a few
strips of the blandest flavor, the one she has on mornings when
her stomach is troubled, and bring them back to her. I watch as
she eats and make sure she drinks plenty of water. When she is
done, I pick her up and carry her—protesting—to our nest of
furs so she can lie down and relax comfortably.

I realize for the first time that we can't stay here. Not if Har-
loh is sick. I cannot imagine how things will be with a kit if
Har-loh is not well. I can take care of her, but I do not know
how to take care of a kit. The knot in my stomach increases.

We must go back.

Harlow

I'm worried about Rukh. He's unnaturally quiet, and I know he has to have questions. He says nothing, though, simply hovers nearby and feeds me small bits of dried meat and makes sure I have plenty of water in my skin. I'm tired and just want to take a nap, but Liz and her mate are coming, and I worry how Rukh is going to react. I can tell he's on edge.

I pat the side of the bed and invite him to come lie down with me. I hate how this day is turning out. Finding out that Kira and the others are alive is wonderful, but weirdly enough, I'm a little resentful that Liz and the hunting party have shown up and upended my life. I like it here with Rukh. I like our little nest beside the ocean.

The baby kicks in my stomach, as if agreeing.

"Hellooo," Liz calls at the entrance of the cave, and Rukh immediately jumps to his feet. All thought of lying down with me is forgotten in the presence of invaders. His long bone knife comes out, the blade wicked-looking as he clenches the handle tight.

My heart thumps loudly. Rukh moves in front of me, shielding me, and even as he does, I'm filled with love for the big guy. My khui starts purring, and I hear his respond. For some reason, it comforts me. Whatever else happens, we have each other.

Liz tiptoes in and I notice her bow is gone. Behind her is a larger shadow, and the way the man stalks in . . . for a moment, it reminds me of Rukh. Then I see the one twisted horn remaining, the stub of the other, and the scars on Raahosh's face as he comes into view. He's taller than Rukh, and leaner, but for a moment, there's a striking resemblance between the two.

I'm not the only one that sees it. The cave falls silent as the two men stare at each other.

Raahosh's eyes narrow and his gaze flicks from me to Rukh. "Who are you? Why do you have Har-loh?"

"Har-loh is mine," Rukh says, a rough edge in his voice. I see his hand tighten on the knife and he moves closer to me, trying to block me out of Raahosh's sight. I think he's going to pounce, he's practically vibrating with tension. Then a moment later, he blurts out, "You look like Father."

"So do you." Raahosh's nostrils flare and his body tenses. "My younger brother was Maarukh. Is that your name? Are you Vaashan's son?"

I gasp. Maarukh? *Rukh*?

Liz gasps, too. "Oh shit," she breathes and her gaze meets mine. "I thought you guys looked similar."

But neither man is moving. They both look stiff and uncomfortable. After a moment, Raahosh speaks. "My father left me with the tribe after you were born." His hand goes to his face and touches his scars in memory. "I went back to look for him after many seasons, when I was old enough to join the ranks of hunters, and his cave was destroyed. There was no sign of life. I assumed both you and he were dead. This is a difficult land for a small kit and a man alone."

Rukh is silent. I touch his leg in a caress, worried about how he is handling this. Overnight, our world is turned over, and now to find he has a brother? This has to be difficult.

"You have a healer?" Rukh's abrupt words startle me. There is no mention of family.

"Not with us." Raahosh's eyes narrow again, and he looks ready to scowl at Rukh. "She does not leave the caves. There are too many that require her assistance."

"Then we take Har-loh to her. We leave now."

My eyes widen and I stare up at Rukh in surprise. "We what?"

He turns back to me and his hand goes to my head, caressing my hair. "You are my mate. We go to see the healer."

"I'm fine," I protest, ignoring Liz's snort.

"You are not fine," Rukh says firmly. "We will go."

Rukh

I do not trust any of this. I am full of suspicion despite the fact that my father has another kit living, and the man looks like a scarred version of him. My father mentioned him often, though I was too young to picture him. But there is no doubt in my mind that Raahosh is of my father. I imagine I look similar in his eyes. Seeing him makes me long for my father, long dead, but it is not the sight of him that made up my mind.

It was Har-loh's soft hand on my leg, a reminder that she is not well.

I will give up everything for my mate and my kit. It no longer matters what I want. All that matters is Har-loh. So I will swallow my worry and take her back to the caves, so the healer can ease the hurts from her belly and make her feel better.

And then we will return here, to our home, and raise our kit alone.

I do not want to stay with the bad ones. That has not changed.

Off to the side, Raahosh argues with his mouthy human

mate. They are arguing over when to travel, and who will go back. I fill my worn shoulder sack with dried meat and other small comforts, even as Har-loh folds furs quietly in our nest. I won't let her get up so she does what she can within reach. All the while, the other two squabble and I cannot tell if they are truly angry at each other, or if this is like when Har-loh teases me with words and then reaches for my cock. I suspect they like to argue about everything, even in the furs.

"We can all go back," Leezh says again. "Safety in numbers. We all have to go back at some point, right? And the others are going to want to meet Maarukh and see Harlow."

The man called Raahosh—my brother—crosses his arms over his chest and scowls down at his mate. "She is ill. We need to travel fast, and the others still wish to hunt and collect salt for cooking. There is still much to do."

She makes a face. No one has asked me if I wish to travel with the entire hunting party. I do not. "They can come back some other time," Leezh retorts. "No one is going to die if they don't have salt on their food. Most everyone's eating raw at this point anyhow. Harlow is more important."

"And a smaller party will move faster."

"Not if we have a travois!"

I do not know what a trah-voy is. I just want them to cease talking, both of them. I want them out of my cave. I glare at both of them, but they seem oblivious to my expression, caught up in their argument. It is definitely sexual. Leezh's chest is panting and she looks as if she's ready to smile despite her sharp words. "I will carry my mate," I say, interrupting their love-talk. "I no want travel with all. Raahosh is right. We go fast with small group." The thought of walking with many of the bad ones makes my stomach roil.

"I agree," Har-loh says, adding her voice. "Let the others stay and hunt. We can travel back. And I can walk, I promise."

I turn to glare at my mate. "I will carry you."

She sticks her tongue out at me.

"Fine," Leezh says, and crosses her arms over her chest. It makes her own rounded stomach stick out. "But we need to talk with the others. They will be wondering where we have gone."

Raahosh grunts and looks out at the skies. "It will be dark soon. We will meet with the others and explain to them we are splitting off. We will return here in the morning to travel. Is that acceptable to you?" His gaze moves to me.

I nod. He's right. As much as I want to leave right now, it is smarter to wait until the morning. Har-loh can rest tonight.

Eventually Leezh and Raahosh prepare to depart, Leezh looking hesitant, as if she wants to fuss over my mate. I won't let her stay, though. That is my job. Her mate eventually herds her away and then Har-loh and I are alone again. Some of the tension in my body eases and it feels as if a weight has been lifted from my shoulders.

"So we're really leaving?" Har-loh's voice breaks through the silence of the cave. It feels unnaturally quiet now.

I move to my beloved mate and kneel next to her. I study her face, now so dear to me that I cannot imagine being without her, even for a moment. "Leezh is right. You are not well. I want healer to help you. If it means we travel with the bad ones, then we will."

"You don't want to go."

I am silent. It's not a matter of wanting to go or not. I will not allow anything to risk her.

Her eyes fill with tears. "I don't want to go. I like our life here."

I cannot stand the sight of her crying. It makes me feel almost as helpless and frightened as when she was unconscious earlier. I move closer, pulling her into my arms to comfort her.

"I'm scared," she admits, wrapping her arms around me. "I feel like everything's changing and I like it the way it is."

I stroke her soft orange-red hair. "I know." But I won't change my mind. I'm too aware of her faint earlier, her clammy skin and pale face. Leezh's radiant health only makes it worse. I see how my Har-loh should feel and does not. I want to fix that for her.

"Promise me we won't change?" She burrows her face against my neck. "No matter what?"

"I will tear khui from my chest before I leave you," I tell her. "We are together. Always."

She lifts her head and parts her lips in the way that tells me she wants to kiss. I hold her gently against me and brush my mouth over hers. Tonight is our last night alone. I want to claim her as my mate, but not if she's feeling unwell. I pull back, uncertain.

Har-loh grabs me by a handful of my hair. "I'm not broken, Rukh. At least, no more than last night. I want to make love to you. Here, in our cave." Her voice catches. "In our home."

I will be careful with her. I nod and ease her gently back into the nest of furs. We will have to leave some of these behind, and this might be the last night with a comfortable bed like Har-loh likes it. I resolve to add a few of the leather puffs to my shoulder bag for her comfort—

She taps my cheek. "You're thinking about tomorrow."

"I am," I admit, and nuzzle her neck.

"Are you worried about the others?"

I'm not. I worry about Har-loh. The others don't matter. So

I shake my head and lick the base of her throat, in the sensitive spot that always makes her shiver. She moans and presses against me, and we both work on pulling the laces of her tunic free for the next moment. She undresses and then I do, and then we are naked together. I pull a fur over us so Har-loh doesn't get cold. I want to cover her body with mine, but her big belly prevents that. I lie beside her instead, caressing her. My mate loves for her soft skin to be petted, and I stroke my knuckles in the valley of her teats and down an arm.

She shivers and puts her hand on my cock, her thumb stroking along the underside of my spur. The breath hisses out of my throat at the small touch, and I grip her hand in mine, roughly stroking into the tight grip. It feels achingly good, but I don't want to spend there. After a few more tugs, I take her hand in mine and link our fingers together. I push her arm back into the blankets, pinning her there, and claim her mouth. Her tongue strokes against mine, greedy for more.

My Har-loh. My mate. I never get tired of touching her.

We kiss, tongues playing, and my hand caresses her sensitive breast. Har-loh sighs and arches up on the furs, pressing her nipple against me. I break the kiss and move down, trailing the tip of my tongue across her chest and then down to one teat. They're bigger now that the kit is swelling inside her, and I love how full her body is getting. I carefully lick one tip, then nuzzle it. The mewing sound she makes in reaction makes my cock jerk, and I tongue her breasts over and over, my hands roaming her soft skin.

"I love you, Rukh," she breathes. "So much."

"My mate," I say softly. "My woman." I kiss the rounded mound of her belly, and the little bump of her navel that now protrudes outward. Then I move farther down, to her thighs and her cunt. Her legs spread open eagerly, and I can see she's wet with anticipation for my mouth. She moans when I lick her folds, her body shifting on the blankets. She is *mine*. The thought is fierce in my head as I lick her clit the way she likes, and her hands go to my horns, holding me there.

I attack her with my mouth, using everything I have to bring her pleasure. My tongue flicks her clit, my fingers go deep in her cunt, and I stroke her as I work her with my mouth. She moans and wriggles on the furs, but I won't stop until she comes.

Her moans turn into soft, keening little cries, and her hips push against my face. I move my fingers faster, determined. A moment later, she chokes out my name and her fluids drench my tongue. Her body shudders with pleasure and my cock aches and aches.

But I lick her until she pushes my face away. Instead of asking her to get on her hands and knees, I lie next to my panting, sated mate and hold her against me. I wrap my arms around her, mindful of her fragility.

"What about you?" she asks, breathless. She reaches for my cock again.

"Shh," I tell her, and push her hand away. "Let me hold you. You are tired."

She protests a little, but I can hear the exhaustion in her voice. I ignore the needs of my own flesh and hold her closer, and she's content to lie in my arms. Her head rests on my chest and her fingers lightly stroke my arm.

I imagine them stroking my cock the same way and it takes everything I have not to come right then and there.

"The kit is dancing in my stomach," she says after a moment. "Want to feel?"

I move my head down to her belly and lightly press a hand

against one side, my ear and cheek on the other. There is movement in her stomach, though I'm not entirely sure it sounds like much. Then, something pushes against my face and I feel her entire belly ripple.

She giggles as I jerk back and mock-shields her face with her hands. "You nearly got me with a horn there."

"It just . . . startled me." I move down to her belly again, my mind full of wonder. My kit is in there, bouncing and lively. The moment I put my ear back to her stomach, it moves again, and I imagine a smaller version of myself, tail flicking with irritation at being trapped in such a small space.

I . . . have never seen a kit. I try to picture it, but I cannot imagine how the horns do not tear her belly up. Maybe it is like my soft mate and has no horns. I picture a little girl kit then, with freckles and reddish hair, a smaller version of my mate.

I like that thought.

Har-loh's hand plays with my hair, smoothing it back. "I'm still worried, you know."

I caress her belly. "The healer will take care of you."

Her chuckle is soft and she gives my hair a tug. "I'm not worried about that. I'm worried about you and me."

I lift my head then, surprised. I take her hand in mine and kiss the palm. "You and I are for always, Har-loh. There is no need to worry."

Her smile is soft and sweet. "It's going to be a lot for you to take in. Just promise me you'll be open-minded about everything. That you won't attack anyone."

"I will not attack them if they are helping you."

She raises an eyebrow. "You looked ready to attack Raahosh earlier."

Raahosh. The one that looks like my father. I grow silent at the reminder. I have a sibling. "I did not know what to think," I admit.

"It was a lot," she says softly, and pats the blankets, indicating she wants me to lie down with her again. I do so gladly and she moves into my arms. "So your name . . . Maarukh?"

"I do not recall." I stroke her back as she tucks herself under my shoulder. "My only memories are of my father calling me Rukh."

"But it is your name. Just part of it."

I grunt agreement.

"Are you pleased to have a brother?"

"I do not know."

"It's a lot of change for one day," she says again. "Earlier today, it was just you and me and the beach. Now we're leaving and everything is changing."

It's obvious I'm not the only one worried. I hold her close to me.

Rukh

Har-loh sleeps heavily through the night, and the next morning, she looks more tired than usual. She rubs her side when she thinks I am not looking, and swears she is fine.

This only reinforces my desire to take her to see the healer. It is the right thing to do. Before, I was angry that the bad ones showed up on our beach. Now, I am grateful. It feels strange.

As Har-loh nibbles on a bit of dried meat and sips water, I pack up the last of the things we will need for our journey. More meat, more waterskins. More furs for Har-loh, and the puffs she likes. Her tunics, the soft wraps she's made for the kit, and everything I can think to carry. By the time Leezh and Raahosh show up, my pack is bulging.

But I will not leave behind anything that my mate might need.

In the morning light, Raahosh looks even more like my memories of my father. When he turns to the side and his scars are hidden, his profile looks just like Vaashan. I'm hit with a bolt of remembered loneliness so strong it staggers me. My father has been gone a long, long time and yet I still miss him. Perhaps I will always miss him.

Does Raahosh feel the same? Does he remember him like I do?

As I watch, Leezh settles in next to Har-loh and eats her own food, chatting. I study my brother, then set my pack down. "Come."

He glares at me, his own pack on his back. "Why?"

"I will show you something." I wave him forward. "Come."

He looks to his mate, clearly uneasy about leaving her. It's a feeling I understand. Leezh, though, waves him away and leans forward to whisper something to Har-loh that brings a small smile to her face. It is good she has a female friend, one that is also with kit. It will relax her. I know she worries. And then I feel shame and guilt that my mate worries and I cannot soothe her.

But Raahosh is waiting for me, and so I push aside my misery. If he is my father's son as he says, he will wish to see his final resting place. With one last look at my beloved mate, I grab a spear and head out. After a moment, the stranger follows me.

We are a silent party as we head down the beach. True to his word, though, no others are nearby. No one stops to talk to us. It is as if we are alone, though I know many bad ones are waiting close by, just over the next set of cliffs.

Then we are before my father's cave. I hesitate for a moment. This feels very personal. As if I am about to expose my entire world to this stranger that I don't know but who shares my face. Thoughts war within me. He is a bad one . . . yet my brother. Would my father not want this? With a heavy sigh, I lay my spear against the cliff wall and crouch low to enter the cave. "Come," I tell Raahosh, my voice harsh. Whether or not he chooses to follow is up to him.

I crawl into the small room and crouch next to the pile of rocks that covers my father's bones. I still remember the day I dragged his dead body here, the long hours it took, the endless trips to collect more rocks because the thought of scavengers tearing at his bones was more than I could bear. I was just a kit myself, then, and completely alone.

The sorrow of that day fills me and I bow my head. *My father.*

I hear a small hiss of breath and look up. Raahosh is there, his long body folded over to crawl into the cave next to me. His scarred face is turned toward me, and he stares at the neat, orderly pile of rocks that is our father's last resting place. His gaze turns to the necklace hanging from the jut of stone, and raw sorrow creases his face.

"That was my mother's," Raahosh says after a moment. "Our mother's. I remember him putting it around his neck after she died."

My heart aches. "I no have memories of her."

"Her name was Daya." There is a rasp in his voice, and he will not look at me. "I have very few memories of her myself, just that her belly was rounded with you when Father took us away. She resonated for him twice. The first time with me, and then five years later, with you." His gaze flicks to me. "She did not love our father."

My brows draw together. "But . . . they resonated." I think of Har-loh, her chest purring under mine. It fills me with such contentment and joy. I cannot imagine anything but.

"She loved another. I remember that very clearly. She did not like Vaashan."

Vaashan. Father's name. Raahosh's words fill me with anger,

but I want to hear more. He knows things of my family that I cannot, and I am hungry for answers. "But I am here."

"No one can deny resonance," Raahosh says flatly. He reaches forward and touches one of the rocks on Father's grave. "Hektar—Vektal's father and then chief—decided that they must have the kit for the sake of the tribe, but that she did not have to live with him. She could return to her heart-mate."

My mouth thins at the thought. No wonder my father hated them so. They kept his mate from him.

"Our father decided that was not a good enough answer for him. He took Mother and I out with him on one of his hunts . . . and then never brought her back. He just took her farther and farther away from the tribe. Not here." He lifts his head. "I would remember the salt smell. But he kept her and hid her. She was not a hunter and did not know the way back to the tribe. I remember many days and nights of her crying. But Father would not change his mind."

My gut feels as if a stone has lodged there.

"Then you were born, and the tension between them seemed to vanish. Mother was content for the first time, I think, since leaving the cave. She loved you. Her tiny Maarukh. I remember her saying it over and over again. It's one of my last memories of her." His gaze swings away, back to her necklace. "*Sa-kohtsk* are difficult to bring down with six hunters. Imagine trying to bring it down with one man, his mate, and a young boy." He shakes his head and rubs his jaw with one hand. "Mother was determined to help, because she knew if we did not get you a khui, you would die. They felled it, but Mother died in the hunt and I was mauled." His hand touches his face, the deep scarring below the broken horn. "I don't remember much after that. Just

Father taking me back to the tribe for healing and leaving me there. I never understood why he did not stay with me." His gaze slides to me. "Now I know. He told me you were dead, but it was a lie. He just didn't want to bring you back to the tribe. With me, he had no choice."

I do not know what to say. There is much anger in Raahosh's voice. I think for a minute, in silence. It is very quiet at Father's rocky bedside. "He carried much hate for them. Always."

Raahosh nods slowly. "And yet he left me with them and protected you. I do not know why this angers me, but it does. You are not to blame."

I am angry, too, and puzzled as to why. I loved my father. I missed him terribly, but after hearing this, I am filled with confusion and resentment for him. He never told me about Raahosh. He never told me that he had to force my mother to stay with him. I no longer know what to think.

"When did he die?" Raahosh's voice is quiet. "I went looking for him many seasons later, but there was nothing left in his old cave."

I am silent for a long moment, trying to picture which cave Raahosh visited. My father had several he passed through from season to season, and I did the same. It's how I avoided the bad ones for so long while on my own. Yet I find his admission that he came hunting for his father satisfying. I like the thought of this man never giving up on his father. It is what I would have done. "I was young. Maybe . . ." I try to think. "Seven seasons. There was a hunt and he was hurt by a snow-cat. The wound did not heal cleanly and he died of fever."

Raahosh's face twists angrily. "Another thing that a healer could have prevented. Did he want to die?"

I have no answer. Now that I know there is a healer, I wonder this myself.

After a time, he speaks again. "You were alone out here?"

I grunt agreement. Alone for a very, very long time. The thought leaves me aching with more vague resentment, and worry when I think about my mate. I would die if she were to leave me. "When I found Har-loh, I had forgotten many things. She has taught me words again. How to work leather. How to do many things."

He nods slowly. "The humans are clever. They are soft and fragile, but their minds . . ." He taps the side of his head, on a scar. "They are like knives. My Leezh can cut with her tongue." But he grins, as if pleased by the thought.

Har-loh has told me the story of how her people got here. I don't know if I believe all of it. It sounds too incredible to be true, but judging by this man's reaction, the humans are new and different to the bad ones, too.

Raahosh stares at our father's rocky grave for a moment longer, then glances over at me. "It is good to have family again."

Are we family? To me, he is still a stranger. Har-loh is the only one I care for. But Raahosh's oddly familiar presence makes me feel less alone. So that is something.

PART FIVE

Harlow

I feel like crying as we leave our beach cave behind. I've been so happy there for the last year, and it feels like home—more so than the tribal caves we're journeying back to. I feel responsible that we're having to make this decision, like my body's betrayal is somehow a choice I made.

If I'm totally honest with myself, a small, worried little part of me wonders if my brain tumor is back. If my khui can't take the stress of holding it at bay and it's returning, and that's why I've been so sick. I don't tell Rukh this, or Liz and Raahosh. It might be nothing, and Rukh would just worry endlessly. My exhaustion and weakness might just be baby related.

But I still worry.

The travel is difficult. Rukh won't let me carry my pack, insisting that it weighs nothing to him. He simply shoulders it and adds it to his own substantial gear. Me? I can barely lift my feet to put on my snowshoes. The thought of walking for three days seems an impossible trial, made even more difficult by Liz's boundless energy. She's been pregnant for longer than me, but she keeps up with the men and even paces ahead at times to investigate tracks (something that makes Raahosh crazy and over-protective). Rukh grips my hand, and with him at my side, I feel less overwhelmed.

Still, it isn't long before my back is sending shooting pains through me, my belly aches, and I can't walk any longer. Judging from the placement of the twin suns in the milky sky, it's not even noon yet.

I've got to do three days of this. Tears of frustration start to course down my cheeks, and I want to plant my feet on the ground and tell them to go on without me. The trail ahead is uneven and hilly, and it'll only get worse because we're going into the mountains instead of leaving them behind.

My steps falter in the snow, and Rukh is immediately there, cupping my elbows. "Are you well?"

"Just tired," I admit. "Can we take a break?"

Liz and Raahosh are ahead of us, and I don't miss the looks they exchange. I don't care. I can't move another step without taking a break. My back feels like one big mass of sore muscles.

"I have better idea," Rukh says. He tosses our packs off his shoulders and onto the ground. Then, he swings me into his arms and cradles me against his chest. The pressure on my back immediately eases as he snuggles me down against him.

"You—you can't carry me the entire way," I protest. He's strong, but I'm a solid girl and I'm carrying a baby. There's no way.

"Can I not? You are my mate," he says in a low voice. "I would do anything for you."

Raahosh moves to Rukh's side and swings our packs onto his back. Rukh adjusts me in his arms, and then we continue. I wrap my arms around Rukh's neck, worried he might lose focus and drop me. But as he steps resolutely through the snow, I relax.

And then I fade into a nap, too tired to stay awake.

The next few days are a blur. My back and stomach feel like raw agony, and I'm so tired and miserable that I don't want to eat. It seems like every time I turn around, someone is forcing another bit of dried meat into my mouth, until I'm gagging on the taste. I can tell Liz and Rukh both are worried about me, but I'm doing the best I can.

Rukh carries me the rest of the first day, and then all of the second day. By the third, I'm sure his arms must be cramping as he carries me in front of him, but he cradles me as gently as ever against his chest. I doze, feeling feverish. The pain in my side is a constant ache, and the baby kicks and pushes against my organs as if trying to rearrange them. One of us is full of energy, at least.

At some point, I fall asleep again, and when I wake up, the world is quiet. So quiet. Soft, warm fingers caress my brow, and another hand is holding mine tightly. It's dark, and I blink because there's no wind on my face. Where are we?

"Be calm," says a woman's soft voice. "I am going to speak to your khui."

Dazed, I realize we've somehow made it back to the tribal caves. It is Maylak the healer speaking, her fingers tracing my brow. How long have I been unconscious? I look around and Rukh is there beside me, his hand gripping mine tightly.

Good, he's here. He hasn't left me. I give him a small smile to let him know I'm just fine. "I must have fallen asleep again. Have I been out long?"

"A day," he says, and his hand flexes on mine. There's a tightness in his voice that tells me of his worry. A full day?

I want to tell him that I'm just fine, but I don't feel fine. I'm so exhausted and worn out. My head throbs and my throat hurts. Actually, all of me hurts. The baby kicks again and a little bit of tension I've been holding inside me releases—whatever happens, the baby is fine. Our baby.

I squeeze Rukh's hand. This can't be easy for him. "I love you."

"You are my heart," he says thickly.

I know I am. I smile at him again, but then Maylak's gentle song begins and I feel a weird excitement in my chest. Not like resonance. It's something else. My body floods with what feels like endorphins and I feel . . . good. Just good. Relaxed. Happy.

"Rest," Maylak says in her gentle voice. Her fingertips smooth over my eyelids, ensuring I close them and obey her. "I will speak to your khui and heal you. But for now? You must rest."

Rest sounds good, despite the fact that I seem to be doing a lot of sleeping lately. "Is it the baby?" I murmur. I have to know before I can relax.

"Your khui will tell me."

"While you're in there checking everything out," I say sleepily, "can you make sure everything's okay . . . up here?" I touch my forehead. "Just in case? Nothing weird going on?"

Her laughter is like a gentle rainfall, which sounds like such a cliché. But it fits. Just hearing it makes me feel soothed and at peace. "I will check everything, I promise."

I nod and squeeze Rukh's hand again, relaxing. "I'll be fine, baby. You'll see."

And then I fall asleep, sinking back into darkness. In my dreams, I'm holding my child. It has Rukh's horns and tail, and my reddish hair and freckles. Poor kid. I can't stop smiling at the thought, though, because the baby is happy and healthy, and when he laughs, he looks just like his daddy . . .

Rukh

The healer hums softly as her fingertips brush over Har-loh's pale skin. She looks calm, happy, and so at ease that some of my tension melts away. I don't let go of my mate's hand, though. As long as I touch her, some of my fear remains at bay. As Har-loh sleeps, I gently rub her knuckles. I want to touch her face, but I don't want to get in the way of the healer as she works.

"Your khui is not familiar to me."

I look up, surprised to hear her speak. Even as her hands glide over Har-loh, doing seemingly nothing at all, there are small changes. Some of the hollows are easing from Har-loh's face, the tension on her brow relaxing.

The healer gives me a gentle smile and puts her hands on Har-loh's belly. "I know the khuis of each and every tribemate, but you do not sing in a familiar pattern to me."

"I am not of your tribe."

She looks surprised to hear that, her hands smoothing over the hard, rounded belly of my mate. "No? But you look like Raahosh."

"We shared a father."

"But you do not claim the tribe?" Her voice is soft and motherly, for all that she could be the same age as me.

"You have nothing I want." My voice is a near snarl.

She ignores the anger in my response, unruffled. "Yet you are here, asking us to heal your mate." Her gaze flicks to me. "I do not judge your choice. I am just stating it."

I return to silence. If she expects a reply from me, she doesn't seem disappointed.

"I am Maylak," she says after a moment.

I do not give her my name. Not yet. When she leans forward to touch the far side of Har-loh's belly, I notice that the healer is pregnant, too.

"You are with kit?" Is everyone in this tribe pregnant? Leezh is, this one is, and Raahosh tells me that the tribe's leader's mate is also pregnant.

"I am, though I am the only one that will be giving birth to a full-blooded sa-khui. All the others will be half human and half one of our people." She sighs and pats her belly. "I envy the humans their speediness, though. They will not be pregnant nearly as long as I am. Your Harlow does not have much longer."

I rub her knuckles again. "No?"

"The kit is small inside her but seems to be fully formed." She touches Har-loh's belly gently. "It will be different, of course. The humans are very different from our people."

That worries me. How different? In the wild, animals cull the "different" from the herd. But this woman is a healer, and she would know if my kit is going to be too "different" to survive. My chest feels tight, and it takes everything I have not to crush Har-loh's hand in mine. "Is that bad? That the kit is . . . different?"

She shakes her head, and the pressure in my chest eases a little. "The humans have different strengths than we do. I'm grateful they're here. Without them, we only had four females. I do not know how much longer we could have lasted as a tribe. They have given us new life and new hope."

I don't care about the tribe's hopes. All I want to know is if my mate and my kit will be well.

Her hands flutter over Har-loh's stomach, and then her chest, and her mouth thins in a firm line.

"What?" I growl, noticing her expression change.

Maylak pulls her hands back and clasps them in front of her rounded belly. "Her khui is very tired. It is having to work very hard to keep her healthy."

It is not doing a good job, then, because my mate is more fragile now than ever. I hold her hand tightly and press it to my chest, as if her khui can take strength in mine. "Because of the kit?"

She shakes her head slowly. "There is something else it is fighting. Both at once are nearly overwhelming it. She will need to stay here, and stay close to me so my khui can bolster hers." Her hand smooths over Har-loh's cheek. My mate sleeps on, undisturbed. "Otherwise, you risk both your kit and your mate."

I knew this, and yet hearing the words spoken aloud fills me with dread.

To save my mate, we must remain here with the bad ones. My entire body tenses and I fight the anger and helplessness that I feel.

I will do what it takes to keep Har-loh safe. What I need does not matter.

I will not make the choice that my father did and doom my

mate by hiding her away from the world. Even if I cannot stay here, Har-loh must.

My heart is heavy as I press my mouth to Har-loh's small knuckles.

The healer goes back to work on my mate, her eyes closing. Her mind goes inward and she is lost in her healing, gently pressing on different spots on Har-loh's body and humming in her throat. After a time, I realize it is not Maylak that is humming but her khui itself—a different song than resonance, but just as powerful. A healing song. I watch at my mate's side, unwilling to leave her, even to get up for food. I can eat later. For now, I will watch over Har-loh.

"You." The voice is low, male. Unfamiliar.

I turn my head and see a large male standing in the mouth of Maylak's cave. His horns are enormous and curling, his hair dark and hanging in a long tail. He wears a vest and leggings, and crosses his arms at the sight of me.

"We need to talk."

I eye him but don't move. I don't want to leave my mate's side. "Who are you?"

"I am the chief of these people." He nods at Har-loh. "Including her."

Maylak breaks from her singing and casts a frustrated look in our direction. "I must concentrate to heal her."

The chief points into the main cavern, waiting for me to join him.

I look back at Har-loh.

"She will not wake for some time," Maylak says gently. "She is safe with me."

Oddly enough, I trust this female, even if she did make the poor choice of living with the bad ones. After a few moments, I release my mate's hand and rise to my feet. I look at the healer, who has been good to my mate. "My name is Rukh," I give her.

"Welcome home, Rukh."

I do not correct her. I am not home. I turn and leave the healer's cave, unhurried as I stalk past the stranger waiting for me. I am not one of his people and he cannot order me about. She pulls the curtain on her cave shut behind her, closing us out.

As I step forward into the main cavern, the sheer . . . busyness threatens to overwhelm me. There are people *everywhere*. This is nothing like our quiet cave by the salt lake. Humans and sa-khui sit in small groups. Some are eating, some are working on leathers. A few lounge by a sunken pool in the center of the cavern. They look at us as we approach and my skin prickles with tension. It's noisy and crowded and awful.

"Come," the chief says. "We will have more privacy in my cave. We will talk there." He strides forward and scoops up a kit that runs past, then hands him off to a nearby man. He doesn't stop to see if I am following as he makes his way through the busy cavern and then disappears into a smaller cave.

I can join him . . . or I can stay out here with all of these people. There is no choice, of course. I can feel the prick of a dozen eyes on me and I clench my fists, hating how open I feel. How exposed. I duck into the cave after the chief and look around.

The entrance is small but the cave itself opens up to a cozy interior. A few candles flicker on ledges, providing light, and a human woman sits on a bone stool, frowning at a bit of leatherwork in her hands.

"Georgie," the chief says. "I need to speak to Maarukh alone. Can you give us a few moments, my mate?"

She looks up at us and blows an exasperated breath out of

her mouth. "Vektal, I've sewn this stupid sleeve on three times and I can't get my seams straight!" She throws aside the tiny garment and then her lower lip wobbles. Her expression crumples and she begins to cry, face buried in her hands.

The chief—Vektal—shoots me a look and then moves forward to kneel at his mate's feet. He soothes away her tears with murmurs, and caresses her cheek lovingly. I try not to stare at her. She looks similar to my Har-loh: same flat face, same pale skin, but this one has no freckles and her hair is an uninteresting brown to Har-loh's fiery orange.

As I watch, Vektal picks up the small bit of leather and hands it to his woman again. She swipes at her cheeks and nods, then gets to her feet. Her belly is huge, like Har-loh's, and she winces and rubs her back as she stands. "I'm sorry," she says to me, and her voice is accented like Har-loh's when she says the sa-khui words. "It's something we humans like to call hawr-moans."

I grunt. Har-loh has also had crying fits for small things. It is the kit in her belly that makes her irrational.

"I can't stay?" The human turns and gives her mate a pleading look. "I'll be quiet."

"You are my heart, Georgie, but this conversation is not for your ears." He leans in and presses a kiss on her cheek, and they look odd together. The male is enormous and muscled, and his woman is tiny against him. Is that how Har-loh looks next to me? Is that why everyone is so quick to try and protect her?

The human Georgie huffs again, but she picks up her sewing and shuffles forward. "Fine, I'll have Tiffany go fix this for me. Love you, *bay-bee*." She gives me a quick smile as she steps past, even though her eyes say she is curious.

She calls him her *bay-bee*. Har-loh calls me that. Once again, I am hit by a surge of worry so thick it chokes me, and it takes everything I have not to race back to the healer's cave and jerk my mate into my arms protectively.

Vektal moves forward and squats by the firepit. He gestures across from it. "Sit."

I contemplate turning and leaving. This man is the chief of the bad ones. My father would have despised him. I watch him, trying to decide. His face is hard and his form is fierce, but I remember the tender way he kissed away his mate's foolish tears. I have done no less for Har-loh . . . and right now, they are healing her.

So I sit across from the firepit. My body is tense despite the cheery homeyness of the cave. There are hunting weapons neatly organized against a wall, next to two pairs of snowshoes and a cloak. There are furs and baskets in every inch of space, and I see a smaller bed made in one corner for the upcoming kit. This is a man anticipating his family.

He will be ready to defend them at all costs. I must remain on my guard.

Vektal raises his chin at me. "Your name is Maarukh?"

"That is what Raahosh says."

"And who are you?"

He knows who I am. My eyes narrow. "I am no one."

Vektal rubs his chin, expression thoughtful. "Leezh tells me that Harlow won't say how you met. She changes the subject every time she is asked. I assume that it is because it is not a good story, yes?"

I say nothing.

"You know she was on a rescue mission to save two sick men when she disappeared? My tribemates were heartbroken, thinking she had died."

Har-loh has told me pieces of this story. She worried they had died because of her. And yet, because she loves me, she will not share with anyone the story of how I hit her over the head and stole her away. My heart swells with love for my mate. This only furthers my resolve that she must be safe no matter what.

"In fact, they nearly died. One of my men was very injured." He looks at me, waiting for an answer. "I assume you prevented Harlow from returning, so you nearly cost him his life."

Silence.

"And since Harlow is pregnant, I assume you resonated for her. Did that happen before or after you stole her?"

He speaks as if I had a choice. The moment I saw Har-loh, she was mine. It was that simple.

"I am not pleased," Vektal says. "You stole her and resonated to her. I wonder if she would have resonated to someone else if you had not? Have you stolen the chance to have a family from one of the men of this tribe?"

I bare my teeth at him. The thought of Har-loh being touched by another man or carrying his kit? It fills me with rage. It takes everything I have not to lunge for Vektal's throat.

We stare at each other, bristling with tension.

"I do not remember much of your father," he continues after a moment. It feels as if he is spitting the words at me. "Just that mine was responsible for his exile. Vaashan told us all that you perished along with his mate." He watches me to see my response. "He lied because he did not trust us."

I remain quiet.

"You are silent?" He snorts. "Just like Raahosh. As if I needed two of you in the tribe."

That coaxes an answer from me. "I . . . do not intend to stay." I cannot. Being around these people makes my skin crawl, yet the thought of leaving my beloved Har-loh here? It destroys me.

"You cannot take Harlow," Vektal says, his curious look darkening to one of irritation. "She is not well. I will not let you take her."

I get to my feet. She is my mate. It does not matter that his words make sense or that they match what I have already decided. He is telling me that I cannot have her. Raahosh's words of my father and mother's story circle in my mind. They would not let him keep her, so he stole her away and she died.

This cannot happen again. This will not. My plans of bringing Har-loh to the healer never went beyond "get better." The thought that she might have to stay here? It is destroying me. A snarl comes to my mouth.

He does not decide to separate me from my mate. It is not his choice. My fists clench.

Vektal gets to his feet, his expression menacing.

"Yoo-hoo," a voice calls. "Knock knock." A familiar human with yellow hair sweeps in. "Hey, Vektal! Rukh. Am I interrupting something?" Liz comes and stands between us, beaming as if she hasn't stepped between two furious males.

"Now is not the time, Leezh." Vektal's voice is an angry growl.

"Actually it is the time," she says, utterly fearless. She links her arm in mine and smiles at the chief. "I just made stew and poor Rukh here hasn't eaten all day, he's been so worried over his mate." She pats my arm. "And Raahosh is wanting to spend some quality time with his brother."

"Leezh," Vektal warns.

"Oh, come on. You guys weren't speaking anyhow, right? He's not going anywhere, not with his mate in the next room. At least let me feed the man!"

Vektal's nostrils flare.

Leezh is not blind to the tension simmering in the room. Why is she pretending otherwise? Vektal looks furious and I know I'm shaking with anger at the thought of him taking my mate away from me.

She is mine. I will steal the healer and bring her to our sea cave if I must, but Har-loh is mine.

"Besides," Leezh adds. "Georgie's crying over her sewing again."

The man's expression changes from stony anger to concern. He rubs his brow and pushes past us.

"There we go," Leezh whispers. "Problem solved."

"No problem has been solved," I growl at her.

"You kidding me? If it turned into a dick-swinging contest, you were not gonna win, buddy. I admire your tenacity and all, but he's the chief and what he says goes. Now, come on. I'm seriously going to feed you."

I want to tell her that I'm not hungry, that I want to go back to my mate and sit at her side. But as we emerge from the chief's den, I see the healer's curtain is still pulled shut, keeping us out. At the sight of it, all the strength leaves me. My legs feel weak and I stagger. How long has it been since I slept? Ate? I cannot remember.

She steers me forward, toward another cave off to the side. In the center of the cavern, I see the chief's mate wiping her eyes, and Vektal puts his arms around her. He holds her close and strokes her hair, and she burrows against him. The chief looks tired, concerned, and confused by his mate all at once.

"Pregnancy hawr-moans," Leezh whispers. "Georgie has 'em baaad. Poor Vektal. She's been making the man crazy for weeks now." Her hand squeezes my arm. "Another reason why we needed to get you out of there. Didn't want anyone saying something they'd regret later when all the baby stuff isn't in play. You can come hang at me and Raahosh's fire tonight. I made an extra bed with some spare furs if the healer stays occupied longer than we hope."

"I will wait for my mate," I say, straightening my tired body.

"Which you can do while eating and saying hello to your brother."

I waver. My need for my mate wars with my exhaustion.

"That's what I thought," Leezh says, patting my arm. "You're irritated with me now, but I'm just being a good sister-in-law. Now come on. I made some stew and you and Raahosh can sit by the fire and glare stoically at each other."

I snort. Raahosh was right—his woman does have a tongue that could flay the hide off a quilled beast.

"Whether you like it or not," Leezh says as she leads me into her cave. The air is warm with the scent of cooking food, and smells like one of Har-loh's dishes. "You need family. And Raahosh and I are here for you."

Rukh

Despite my exhaustion, I cannot sleep. My sweet Har-loh's warm body is not curled up against me, and everywhere, there are sounds. Not the normal sounds that invade the quiet evening hours, but the sounds of people. Someone coughs. A man snores. People whisper. The furs rustle as Leezh and Raahosh move around in their bed. They are all small noises, but to me, it is an endless stream that sets my nerves on edge.

These people are never alone. There is always someone nearby. I cannot imagine such a life, and it fills my gut with dread that to be with Har-loh, I must consider it. I tell myself she is worth it, but every time I do, another sound grates on my frayed nerves until I am twitching and restless.

I jump up from the furs, unable to relax. I must see my mate. I must know she's all right. I can't stand the thought of her reaching for me and me not being there. I move silently out of Leezh and Raahosh's cave and into the main cavern, now deserted. The healer's den is no longer blocked off, and I head toward it.

When I duck inside the den, the small area is quiet. There is a male sleeping in the furs at the back of the den, but the healer herself sits beside Har-loh's bed. A child is cradled in her arms, and she rocks it gently as she watches over my mate. This is a good woman, this healer.

She looks up at the sight of me and puts fingers to her mouth in an indication of quiet. I move to my mate's side and take her hand. Her fingers are warm and she doesn't look quite so fragile as before. I breathe a sigh of relief.

"She is a little better now," Maylak whispers. Her hand smooths the hair of the sleeping child curled against her rounded belly.

"You have my thanks," I tell her. The exhaustion that was in Har-loh's eyes seems to have transferred over to the healer. No doubt the woman is exhausted from caring for my mate all day.

She nods slowly, and her gaze moves to Har-loh. "Her khui is still very tired." Her voice is so soft I can barely hear it, and I lean forward so I do not miss a word. "Her body . . . it was not doing well before she took on the khui. It has had to work hard to keep her healthy. Now with the baby, it is struggling."

I nod. She told me this earlier, though it is no less terrifying to hear it a second time. "What can I do?"

"The kit will probably come early," she says, reaching a hand out as if to touch Har-loh's stomach. "Her body cannot make enough nourishment for it, and when it grows hungry enough, it will seek its way out. We must be ready."

I nod slowly. Then Har-loh must stay here, with the healer.

And I must stay with her.

I gently stroke Har-loh's hand, even as Maylak gets to her feet and settles her child in a nearby bed, then crawls in the furs next to her mate. Now it is just me with Har-loh, and my searing thoughts. Her khui struggles to keep her well. What if she were to become hurt out at our sea cave? Or what if we resonated again? The healer herself carries a kit in her belly and one in her arms.

If I take her away from here . . . it will be her death.

The thought is agony. And I think of Vektal's hard face, and his reminder that he will make the decisions for Har-loh, even if they are not what I want.

To save my mate, I might lose her.

I hold her hand and brush my lips against her skin, aching at the thought. My life was nothing but loneliness before her. The thought of losing my sweet mate?

It will destroy me.

Harlow

A big, warm body is curled up next to mine as I wake up, and for the first time in what feels like forever, my side doesn't ache. I open my eyes and stare at an unfamiliar ceiling, then touch my belly to make sure my baby is still there. It flutters under my touch, reassuring me, and I turn to look at my mate.

Rukh sleeps on, oblivious to the fact that I'm awake, and I simply gaze at him, soaking in his peaceful sleeping expression. His fingers are linked with mine, and he's squeezed in against the rock wall, which doesn't look comfortable. Meanwhile, I'm lying on a padded wealth of furs and feel really good. I wiggle my toes, unwilling to get up and face the day just yet.

There's a soft hum of voices in the distance, at once familiar and yet strange. It's been a year since I woke up to the sleepy sounds of the tribe. They're so strangely . . . noisy. I absently squeeze Rukh's hand. It can't be easy for my poor loner to be here. Being around me was a shock to his system. Being around a tribe of forty-something? It must be making him insane. I feel a twinge of unhappy guilt at the thought.

Lips nuzzle my ear, and I feel the flick of a ridged tongue against my earlobe. "You're awake," Rukh says, voice gruff and sleepy.

I snuggle closer to him—or at least, as close as my ungainly body will allow. "Did you sleep okay?"

"No."

Always honest, my mate. Heh. "Too many people around?"

"They are everywhere," he says thickly. His fingers caress my cheek. "I am surprised they do not stumble over one another."

I chuckle. "It's not that bad, but I will be ready to go back to our home soon, I imagine."

Rukh is silent. He kisses my temple and gets up from the bed. "I will wake the healer."

"No, I'm fine," I protest, but Maylak is already rising from her bed across the cozy den. She gives me a sleepy smile and adjusts her leathers around her body, smoothing the round bump of her belly. It's so weird to see her a year later and she's no more pregnant than she was the last time I saw her. I sincerely hope I don't carry my baby the full three years that the sa-khui do. I don't know if I'll be able to stand being pregnant and swollen for much longer.

"How do you feel, Harlow?" Maylak asks.

Rukh lowers to a crouch next to my bed, as if guarding me. I move to sit up, and my mate is immediately there, arranging the furs and adjusting things to try and make me more comfortable. "Do you need more cushioning? Shall I get you more furs?"

"I'm just fine," I tell him. "Really." The worried look doesn't leave his face, and I'm torn between exasperation and sympathy. This is all new to Rukh, I remind myself. He's not familiar with the hospital bed situation.

Me? I'm all too familiar with it. This is different, though. I tell myself that even as I sit up and give the healer a brave smile.

Maylak's expression is relaxed as she folds her legs and sits down next to me. "Rukh, do you know of the green tri-leaf plant? When you crush the leaves, it smells foul, like three-day-old meat."

He gives her a brief nod.

"Could you get some? It makes a strong tea that is good for the kit, and it is best taken fresh from the plant. There are bushes nearby." The healer's gaze is direct as she stares down my mate.

He looks to me, and then gets to his feet. "I will be back soon."

It's silent until he leaves the cave, and then Maylak turns to me. Her gentle expression is apologetic. "The tea is quite awful, I must warn you, but it is beneficial."

"You weren't just trying to get him out of here so he wouldn't—" There's no word for "hover" in their language. "Um, be in the way?"

"There is that, too," Maylak says. Her hand grips mine. "Does the tribe need to intervene?"

I blink at her, not sure what she means. Intervene with what? Then I realize what she means—do they need to intervene and get Rukh away from me? I gasp and jerk my hand from hers. "What? No! I *love* him."

"I just wanted to be sure this was of your choosing. Males do not tend to see reason when they resonate." She smiles to take the sting out of her words. "I did not wish to offend you, but I had to know. His father—"

"I know about his father," I snap, still reeling. Do they all think this is crazy Stockholm syndrome? That because Rukh is devoted and caring that he's fucked the brains out of my head? I love him. Maybe I was scared of him at first, but that was because he didn't know how to act around people. He's come so far, and I couldn't ask for a more attentive, thoughtful, funny, smart, handsome, intelligent mate. I know I'm being rude to Maylak, who's exhausted herself trying to heal me, but I'm still offended. "I'm sorry if I yelled. I just feel protective of him."

She nods and pushes the blankets off my belly, all business once more. "I thought so, but I had to ask. Sometimes it is hard to tell." Her fingers prod the side of my stomach, and she looks up at me. "Any pain here today?"

I shake my head. For the first time in what feels like forever, the nagging ache in my side is gone. "No. It feels good."

She nods. "Your child is healthy, but your body struggles to create enough food for it. There is a . . . thing the body creates when a kit comes out of the mother. We call it the 'life meat.'"

Well, that sounds gross. I'm growing a baby and "life meat" inside me. "The placenta?"

"It is not nourishing your kit as it should. Your child will come early."

My hands go to my belly, caressing it. "Is that bad?"

"No. It just means you will be with us for a while longer."

I relax. "I'm ready to stop being pregnant."

Maylak grins, her sharp teeth showing. "I know this feeling well. But for you, it will not be much longer now."

I can hardly wait.

⚫

The next week crawls by slowly.

I sleep a lot, thanks to the baby and Maylak's healing. Since I'm confined to the caves, there's not much to do when people aren't visiting. And since my mate is skittish around all these people, I do a lot of shooing off even the most well-intentioned of visitors.

Much has changed in the tribe since I was here last. They've split into two caves, with half of the group living in a network of caves to the south. Kira and Aehako are there, along with a lot of the single women and men. Tiffany, Josie, and Claire are the only girls that haven't mated yet, and so they are there as well. The main cave is full of pregnant couples, since they need to be close to the healer.

Rukh and I are made comfortable in a cave that is used for meat storage, and everyone stops by to bring us extra furs or additional food or even baby clothes. My mate is clearly uncomfortable whenever people arrive, and he takes to spending a lot of time with Raahosh, hunting. The two men leave at dawn every morning and go out to provide meat for the tribe. Rukh has confessed to me that he feels obligated to Maylak for her help, and so he hunts not only for us, but for her and her family. I personally think a lot of it is stress relief, and I'm happy that Raahosh goes with him. Every time Rukh disappears, there's a nagging worry in my mind that he won't come back. That he'll just walk and keep going, deciding that life alone is less of a hassle than a pregnant mate and people constantly in your face.

At least Raahosh is with him. Liz comes over every day to keep me company, grumbling that now that I'm cave-bound, he wants her to stay with me. She thinks he just wants her to stick around in the caves because he worries she'll end up like me. I want to point out that it's likely she never had a brain tumor, but then my secret would be out, and I don't want to be treated weirdly by the others.

Aehako and Haeden stop by from the South Cave one day,

and I'm thrilled to see both of them looking so healthy. It eases my lingering guilt, especially when Aehako wraps me in a bear hug and tells me all about Kira's pregnancy and how happy they are.

Days pass, and still the baby doesn't come.

I start to relax, because I'm feeling a lot better. The endless nagging pain in my side is gone and I no longer feel stretched to my physical limits. I suspect that maybe my baby won't be coming early after all. Georgie's further along than me and she shows no signs of going into labor anytime soon.

Since there are so many of us heavily pregnant, we tend to gather by the bathing pool. The water's heated from one of Not-Hoth's many hot springs, and it feels wonderful on my swollen feet. I'm happy to see that Marlene also suffers from puffy feet, and it makes me feel less like I drew the short end of the pregnancy stick.

Today, several of the human girls are sitting around the pool. It feels a little cliquish, but then I remember that there are practically no sa-khui women in the tribe. There are two women our age, and two elderly women. Oh, and Farli, who is the Earth equivalent of a preteen. So I guess it's okay if we huddle together.

Megan holds up the leather belt she's braiding. "See? You thought being a Girl Scout wouldn't be handy at all. Who knew that I'd be using macramé skills on a daily basis in the future?"

Nora snorts and wiggles her feet in the water. "When you're done with that, make me one. I'm all thumbs."

"You are?" Georgie kicks a bit of water in Nora's direction. "Have you seen my attempts at sewing? I can balance a checkbook like nobody's business and can count a drawer of money in a heartbeat. But crafty shit? Not in the slightest."

I'm seated next to Megan, between her and Stacy. She's trying to show us how to macramé leather together into knotted creations. It looks useful, and I think of the things I could make—a sling to carry the baby in, and Rukh's shoulder bag looks as if it's about to fall apart it's so worn. Hell, maybe I could macramé a bra, because right now? My boobs hurt like there's no tomorrow and the leather band I wear around them tends to slide.

Liz sits nearby, sharpening and resharpening the tips of bone arrows. Marlene's with the group, but she's quiet, preferring to listen while others chatter. Ariana's sleeping back in her cave, and the men are out hunting to stock up. Last "winter" apparently cleaned the storehouses out, and so they're working extra hard to make sure everyone has enough to eat for this upcoming winter, when the snows get so high they sometimes can cover the cave entrance entirely. Liz has plenty of stories about the insane amounts of snow, and they make me shiver. It was cold by the sea, but not nearly as cold as that.

I concentrate on working the cords together like Megan's showed me. "I'm afraid you're going to be disappointed," I tell her. "I'm not good at craft stuff, either. Cooking, yes. Mechanical stuff? Yes. Crafts? No."

Liz looks up at that. "Oh, I forgot. Your dad was a mechanic, right?" At my nod, she continues. "Kira said that before you disappeared, you were trying to put together some stone cutters out of the ship's old parts. You think we could still do that? Cut a few more caves? The south ones are nice, but I miss having Tiff and Josie and Kira and Claire here."

"Maybe," I say, twisting my leather cords. It looks wrong and I immediately untwist them again, frustrated. "I never got to finish the stuff from before. Things . . . happened."

"Yeah, we know," Nora chimes in. "Rukh happened."

Georgie bats her arm. "Be nice."

"That was nice!"

Georgie lifts her chin at me. "Speaking of Rukh, have you guys talked about baby names?"

I make a knot with the cords, and Megan immediately pulls them back out of my hands and proceeds to redo them. Maybe I'll just ask Megan to make me a sling instead of doing it myself. Crafty, I'm not. "We hadn't really thought about it, no. I thought there would be plenty of time. And then, well . . . other stuff happened." Other stuff like Liz and Raahosh showing up, and me getting sick, and and and . . .

"We've been talking about it for a while, and a lot of us are going to go the Brangelina route," Georgie says. "Combine our names with our mate's names, since the babies are going to be the first of their kind."

"Yeah, it'd be a little weird to have a horned kid running around named Joe or Billy when everyone else is named things like Raahosh and Vektal," Liz adds.

"So like . . . Georgie and Vektal would be . . . Georgal? Or Vektie?"

Georgie makes a face. "We have a name picked out and it's not as bad as that."

"Oh, come on. It could be worse." Liz's lips twitch. "It could be Raahosh and Vektal's names we're mashing together. Their kid could be . . . Rectal."

Laughter explodes in the cave, and for the next few minutes, we crack up trying to make awful pairings of names. Liz jokes that their kid will be called Ho-shiz and Kira and Aehako's called Crack-ho, and we all lose it again.

"Stop, stop," Nora gasps, clutching her sides and giggling madly. "You're going to make me pee on myself."

"Easy for you to say," Stacy chimes in, wiping tears from her eyes. "I had this discussion with Pashov last night when we were in bed. He told me that he thought our baby should be called Shovy. For Stac-y and Pa-shov."

"Shovy!" Liz howls. "Oh God, that's the worst!"

"You guys be quiet!" Ariana bellows at us from her cave. "I have a stinking headache!"

We sober up, but a few giggles still escape the group. I'm grinning so hard my face hurts. It's moments like this I've missed while being alone with Rukh. The seaside cave is quiet and lovely and spacious . . . but it's lonely, too.

But if things hadn't happened like they did, I wouldn't have my Rukh and my baby on the way. I pat my stomach and the baby kicks me in response. I like how things turned out. "So, how is Kira?" I ask. "She's at the other cave, right?"

Georgie nods and rubs her belly absently. "She's great. She's so stinking happy with Aehako. You've never seen someone smile so much, really. It's wonderful to see."

I don't know Kira as well as Georgie and Liz, but I'm glad to hear that. "And Claire?"

Nora wrinkles her nose. "She moved in with that pushy Bek guy."

"Oh, so they resonated?"

"Didn't say that," Nora corrects me. "He's just so determined to have her as his mate that he moved her in anyhow. He's super bossy. No one likes him."

"Maybe he's good in the sack," Marlene chimes in.

Stacy breaks out into the giggles again.

Marlene shrugs. "Maybe so. It is not the worst reason to have a mate."

Georgie doesn't look quite so convinced. She glances over at me again. "Tiffany's doing awesome, of course. Last time I saw her, she had three guys dancing to her tune. She never picks one over another. Just lets all three of them pay attention to her. They give her all kinds of gifts, too. Girl's got it made. She doesn't have to hunt, doesn't have to do anything. She could lie in bed all day—"

"Like Ariana," Nora whispers.

Stacy elbows her.

"But you know that's not how Tiff is," Georgie continues. "I swear she loves this roughing-it shit. Last time I visited their cave? She told me she was saving her pee because she read in a book that pee made a good leather curing agent." She wrinkles her nose.

"Remind me not to ask her to make me any clothing," I murmur.

Stacy giggles again.

A sharp cramp shoots up my belly and I shift in place, uncomfortable. I'm used to things cramping and flexing and adjusting with the pregnancy, but that was a particularly sharp one. I barely pay attention to the conversation as Georgie talks about Josie, and how she and Haeden still hate each other and it's a source of amusement for the tribe to watch them bicker. Georgie looks at me as she talks and I smile, but I mostly want to get up and walk out this cramp.

"Well?"

I glance over at Georgie. I missed what she was saying. "Hmm?"

"I asked if you're going to stay with the tribe or if you're going to go when Rukh leaves?"

I stare at her in shock. "He's leaving?"

Her expression grows worried. "He told Vektal that he wouldn't stay here."

I don't know what to say. Rukh hasn't discussed anything with me. In fact, every time I bring up when we're going back to the seaside cave, he changes the subject. Dread fills me. Is . . . is he going to leave me behind? I thought he loved me. "I don't know," I whisper to Georgie.

She reaches over and squeezes my hand. "It probably just hasn't come up."

It hasn't come up because my mate's avoiding the conversation. I nod absently and rub at the cramp in my belly again.

Georgie gets a weird expression on her face as she looks at me. "Hey, Harlow?"

Oh God, what now? "Yes?"

"I think your water broke."

PART SIX

Rukh

I won't stop running until I get back to the tribal caves. It doesn't matter that I've been running across snowy hills for hours. All that matters is Har-loh. I can't stop thinking of the sickening way my gut churned as one of the hunters crested the hillside and headed straight for Raahosh and me as we hunted a dvisti herd. He scared away our prey, and Raahosh snarled at him . . . until we found out the reason why he'd chased us down.

Har-loh is in labor.

Raahosh stayed behind with the exhausted hunter, who'd run a long way to find us, and I raced back alone. My mind rips through all the hours that have passed since they sent the runner. Is my Har-loh in pain? Is the kit well? Did something go wrong that caused her to give birth today? A thousand worries crush me until I can't breathe.

But I still race forward.

Relief shoots through me when the rocky cliffside that houses the tribal caves comes into view. I race a little faster, the end in sight.

I skid into the cave a few moments later, flinging aside my pack. There's a crowd of people hanging around in the caves, but I ignore them, heading straight for my cave. The curtains are shut and Vektal paces just outside, a concerned look on his face. I move right past him and push into my cave.

Har-loh is there, seated on the blankets. Georgie, the chief's mate, is at her side, gripping her hand. Maylak is on the other side of her, and her expression is so calm that some of my panic disappears. The moment Har-loh sees me, she cries out. "Rukh!" She releases Georgie's hand and reaches for me.

"I am here, my mate." I move to her side as Georgie gets up, and I brush the sweaty hair off of her smooth brow. "Everything is all right."

She pants, and her hand grips mine tight, her nails digging into my skin. "You're sweaty, too. Did you run all the way here?"

"All the way," I agree.

She chuckles at that, and her laughter turns into a groan a moment later. Her face scrunches up and she grips my hand so hard it feels as if she will snap the bones.

"What is happening?" I snarl at the healer. "Why is she hurting?"

Maylak frowns at me. "This is normal, Rukh."

"Con-track-shuns," Har-loh adds between pants. "They're coming really fast now."

I press my mouth to her hand. "How can I make them stop?"

Har-loh stares at me, confused.

"You are in pain," I explain. "I want to make it stop."

"Then get this bay-bee out of me!"

I look at the healer. "How do I do that?" I feel useless.

Maylak just shakes her head. "The kit will come out on its own. Just hold her hand and support her. That is all you can do."

I'm relieved that there is not something I'm missing, but at the same time, I hate that I cannot take the pain from my mate. She has suffered so much.

"Water, please?" Har-loh asks a moment later.

I nod and scramble for my waterskin, frantic. It's empty, and I stumble out of the cave, looking for more. "Water!" I bellow at Vektal and Georgie, still nearby.

Vektal silently hands me a waterskin. It is good that he does not smile, or else I might shove him. I snatch it from his hands and race back into the cave, drawing the curtains closed.

As I step back inside, I notice that Maylak is helping Har-loh into a squatting position. My mate is naked, I notice for the first time. "What are you doing?" I ask. Is she getting up? She can't get up. She's having our kit.

"The child is coming," Maylak says. "She is getting into position."

I watch, helpless and clutching the waterskin, as the healer coaches her through. The healer rubs Har-loh's shoulder and whispers encouraging words. My mate groans, and as I watch, she bears down, her hands curling into fists against the stone floor of the cave. Maylak moves the furs between Har-loh's legs. "It's coming. One big push."

Har-loh screams, the cords of her neck showing, and I clench the waterskin so tightly in my hand that it spills over. She sounds as if she is in such pain. I feel helpless at the sight of it. I remain frozen as the healer reaches between my mate's bent legs and pulls something free.

A moment later, a kit cries out, the wail overloud in our cave.

Har-loh pants and laughs, tears streaming down her face. She looks up at me, exhausted and happy all at once.

Maylak cuts the cord, wraps the child in furs, and then holds it out to me. "Take your son while the mother and I finish."

My son?

I step forward, numb, and drop the waterskin. The child is thrust into my arms a moment later and then Maylak turns back to Har-loh. I stare down at the bundle I hold.

It's so . . . tiny. So small. The face is small and scrunched, the forehead with two small buds that will one day become horns. His nose is small and smooth like Har-loh's, but his forehead holds traces of the ridges that mine has. And he is a pale, pale blue, a color between my skin and my sweet Har-loh's. He is bald, and I'm torn between thinking he is the ugliest, weakest creature I have ever seen . . . and the most wonderful.

I unwrap him because I have to see all of him. I have to know he's fine, he's healthy . . . he's just so small. The moment I unwrap him, he begins to wail even louder. I stare down at his tiny body. Skinny legs flail, and his tiny tail flicks with anger. The cut cord is still bleeding, limp against his rounded belly. His arms reach out as if looking for something, and I give him my finger to hold on to. He clutches it and I notice his grip is three fingered, like mine. Even his tiny cock has a spur.

My son.

I catch a glimpse of his eyes, wrinkled slits that scrunch as he wails. They are dark, no blue spark of life in them. That worries me. His size worries me, too. He's so small that he fits in the palm of my hand. I'm awed by him, but I'm terrified. My Har-loh brought this tiny life into being and now I must ensure that he is safe and well-fed. A fierce surge of protectiveness wells inside me, and I wrap the baby tightly in the furs again and hold him to my chest.

I would do anything for him. Anything. I'm choked with

emotion. Helplessness, joy, fear, and utter happiness war inside me. Is this how my father felt at my birth? Like he would destroy anything that came between him and his child?

Is this why he fought so fiercely to keep me away from the others?

But . . . then why deliver Raahosh to them? For the first time, I truly understand Raahosh's feelings of betrayal and hurt. I hold my son close to my breast and silently promise that I will do whatever it takes to ensure his happiness.

Har-loh groans again, and when I look up, she's lying back down on the furs. Maylak is calmly folding up the birthing fur into a bundle nearby. Har-loh smiles at me, tired and sweaty. "Can I see him? Is he healthy?"

"He is wonderful," I tell her, and my voice catches in my throat. "He is a mixture of both you and me."

She holds her arms out, and I kneel down to gently hand her my son. Our son. Our child. My heart overflows with emotion. Never have I felt so content and so utterly terrified that it will all be ripped from me.

Har-loh's eyes widen at the sight of him, and then she begins to cry. "He's so beautiful."

I chuckle. "No, he's not. He is wrinkly."

She bats my arm but doesn't look up from the kit. "Shut up. I thought he'd have red hair. Can you imagine a blue baby with red hair? Horrible. But he's perfect." Her hand smooths over the small head, the tiny horn nubs, his nose, his cheek. In response to her touch, the baby turns his face toward her breast. She fits him there against her, and more tears fall down her cheeks as the baby begins to suck. The tiny mouth fits against her nipple and the baby quiets.

I could watch them forever.

"Take this," Maylak says, and hands me the bundle of the birthing furs. "Go and bury this as far from the cave as you can."

I nod and look at my mate. Har-loh's gaze as she watches me is worried.

"What is it?"

"Will you . . . will you come back?" Fresh tears spill from her eyes. "To us?"

The hurt in her voice is like a knife in my gut. Why does she doubt me? How can she think I would abandon her and my child—my son—at this moment?

But then I remember Vektal waiting outside in the main cave. And I remember that my Har-loh must stay here if she is to be healthy. And my happiness is crushed. If I stay here with them, I will be going against everything my father taught me. And yet, how can I abandon them? They are my heart, more than the khui that vibrates in my chest whenever she is near.

I nod slowly. "I will return." I want to say more, but there's so much worry and emotion in Har-loh's big eyes that I can't speak. I clutch the bundle of bloodied furs against my chest and leave the cave. We will talk more when I can think clearly.

Vektal is waiting the moment I exit the cave. I stalk past him, not wanting to talk, but he walks alongside me as I exit the cave.

"Well?" he says when I remain silent and head out into the snow. "Is it healthy?"

I nod. For some reason, I'm glad his first question is asking about the child's health.

He exhales in relief and claps my shoulder as if we are friends. I stiffen but say nothing. Har-loh must remain with these people no matter what, so I cannot snarl at him.

"And Harlow? Is she well?"

"She is tired, but well."

"The child—a female or male?"

"Male."

He grunts. "Does it look as the humans do?"

I think of the kit. I held him in my arms for seconds only, and already I want to race back in there and hold him again. I want to stare and count his fingers and toes and check him over once more to ensure yes, he is whole. "It looks like both myself and Har-loh." I pause and then remember the size of the child, no bigger than my hand. "It is very small. Very small."

And his eyes are dark.

Vektal makes a worried sound. "We will need to get a khui inside him soon. Right now he is fragile without it to protect him."

I swallow hard and nod. I haven't even thought that far ahead, but he's right. The baby will need a khui or he will weaken and die within days. Terror clutches at me. My mother died on a khui hunt right after I was born. What if I can't bring down a sa-kohtsk by myself?

I need the tribe to help. I cannot do it on my own. Har-loh is incredibly weak and I cannot ask her to help me hunt one. She needs rest, not a hunt.

Not for the first time, I'm filled with helpless anger toward my dead father. How could he ask such a thing of my mother, fresh from giving birth to me? Was his pride so great that he did not want anything to do with the tribe and so he risked her life? Are they that awful? Am I yet being deceived by their helpfulness?

Vektal claps a hand on my back again. "I will send out the fastest hunters to track one of the sa-kohtsk."

The lumbering giants could be anywhere. I pause and look over at the chief. "And my mate and kit? How will they get there? Har-loh is too weak to walk."

He nods as if expecting this. "Raahosh has a sled he uses during his hunts with Leezh. We will use that to carry Har-loh and the child with us."

What would I do without the tribe's help? Even if I don't like Vektal, he is putting his people's lives on the line to help me and Har-loh.

I do not know what to think anymore. All I know is that I must bury my bundle quickly and return to my mate's side.

Harlow

I sleep for a few hours, my dreams fitful and strange. I wake up to the sound of a baby crying, and it takes a moment of disorientation—and the leakage of my breasts—to remind me that it's my child. Oh. I sit up and reach into the basket next to my bed, pulling my baby into my arms. The leather wrap around his bottom is wet, so I change that, wishing fervently for disposable diapers. I'll just have to become a real expert at wiping down leather, I suppose. I pull the baby into my arms and tuck him against my breast.

The little rosebud mouth immediately seeks my nipple and he latches on.

God, he's so beautiful. I watch him nurse, amazed and overwhelmed. He looks like Rukh, but there're enough of my features there, too. The mixture of Rukh's alien appearance with my human one should create an ugly mixture, but the baby is beautiful and I feel like he's going to be even better looking than any child I've ever seen. Of course, that might be the proud mama in me talking.

The only thing that worries me is his size. He's not a plump baby. He's long, but his legs are skinny and his belly should be more rounded. He stops eating too soon, and dozes back to sleep, and I want to wake him up and make him drink more. I worry he's not getting enough.

The leather curtain over the cave entrance parts, and Rukh enters, looking tall and handsome and so wonderful that my entire body aches with love. He's got a small bowl of Liz's stew with him, and a waterskin. I'm hungry, but I'm not ready to let go of the baby yet. I trail my fingers over his tiny head. There's a faint down but it's too pale to see what color it will be. I hope he has Rukh's gorgeous, thick black hair instead of my limp red hair. Actually, if he looked a hundred percent like his daddy, I'd be in heaven.

"You are crying," Rukh states after a moment. "Are you hurting?"

I ache all over and certain parts of me don't feel great post-birth, but I haven't given it a second thought. There's a sweet little baby taking up every bit of my attention. "Am I?" I brush the back of my hand over my cheeks, and sure enough, I'm crying. "It's just emotion, I think. I . . . never thought I would have all this." I look over at him and realize it's true. I never thought I would have a gorgeous mate that loves me and a baby. A family. Anything. Before the aliens grabbed me for their spaceship? My days were numbered.

"Because of the problem with your head?"

I still at his words. "My head?"

He nods slowly, his gaze fixed on me. "The healer said that your khui works hard because of a past issue in your head. That it is one reason why you struggled with carrying the kit. Your khui was tired."

Oh. I nod slowly and stroke my fingers down the baby's sleeping cheek. I keep my voice low and modulated so he can sleep. "There was something growing against my brain that should not have been there. It was going to kill me within a few months. I was terminal. I had no hope."

"You never told me."

"When I talked with the ancestors' ship, it said I was healed. I didn't think it would continue to be a problem." I keep stroking my baby's soft cheek. Of course, I also didn't think I'd become a mommy.

"This means you must stay here, Har-loh." His voice is soft and agonized. "I cannot take you away, not when you must be close to the healer. What if your khui grows tired again?"

"Oh." I think of our seaside cave and I'm a little sad. I liked it there, but our current cave is cozy and there are so many people around to help out. "But I thought you didn't like it here, Rukh."

He's silent.

The horrible worry gnaws in my belly and I remember what Georgie said. "You're not planning on staying, are you?" I whisper.

The look Rukh gives me is agonized. "The thought of leaving you and our son tears me apart."

"But you're still considering it." The words that come out of me are bitter, hurt.

"If I know the two of you are safe . . . maybe I can bear it then. All I know is that if I take you away with me again, I am destroying you."

"The thought of you leaving destroys me, too, Rukh. Are these people so very bad?"

"They are not my people."

"They're not mine either!" I gesture at my pale, freckled skin and red hair. "Do you think I chose to show up here? I didn't! But these people are good, caring people. We could have a good life here! Together!"

He hangs his head. "The only memories I have left of my father are of him and his words of caution. Telling me to stay away from the bad ones. That they will destroy me."

"But he's dead and I'm here now." I hold our son out to him. "Our baby is here now. How can you leave us?"

"I don't want to." He moves forward and takes the baby into his arms, and I see the love on his rugged face. It breaks my heart anew. Our family is so perfect—why doesn't he see it? "But if I stay, does it mean that my father died for nothing?"

I know he's attached to his father. I know his memories of him are the only memories he has of anyone at all. Of course he's incredibly emotional about them. But what about me? Our child? I want to scream a protest. It's clear that Rukh's warring with his own internal demons. He moves closer to me and curls up next to me in the furs, and we cuddle, watching our baby sleep.

"Everything in me, everything that I am," Rukh murmurs. "It tells me that I should be here, with you. Taking care of you and my child. But when I close my eyes, I see my father's angry face. And I wonder how long it will be before someone pulls us apart like my father and my mother. To live here and not have you? That will destroy me more than leaving."

I nestle my head against his shoulder, my heart hurting. He doesn't trust these people not to hurt him, not to destroy his fragile happiness. I get it.

But at some point, he's going to have to trust, because I don't know what I'll do if I lose him.

Harlow

The next day, one of the hunters returns with the news that he's found a small herd of sa-kohtsk, seven in total. One of them is a kit. It is this that will provide the khui for my tiny child. I worry every time he drifts to sleep, because he's not thriving. Not yet. I think of the poison in the air, and I am frantic to get a khui inside him. I want to hear him crying out with strength, not with a weak, feeble wail.

I worry that he won't have many more days left.

Because I'm still recovering from the birth, they load a sled—normally used for hauling meat—with furs and cushions, and the baby and I are settled onto it as the hunting party readies. Liz is at my side, practically bouncing with anticipation as the men go through last minute weapon checks. She flexes her hands. "Can I hold him? Please?"

Even though every inch of me wants to clutch the baby and shove my breast into his mouth again in the hopes he'll feed a bit more, I reluctantly part with my bundle. She takes him in her arms and her expression softens with delight. "Oh my God, he's the cutest."

I feel a warm flush of motherly pride at that. "He is."

"Look at those teensy horns! And the teeny-weeny brow ridges!" Her voice turns into a coo. "You are just the most precious, aren't you?"

The baby cries, weak and dispirited.

I hold my arms out, my breasts automatically starting to leak, and open my wrap to feed him. "He's not as strong as he should be," I tell Liz when she hands him back. "I'm so worried."

"The cootie'll fix that right up," she assures me, patting the bow slung over her shoulder. "Did you guys decide on a name?"

I nod, pleased when the baby latches onto my breast and begins to feed hungrily. Every meal feels like a success. "We took the first parts of both of our names and came up with Rukhar."

"Oh, I like it!"

"Me too." It seems like a big, fierce name for such a tiny, scrawny baby, but he'll grow into it.

"I wonder what mine will look like." Liz pats her stomach dreamily.

"Bigger, I imagine," I say, and try not to be envious of the thought. It's not Rukhar's fault he's early and tiny. My body just couldn't handle nourishing him for much longer. I feel like a bit of a failure at that.

But then Rukh comes to my side and touches my cheek, and it doesn't matter. We're going to get our baby a khui, and it will fix him.

Like it fixed me.

We travel for most of a day. Rukh pulls my sled and the other hunters keep pace with us, though I know they could go much faster. Liz walks beside me, chatting my ear off and holding the baby whenever I let her. I hand him off more often as the day goes on, because even just riding in the sled is exhausting, and "Auntie" Liz is eager to get in her share of baby time. I doze fitfully, and my dreams are terrible ones full of worry and fear.

The slow thud and subsequent shake of the ground is what wakes me up. I sit up on my sled as another thud rocks the world, and realize we've stopped. It's twilight, the suns fading into the purplish skies.

"Found 'em," Liz whispers.

In the distance, at the tree line, I see a few of the enormous heads of the sa-kohtsk. One grazes on the feathery tips of one of the pink trees. Another slowly rambles past, the thudding of its feet shaking the earth. They're enormous, each as big as an airplane, and I worry all over again. I've seen them before, but I've forgotten how big they are. They're grazers, but their sheer size and strength makes them dangerous.

Raahosh turns to the hunters, and his gaze flicks to Liz. "We'll circle, look for the small one. If we can wound it, we can separate it from the herd. If not, we can try and run it down, corner it." He nods at Rukh. "Are you ready?"

Rukh lets go of the sled pull and glances down at me. I want to protest that he doesn't need to go, but he has to. This is for our baby.

Liz hands me Rukhar and I clutch him close. "You don't want Rukh to stay with his mate?" Liz asks.

"Rukh is strong and fast. We need him," Raahosh says. His gaze fixes on Liz. "You will stay with her."

"You're sidelining the vaginas?" Liz bellows. "The fuck, babe?"

"You cannot run, my mate." He moves forward to her and

pats her stomach, even though she tries to swat his hand away. "You are an excellent shot, but you do not need to race with the hunters to use your bow." He kisses her brow. "Guard her."

Liz grumbles, but doesn't say anything else. I look over at Rukh and he touches my cheek, then joins the others. *I love you,* I think quietly. *Stay safe.*

It's impossible not to think about the hunt that killed his mother and maimed his brother. Judging from the tense expressions on both Rukh and Raahosh, I'm not the only one thinking about it.

The men melt into the trees a few moments later, and then it's just me and Liz sitting in the snow. Rukhar lets out a tiny wail and I automatically tuck him under my poncho-style tunic and offer him my breast.

"Well," Liz says, and grabs the lead on my sled. "Let's see if we can get a seat on the sidelines, I guess, and hope for a good show."

I don't care if the show is good. I just want to save my baby and have my mate come back to me in one piece.

Rukh

Raahosh has done this before, the others tell me. When May-lak's little Esha was born, when the women received their khui, and earlier, when Farli was born many, many seasons back. But each hunt is equally dangerous, and some of the hunters were out on the game trails and we could not wait for them to return. Every day is another that puts Rukhar at risk, so it must be now, and it must be this herd.

We approach. There are six strong men. I do not know all their names, and for some reason, that shames me. They all risk their lives for my son to have a chance at his. This realization goes through my mind over and over again. My own brother leads the pack, his spear at hand, a "bow" like the one Leezh carries strapped over one shoulder.

The sa-kohtsk herd is fearsome up close. The creatures have enormous mouths that gape open as their heads swing back and forth, sifting the air. There are several adults, each one so large that one foot can crush a grown man. In the center of the herd, the kit stands near its mother. It is only half the size of the others, and it is our target.

Raahosh stops, and as the hunters gather, he gestures at the kit. "I have a clear shot of it from here. We can wound it, then stampede the herd. It will be left behind." He motions for the men to pair off. "Chase the adults. Make noise but be cautious you do not risk your life."

The men nod.

"Make sure they do not turn. The women are behind us, and we do not want the sa-kohtsk running in their direction."

A trickle of fear traces down my spine at the thought. Harloh is weak, and Rukhar small and helpless . . . and both are far too close nearby for my liking. But they must remain close so Rukhar can receive his khui. My gut churns uneasily at the thought. The dangers are many.

The hunters ready their weapons. There are spears, slings, and several men carry wickedly sharp bone knives like my own. One of the sa-kohtsk lumbers past, ignoring us as small and insignificant, and I think of my father and the hunt to get my khui. Did he feel the same heart-pounding terror as I do? Did his gut clench when he realized he was putting his older son and his mate in danger? Or was he too reckless to care?

I can't imagine why he didn't return to the tribe to get their help. He had to know the danger. Or did he just not care?

Raahosh pulls his bow free and carefully places an arrow. He aims it, and I watch as he launches the arrow. A moment later, the sa-kohtsk kit bellows in pain, and one of the adults bugles in distress. Feet move and the ground shakes. The hunt has begun.

The men split off, yelling and shaking their spears as they surge forward, chasing the confused animals. One lumbers into a trot, and the ground feels as if it is about to shake apart. Another follows it, and then the herd is moving forward, prodded by spears and screams from our hunters. We are small against them, but it is working.

At the center of the herd, the kit staggers. The mother noses it, trying to get it to move, and when it collapses to its knees, she bellows and then turns away from it, abandoning her child in favor of self-preservation. I see this from my vantage point next to Raahosh, and I'm suddenly frozen. My memories turn back to my father. This is what he chose. He sacrificed his own child—his firstborn son, Raahosh—when he was too injured. For a moment, I want the mother sa-kohtsk to turn around, to nudge her kit to its feet.

Instead, she gives a plaintive howl and lumbers away from it, abandoning it to us.

My heart feels as if it shatters in my breast. I think of Raahosh and his scarred face and come to a devastating realization.

My father was so broken that if I had been wounded like the sa-kohtsk kit before us, I suddenly have no doubt in my mind that my father would have left me behind like the mother beast does now. He would have abandoned me like he did Raahosh, to the ones he deemed as "bad." Or worse, left me in the snow one day and turned his back on me.

I think of doing that to my own son—my Rukhar—and want to vomit.

Never.

I would never leave him or Har-loh behind. Ever. My father was wrong. He did what he thought he had to do to survive, but I realize now that it was not survival. It was mindless instinct. The man I have imagined as my father for so long in my bits of memories? The man I have revered? It is not the man I should be looking to for answers. It should be the man at my side, my brother. My brother who has tirelessly hunted at my side and given me company even when I did not want it. Who brings his pregnant wife and has her sit with mine so she will not be lonely. Who risks his own family to help me protect mine. Who opened his home to me without question, and has never expected thanks.

These are not the bad ones.

"*Move*, Rukh," Raahosh says, and gives me a shove.

I stagger off to the side, just as another one of the sa-kohtsk lumbers past, lowing in anger. I've been standing like a dazed fool in the midst of the hunting fields. Even as I roll away, another hunter moves between myself and the animal, driving it away. Protecting me.

These men all risk themselves for my Rukhar. For my family. I am humbled.

The rest of the hunt passes in a daze. I join the hunters as we circle loosely around the kit, bleating in pain and anger. Even though it is a young creature, it's still twice my height, and could easily crush a man. It moves faster than the adults, limping as we surround it.

In moments, it is over. It is not a glorious hunt, but an effective one. I give silent thanks to the creature that died so that my son might live, and kneel near its chest. With my knife, I slice open the ribs and pry them apart, revealing the pulsing heart full of glowing blue slips of light.

"Is it safe to come?" Liz calls out from afar.

Raahosh waves her forward and one of the young hunters pulls Har-loh's sled. My brother looks over at me and scowls. "You are an idiot. You nearly let one of the herd trample you."

He's mad at me. He's mad like I would be at Har-loh if she

did something so foolish . . . and it's because he's my family and he wants me to be safe. I'm oddly pleased by this, and I reach out and enfold him in a hug.

Raahosh is stiff, and eventually returns the hug awkwardly.

"Thank you," I tell him.

"You are my brother," Raahosh says in a low voice. "I will always help you."

"Oh my God," Liz cries out. "Can you two make out? For me? That would be so hot."

Har-loh giggles. Raahosh shoves me, and then I move to my mate's side, smiling. Har-loh gets to her feet and then she hands me the baby. "Is it time?" She seems nervous, smoothing her hands down her loose clothing.

I hold my son close. Even though it's cold and his tiny face is scrunched up with anger, he's not crying. It worries me. I look to Raahosh, because I've no idea how I get the khui in him.

"Make a cut at the throat," Raahosh says. "Shall I hold him?"

"I'll do it," Har-loh says. "He's my child." She steps forward, her movements slow and tired, but determined.

I reluctantly hand my son back to her and then give her a kiss. "He will not remember the pain," I tell her, though it's half to convince myself.

"I know." She gives me a wry smile. "Remind me to tell you about something humans call 'sir-come-si-shun' sometime."

Liz cackles behind her.

I touch my son's cheek one last time, and his eyes open. So dull and lifeless. They don't sing with the vibrant blue that radiates from Har-loh's eyes and from the eyes of every other person with khui. *Do not worry, my son*, I quietly tell him. *You will be better soon.*

I move to the slain sa-kohtsk and cut the heart free. The slivers of blue wiggle madly, as if trying to break out of the dying organ. It pumps slowly once more, then stops once and for all.

"Just one is needed," Raahosh instructs as I gaze down at the heart.

I nod and turn to my mate. Her face is resolute, and she pulls the furs away from Rukhar's small chest, exposing his upper body.

I clutch the heart against my chest and pull my bone knife free with the other.

"A small incision at the neck," Har-loh instructs me.

My mouth is dry. I hold the knife over my son . . . but I can't do it. His big, dark eyes blink up at me and his tiny fists move. I can't hurt him. "I am weak," I admit to my mate, hoarse. "Raahosh—"

"I'll do it," Har-loh says, and I'm humbled by my mate's strength. She takes the blade from me and sucks in a breath, then nods. "Get one of the khui ready."

By the time I pull one of the wriggling slivers free, it is done. The child's cry is weak, more of a hiccup than a yell, and Har-loh wipes the blood from his neck, soothing him with soft clucks. Gently, I place the khui against the baby's neck—

It writhes and slides into the wound before my mind can grasp it. A moment later, the kit shudders and jerks, and Har-loh clutches him close, her body stiffening with worry.

"Is he . . ."

I clasp her shoulder, both of us intently watching our son. Moments pass. Long, tense moments in which no one breathes. The laughing, boisterous hunting party is utterly silent, even Leezh.

Then, the baby coughs. A moment later, he breaks into a loud wail and his fists raise in protest. Har-loh breathes a happy sigh of relief, but I don't release my breath until he opens his eyes and I see the bright blue glow in them.

At that moment, I know it will be all right. Relieved, I sink to my knees.

The others break into cheers.

Har-loh kneels next to me and offers me the angry child. "Do you want to hold your son?"

I take him in my arms and stare down at him. Already the wound in his neck is healing and his fists move vigorously in the cold air. I hold him close. My son. I look at Har-loh, and my heart overflows when she smiles at me.

My mate.

"Let's go home," I tell her.

Her brows furrow. "Back to the sea cave?"

I shake my head. "Home. With the tribe. Together."

She bites her pink lip. "You're staying?" Her voice is shy, full of hope.

I reach out and touch her cheek. "I could never leave you. Not you, nor our son. We are a family."

Her radiant smile is better than a thousand memories of my father.

EPILOGUE

Harlow

"Ow!" I wince as Rukhar's little gums bite down hard on my nipple. His tiny fist holds on to my finger like he will fight me if I even think about taking my breast away. "Your son is a biter."

"My son is a warrior," Rukh says lazily next to me. He plays with Rukhar's small foot and grins up at me from our furs. "He wants what is his."

I snort, but I can't complain as the baby gazes up at me with bright blue eyes as he feeds. Ever since he got his khui, little Rukhar is not so little anymore. The baby has nearly doubled in size, which is shocking to me. He's now plump and happy and a lot stronger than I expected. The tiny tail lashes back and forth as he feeds, impatient, and I wonder if I'm going to have to go see the healer again to increase my milk production. I switch breasts and the freed one dribbles milk and still feels heavy. Nope. Rukhar's just a little piggy. Strangely enough, I'm fine with that. He's so healthy it makes me beam with happiness to see him. Even his tiny horns are growing.

Rukh's hand brushes over the blondish fuzz on the baby's head and then strokes my arm. I still, because his touchy-feely-ness is something I've sorely missed in the last month. We've been caught up with the new kit and adapting to the tribe, and my body adjusting to post-baby. There hasn't been a ton of time for sex.

Okay, there's been no time for sex. And I'm dying for my mate to touch me again.

Rukh's fingers trace up the curve of my arm, to my shoulder, as he watches me feed our son. Maybe I can put the baby down and we can—

Someone rattles the string of shells in front of our "door." It's a curtain, but since you can't knock on a curtain, I made the next best thing. It allows Rukh to feel like we have a bit more privacy. I pull a leather throw over my body as I nurse, and Rukh sits up. "Enter."

Vektal comes in, and Rukh gets to his feet. The chief looks harassed. "Leezh's kit is coming. Raahosh is . . . not himself."

Which means he is panicking. Not surprising, considering that over the last few weeks, Liz has gone from sharp-tongued to downright crabby as her belly expanded and she grew nearer to giving birth. Raahosh has hovered over his mate and obsessed over the smallest things to ensure that his Liz is happy. Consequently, he is driving everyone else in the tribe crazy. Vektal and Rukh have talked about taking Raahosh hunting while Liz gives birth so he won't drive poor Maylak insane with his questions and nitpicking.

Rukh immediately grabs his spear and his hunting bag. He looks at me, hesitating.

"Go," I say, waving a hand at him. "I'll bring Rukhar over

to Liz and see if we can't distract her. You take care of the father-to-be."

My mate moves to my side and caresses my cheek. "I will bring you home your favorite. With the new birth, the tribe will want to feast tonight."

I chuckle, nuzzling his hand. "Just bring home a calmer Raahosh and that alone will be worth celebrating."

He looks as if he wants to say more, but then nods and heads out after Vektal. I finish feeding the baby, burp him, and then change his leather swaddling out for fresh wraps. Funny how Vektal, Raahosh, and now Rukh have become such close friends. They argue and bicker like brothers, but they also support each other quite a bit more than I expected. Rukh has adapted well to living in the tribe, though when he is in a bad mood, he complains about the noise. But hunting with Raahosh and Vektal helps, and I think he's growing to enjoy the company instead of being irritated by it.

When Rukhar is changed, I put on my prepregnancy tunic dress and am pleased to find it fits. I'm feeling more like myself, though I still miss the touch of my mate. I've stopped bleeding, though, and everything feels like it's back to normal. That means *everything* can go back to normal, right? I hope so.

Because I sure do miss sex. I love Rukhar, and I love being back with the tribe . . . but I want my mate back, too.

I tuck Rukhar under my arm and head over to visit Liz's cave.

She and Raahosh are near Rukh and me, at the back of the spacious cavern system that houses the tribe. I'm not surprised to see Georgie there, though there's no sign of the healer. "Where's Maylak?" I ask as I settle in to join the women.

"Taking a nap," Georgie says. "It'll be a while yet, according to her. Liz is barely having contractions." She pats her own enormous belly with a sigh. Georgie's more than ready to give birth, though the child in her stomach doesn't seem like it's in any hurry.

Liz makes a face at Georgie. "The moment you feel anything close to a cramp, you're going to scream bloody murder yourself, so don't give me shit." She raises her arms. "Now, gimme my favorite nephew."

I hand off Rukhar and settle in to wait with my friends. I'm a little annoyed Maylak isn't here, because I want to ask her about sex and if I'm okay to have it again. She's the closest thing we have to a doctor, and I'm impatient to make a change.

It's time, I think.

❧

Day passes into evening, and evening becomes night before Liz's baby makes its way into the world. Raashel is a fat, healthy baby with a shock of her father's dark hair and her mother's pale coloring . . . and no tail. It's different than Rukhar but she seems otherwise perfect, so even Maylak isn't worried. Liz sobs happily and holds her child as if it might break. When Raahosh enters to see his mate and their child, I swear the man looks as if he'll burst into tears of joy. Georgie, Maylak, and I quickly exit the cave to give the new family some private time.

Outside in the main cavern, someone has broken out the *sah sah* and is passing it around. It's a fermented drink that the sakhui like, but I'm not a fan of it. Plus, I'm nursing and I'm pretty sure that's not good for the baby. There are rowdy drunks and someone drums a song. Georgie yawns and makes a face. "I am happy for Liz, but I can't say that I don't wish it was me at this point."

"You are close," Maylak says, reaching out to touch Georgie's swollen belly. "Your kit has dropped."

Georgie brightens. "You think so? I'm so ready to give birth." She rubs her enormous stomach. "I feel like I should have been the first one to have a baby, and you and Liz are ahead of me."

"Babies come on their own time I guess," I say, holding sleepy Rukhar against my shoulder. He's just finished feeding again and is ready to nap. "You'll have plenty of time once he gets here. Or she."

Georgie nods and holds her arms out. "You want me to take him for a few hours? Give you and your mate some alone time?"

It's like she can read my mind. I blush and hesitate, looking at my sweet baby's face. He won't need to feed for a bit, and I wouldn't mind getting Rukh alone. I look over at Maylak as if asking for permission.

She puts a hand on my now-flatter stomach, which startles me. Her eyes glow bright for an instant, and then dim again. She nods. "Your body is well."

Georgie wiggles her hands, indicating I should pass the baby over. "Were you guys planning this?" I grumble as I hand her Rukhar.

"It's a little obvious that you guys need some alone time," Georgie says with a grin, tucking my son against her with an adoring expression on her face. She cups his little head and then glances at me. "Vektal says Rukh can't stop staring at you every time he sees you, and he's distracted on hunts."

I blush. "Well, we can't have that, can we?"

She winks at me. "Besides, this'll give me an excuse not to party other than 'I'm too pregnant and tired.'" She disappears into the celebrating throng, heading back to her cave. For a moment my entire body itches, and it takes everything I have not to chase her down and snatch my baby back. A few hours away will be good for both of us, and Georgie is more than ready to get some baby practice time in.

Maylak chuckles at my expression and pats my shoulder. "It gets easier, I promise. You will soon be excited for the days when someone offers to take your child for a few hours. For now, enjoy tonight and enjoy your mate." She smiles and hides a yawn. "I'm off to find mine and my bed."

Not the worst idea I've heard so far. I glance around the cavern, looking for a familiar pair of horns and a man that stands slightly differently than the others. I spot him easily—he's off by the central firepit, helping to butcher the kill and chatting with Vektal as he does. They chat with Oshen, one of the elders, as he spits some of the meat for the humans. Even though it's been a year and some change, not everyone can get used to eating their food raw, and kills are divvied up accordingly. I still prefer mine cooked, and I'm guessing that's why Rukh is waiting nearby.

As if he can hear my thoughts, my mate looks up and makes eye contact with me. A possessive gleam shines in his gaze as he watches me. I bite my lip, wondering if I want to wait for food, or if I want to enjoy the time with my man instead.

I tilt my head at our cave, suggesting Rukh meet me there. I'm going to go with "mate" instead of food.

I watch his response, as his nostrils flare and his body stiffens. He cuts Oshen off mid-comment and leaves the group, heading directly for me. Oshen looks confused but Vektal merely grins knowingly as Rukh heads across the cave.

I meet him halfway, admiring how handsome my mate looks. He's come a long way since the first time I saw him. His wild hair has been tamed into long, sleek braids that keep his mane off his face. Instead of the loincloth I had to fight to get him to wear months ago, he now has leggings decorated with dyed quills running up each side and thick fur boots. He wears no shirt, but I don't think he needs one. He's got a gorgeous chest and I'm selfish enough to want to look at it all the time. Heck, I can't seem to stop staring at it right now. My mouth goes dry as he comes closer to me, and I press my hands to that gorgeous blue flesh. "Hello there."

"Are you hungry?"

I smooth my fingers over his collarbones, fascinated by the way his velvety skin feels under my touch. Gosh, it's been a while. I mean sure, we touch every morning and throughout the day, but we don't *touch*. "It can wait."

"Rukhar?"

"With Georgie for a few hours." I look up at him and bite my lip. "We have some time alone."

Around us, people laugh and pass skins of the fermented drink, and they celebrate loudly. We might as well be alone out here for all that we're noticed.

He pauses, and my fingers trace small patterns on his skin. He looks down at my hands, then at me, and then knowing flickers in his gaze. "Not hungry?" he asks, and his voice is low and husky as he moves closer to me.

"Not for food," I whisper.

Rukh places his hand over mine, pressing it to his heart. "Can we . . ."

I nod.

He grabs my hand and tugs me along behind him, heading for our cave. I suppress my laughter, overjoyed that we're getting to steal this time together. Life is so wonderful, and I have my gorgeous mate and a precious baby and a tribe full of friends. I have my health. I couldn't be more content.

We race inside our cave and Rukh releases my hand to draw the curtain securely shut over the mouth of the cave. It's the closest we'll get to privacy, but I've learned that when the curtain is shut? No one comes to bother you. It's an unspoken law of the tribe, and a good one.

The moment Rukh turns around, I kiss him. Not the easy, quick peck of a morning kiss but a hungry, searching kiss that promises all the things we've been missing out on since Rukhar was born. He groans low in his throat and clutches me against his chest, his mouth devouring mine with equal fervor. And here I'd thought I was the only one feeling the need. The way Rukh holds me? It's clear it's been on his mind, too.

But then he breaks the kiss and gently nips at my mouth. "Are you sure you are . . . well?"

I nod, my hand sliding down his chest to cup the bulge in the front of his leggings. "Maylak says I'm perfectly fine and more than ready for mating again."

He groans. "You asked her?"

Is my mate shy? I giggle and stroke my fingers over his cheek. "Of course. I've been wanting you to touch me for forever. Don't you think we've waited long enough?"

He catches my hand in his and gently kisses my sensitive palm. "Har-loh, I will wait forever for you if I must. Time does not matter as long as we are together."

I blink several times to clear my eyes. Just when I think I can't love this man more, he says something new that sweeps me off my feet. I grab one of his braids and wrap it around my hand. The other cups his bulge. "That's a wonderful thing to say, but

I hope you aren't disappointed when I tell you that I'm ready to have sex now."

His eyes gleam wickedly. "Never disappointed."

We kiss again, and he tugs at the ties of my dress. The next few minutes are spent quickly undressing, and then we're naked together. My body's a little different than when we first mated—my breasts are full with milk, my belly's rounded and a little soft, and my hips feel a little bigger than before. But the way Rukh looks at me? I've never felt sexier.

He raises a hand and brushes his knuckles against my nipple, and a bead of milk wells up. "I liked your body before, my Harloh, but now . . . you steal my breath from my chest."

I shiver at the raw need in his voice. I tug on his braid again, indicating that I want him down on the blankets. We can make long, luxurious love in a bit—for now I just want my mate inside me, and I want him to hold me. I crave the closeness that only sex can bring. When he kneels onto the furs, I push him backward, releasing his hair.

Rukh falls onto his back and I bend over him, running my mouth and hands over that gorgeous chest. He touches me as I do, his hands roaming over my skin as I drag my mouth over one hard nipple and then tongue the ridges over his breastbone. I lick my way down his flat, hard belly and then down to his cock.

"I want inside you," he growls, and his hand fists in my hair. "Not your mouth. In my mate. In her body."

I nod quickly. I want that, too. He releases my hair and I slide a leg over his hips, straddling him. It's an awkward position because of his spur, but I rise up on my knees and use my hand to guide him into me, then slowly sink down.

A moan escapes my throat as he thrusts his hips upward, cramming his cock into me. God, that feels incredible.

"Shhh," he whispers. "They will hear you." But then the terrible man reaches up and caresses my sensitive breasts, and it's not like I can keep quiet.

I moan again. I don't care if anyone hears us. They're having a party and I doubt anyone would care. Meanwhile, my mate—my gorgeous, glorious, handsome mate—raises his hips up again and thrusts into me, his hand moving to my hip to hold me steady on him. The spur slides through my pussy lips and brushes up against my clit with every stroke of his cock, and it just adds to the intense pleasure. Having sex with Rukh is always mind-blowing. I move my hips faster, until we're slamming against each other, and the orgasm I'm chasing starts to bloom in my belly. It's not quite there, and I grit my teeth, pushing harder against him, rocking my hips even more.

And because he knows me so well, he reaches between my legs and pinches the top of my pussy. Now, when his cock shuttles into me, the spur slicks against the lips of my sex harder than ever. I cry out as the orgasm takes hold, and I'm oblivious to everything—Rukh trying to shush me, my mate's roughly jerking hips, the party going on in the other part of the cave—as the sweet rush of the orgasm rolls through me. I ride Rukh until the last ounce of the orgasm is wrung from my body and I go limp with pleasure. He rolls us over until my back is to the furs and he hitches one of my legs up, and then fucks me hard until he comes, and the force of his orgasm sends happy little aftershocks of excitement through my body.

He collapses on the furs, panting and sated, next to me. I immediately roll against him and snuggle against his chest. My nose burrows against his neck and I inhale his scent—wild, sweaty, and wonderful. "I love you."

"You are my heart," he tells me, brushing my tangled hair from my face.

I smile and cuddle against him for a moment longer, enjoying the sounds of our breathing mixed together. It feels weird not to have to tense for a baby noise—a wail, a restless hiccup, anything. It's nice but at the same time, I can't wait to get Rukhar back. Well, soon. My hand strokes down Rukh's chest, over his suede-like skin. "Are you happy?"

"Of course."

I sit up on my elbows and peer at his face. That's a quick answer. "No, I mean, are you really happy here? I know you loved the cave by the sea. I know it's hard when there are so many people around. Are you really and truly happy?" The tiny worry that's been gnawing at me for the last month has finally surfaced. "Or are you just putting up with it because of me and Rukhar?"

He gives me a strange look, as if I've asked a weird question. His big hand brushes the tangled hair off my shoulder. "Am I happy to be here with the bad ones?"

I try not to flinch at his expression.

He sees it, and he taps my chin with his finger. "My father filled my mind with his ideas. His thoughts of good and bad. I never thought that he could be wrong. Now that I have you, and I have met the others? Sometimes it is frustrating, but more than anything, I am relieved that we are not alone. That you are not in danger because I cannot be everywhere at once. That we have others to lean on." Rukh looks thoughtful. "And it is strange to have a brother . . . but I like it."

"So even if we could leave for the sea cave tomorrow . . . ?"

He shrugs. "I would choose to stay here. They are not bad

people. They are just people. And they are willing to go to any length to help each other, because they are family. Even if they do not share blood, they are family. I like that." He pauses, and then gazes at me. "We will stay. Our son will need friends. You will need the healer. And I," he says, grazing his thumb over my mouth. "Will always need you. A male cannot exist apart from his heart."

Neither can a woman, and it's clear that Rukh has mine. I lean down and kiss my mate again, determined to enjoy every moment of this time alone.

BONUS STORY

FATHERS

Rukh

I jerk awake in silence.

Always in silence, just as my father taught me. *Do not make sounds. Do not make unnecessary noise, or else the bad ones will hear you.*

I rub my eyes, staring up at the ceiling of our cave, trying to orient myself. I am not a kit alone, forced to bury his father. I am not by the great salt lake.

I am here with the tribe—the bad ones my father warned me about—and here with my mate.

I hold my mate against me in our furs, listening to her quiet breathing as she sleeps. I gaze at her pale body, admiring each brown spot—each freckle—on her skin. Sometimes it does not feel as if I belong in this life, with a mate and a healthy kit. Sometimes I wake up and I think I am still that lonely hunter, unable to join the others because they are "bad ones" as my father taught me all my life. I did not know what it meant to be so happy. To wake up and feel joy at facing the morning.

There was not joy in my dreams last night, though.

My father was in them. I worry his spirit is trying to tell me something. If I close my eyes, I can see his face clearly, the firm disapproval of his mouth glaring at me. I fear I have disappointed him. All his days, he sought to protect me from the "bad ones" and to keep me safe, yet the moment Har-loh is in danger, I race back to them. Now I have promised to live with them for all my days.

My father would hate that. He would hate me for choosing it. Perhaps that is why I dream of him.

Troubled, I press my mouth to my mate's soft mane, breathing in her scent. She is tired, sleeping through my pawing, but I hold her anyhow. Har-loh is the best thing I have ever had. She has made my life so much better—and so much less lonely—ever since I saw her bright orange mane and my khui throbbed in response. I hold her close, letting her chase away the bad dreams. I love my mate's scent, and this morning her teats smell like milk, a sure sign that our son will wake soon and demand his food.

Thinking of Rukhar makes me slide to my feet, gently releasing Har-loh into the furs. Only one thing can pull me away from my mate, and that is my son. He sleeps in a nest a few steps away, because Har-loh worries she will roll on him if he sleeps with us. I move to his side, not surprised to see that he is awake, blinking bright blue eyes at me. He sucks on his fist, kicking his small legs in the air, and my heart fills with such joy at the sight of him that I feel I cannot breathe.

"Ho, my son," I whisper as I pick him up. His wrap is wet, so I quickly change it out, cleaning his soft little bottom before putting a new one on him. He is not yet crying for food, so we will let his mother sleep a bit longer. I cradle him in my arms, and when he reaches for my mane, I give him a handful, ignoring that he yanks hard on it. He cannot do much damage with his weak grip, and even if he could, I would gladly give him every strand on my head.

Rukhar burbles, making soft noises that are not words.

"Mane," I whisper to him as he tugs again. "Mane." He did not come out of Har-loh speaking words, so we must teach him, just like Har-loh has taught me. Rukhar does not seem very interested in learning, though. He smacks his lips and waves his fists again. "We must speak your mother's words so we can all understand one another."

He does not like that. His face screws up, and a little wrinkle forms on his brow. It is a sign he is about to wail, and I wince, pushing a finger into his mouth. He sucks on it for a moment, confused, and then makes a stuttering cry that is loud enough to wake half the cave.

Har-loh immediately shoots upright. "M'up," she mumbles, shoving her orange mane out of her face. "Mommy's here." Her eyes are closed, her expression that of one about to drift back to sleep.

"You still tired," I say in a gentle voice as I kneel next to my mate, offering her our wailing kit. "You feed Rukhar, I do rest."

Har-loh gives me a sleepy smile. "You are amazing, Rukh. I love you."

I prop up a few pillows behind her back as she settles Rukhar against her chest, offering him one full teat to suck upon. Once he latches on, she sighs and leans against my side, her eyes drifting shut again. When my son releases her nipple, Har-loh yawns and switches him to her other teat automatically. As he finishes, she lifts him to her shoulder, and she looks so very tired that my chest aches with fierce devotion. "Rest, Har-loh. I take Rukhar."

"Mmmm. Love you." She pulls the pillows against her and

snuggles down, then drifts back to sleep. I take my sleepy son and put him on my shoulder, gently rubbing his back as I get to my feet. I know this part well. I must rub a belch out of my son or he will spit up his meal. With one hand on my son, I move the screen away from the front of the cave and step out.

It is strange to emerge from my sleeping cave and see so many others about. The myriad scents clash and run together, as if I have my nose down on a busy game trail. The noises of others intrude, too, but they are less offensive than scents. Someone makes food. Someone is working on skinning and the scent of urine mixed with animal brains leaves an acrid tang in the air. I smell the milk of another new mother—probably Har-loh's friend Leezh. I smell many, many humans.

Sometimes it feels like too much.

Rubbing Rukhar's back gently, I move toward the front of the cave with him. "This good place," I remind my son. "You will have good life." I did not have such things. It was me and my father, for as long back as I can remember. Then, when my father died, it was just me, alone, and I did not know what to do with myself.

All I remembered were his warnings. *Avoid the bad ones.*

Yet here I am, living with the bad ones. But they have not been bad to me. And Har-loh needs them.

And I need Har-loh and my son more than I need anything. So here I stay. But some days, I do not like it. Some days, I am reminded that I am disappointing my father. Am I doing wrong for my son? I wonder. Should I take Rukhar and Har-loh away from here? Raise Rukhar as my father taught me? To be silent even in pain, to hide from others at all costs, because they are not safe? I rub my son's back, my mind full of jagged thoughts, and I am startled when the tiny kit lets out a large, hearty belch.

"Ah," says a voice behind me. "You are good at that! We should all pass you our kits and let you belch them."

I turn to see a smiling elderly female. She has a name. I am sure she has told it to me several times. Her mane is streaked with gray, and her face is sharp, her chin pointy. Her eyes crinkle as she smiles at me, a gathering basket on her hip.

I do not trust her. Why would I wish to burp all of the kits in the cave? I only wish to tend to my son. Does she think I am at her call now that I have agreed to stay? I bare my fangs at her, growling. "Leave."

She does not scuttle away with fear, like a metlak would. Indeed, this one must be less intelligent than a metlak, for she ignores my snarl and simply studies me. "I knew your father, when we were young. You are very much like him."

This female knew my father? But if that is the case, then she is one of the ones he wished to avoid. I glare at her, patting Rukhar's back.

My son begins to hiccup, and the female clucks her tongue. She sets down her basket, reaching for him. "There is a trick—"

"No!" I stagger backward, cradling my small son against my shoulder protectively. "You do not *touch*!"

The female raises her hands in the air, giving me a mild look. "Just like your father. You think you can do it all yourself." She shakes her head. "We are here to help you, my friend. We are family here."

Family? My family is dead in a cave by the shore. My family is Har-loh, who sleeps in the furs, so fragile that she must remain close to the healer always. This female with her knowing eyes and gray braids is not my family. She is no one to me. And she *cannot touch my son*.

Furious, I storm away from her, looking for a quiet spot in

the cave. There is none to be found. People are everywhere, making noises, smelling, laughing. Someone splashes in the pool, and it is a happy sound, but it is all too much. It is too much for me this morning, when I have always been alone. When the quiet has been my friend.

With an angry growl, I race outside with my son. Outside, at least, it is quiet.

Harlow

The moment I emerge from my cave, Kemli races over to see me.

Well, that can't be good.

I manage a bright smile as she takes me by the arm. "Morning, Kemli. How are you today?" She and her family are visiting for a day or two from the South Cave. Normally I'd be happy to see her, but the concern on her face has me internally bracing.

"I am worried," she says, lowering her voice. "Your mate ran outside with your kit. Have I offended him somehow? Is he upset at me?"

Wincing, I give her arm a squeeze. "It's not you, Kemli. It's just a lot for him some days. If he comes across as prickly, he doesn't mean it."

"Prickly?" Kemli chuckles, waving a hand in the air. "I knew his father. Compared to him, Rukh is as soft as a hopper. I just fear I have hurt his feelings somehow. I want him to feel welcome, but I worry he thinks I am not his friend."

"That's not it at all," I exclaim. Rukh seemed fine to me this morning, but I know he's been dreaming about his father lately, and when he dreams about his father, he gets . . . erratic. It's like his father didn't want him to be happy, and so every time Rukh feels content, those memories of his father surge up to sabotage him. "I'm sure you did nothing wrong, Kemli. Everyone's been so kind."

The elder clucks, shaking her head. "Perhaps I asked for too much. Borran says I am always sticking my nose in, trying to help. But there have been so many young hunters without mothers that Sevvah and I have tried to mother all. I cannot just turn that off." She gives me a sad look. "Am I pushing too hard, do you think?"

It's hard to say. With Rukh, even saying hello might be perceived as "too much." I keep reminding myself that his father died when he was young and he grew up more or less alone. He doesn't know how to be around people. It took him time to be around me, so it's going to take him just as long to figure out how to be around the tribe, maybe longer. It's not something that can be rushed. "I'm truly sure it's fine, Kemli," I tell her soothingly. "I'll go out and talk to him, though. If you did offend him somehow, I'll be sure and let you know and we'll come up with a plan to ensure we don't ruffle his feathers again."

Kemli brightens. "My thanks. Let me know what I can do to help."

I nod and head toward the front of the cave, tightening my leathers around my body as I do in preparation for stepping outside. It's a chilly day, but I know it affects me as a human way more than it does Rukh or my tiny little Rukhar. I'm more concerned that Rukh is hiding away from the tribe, or that he's going to get upset with the elders being nosy or fussing over him and the baby. Kemli has the best intentions, but she's used to actively mothering all around her, and Rukh doesn't know how to take that.

Part of me still worries that he's going to bolt. That this is going to be too much, and one day he'll snap and I'll never see him again. But he's promised to stay, and if he's so miserable here, I hope he'll talk it through with me before he makes any drastic decisions.

I just want him to be happy.

I head to the front of the cave, to the large entrance where the cold wind blasts inside. Shivering, I tighten my leathers around me and peek outside. I don't see anyone right out front, but of course Rukh would go a little farther away. He wouldn't pay lip service to leaving the cave. He'd go as far as he could to get away without actually leaving. So I trudge up the hill, tucking my bare hands under my arms to keep them warm.

Sure enough, Rukh is up on the rise. He's naked, and his kilt is on the snow, with Rukhar laid out on it on his belly. The baby is swaddled well enough, and he looks happy, so I try not to panic about the cold. Rukh turns as I approach, glancing over his shoulder. "I was not leaving."

"I know," I say, and touch his mane, stroking it as I approach. His accent is thicker today, like it always is after bad dreams, as if he's forgetting his ease with the language. I crouch next to him and brush my fingers over Rukhar's tiny foot. It's warm, his little toes toasty. He's inherited his father's invulnerability to the cold, which is a good thing. I give the foot a little shake, smiling. "Was it too much this morning, love?"

Rukh is quiet for a long moment. Then, he sighs. "It was loud and noisy. Everyone talks at same time. And smells . . ." His nostrils flare. "So many smells. I wanted fresh air."

"I understand." I run a hand lightly down his arm, trying to comfort him. Rukh grew up alone. Some days it's really hard for him to be around a lot of people. "How can I help?"

He shakes his head. "There is no help. I must get used to it."

That sounds depressing. He just has to learn to accept it? I rub his arm again, wishing I could help him along with this. It's such a radical change from how he was living before that of course there are these moments of frustration. They're bound to come up, and sometimes I admit the tribe is too noisy even for me. It's an adjustment living in a cave with a dozen other families, but it can also be good. There are always hands reaching out to help, and someone always has food cooking. There's always a fire to borrow a coal or two from, and clothes handed down. I know Rukh wants to be here for me and the baby. I just wish . . . well, I guess I wish it was easier for him. I press my cheek to his shoulder. "I'm sorry, love."

"No sorry," Rukh says, his language becoming rougher with emotion. "Here is best for you and Rukhar. Here we will stay."

That doesn't soothe my worries. I know sometimes he thinks being alone is what's best for him, but it's no way to live. He needs people to love and care about him . . . he just doesn't know how to handle it yet.

We return to the cave, and I decide I have a "craving" for fresh fish. Rukh is all too happy to head out to the nearest stream to find me something to satisfy my needs. I suspect he's relieved to get out of the cave for a while, because he's used to traveling and being out in the open, spending time wherever. He hasn't traveled all that much since he met me, but I know he gets restless when forced to stay inside for long periods of time. I can't keep finding errands to send him out of the cave so he can breathe, though. He has to come to grips with how he feels on his own. I know he wants to be here with me and Rukhar. There's no doubt of that in my mind. I think sometimes just the reality of it is hard for him to settle into.

So I scoop up my son, and head over to Liz and Raahosh's cave.

The screen is to one side, and as I approach, I can see Liz and her mate. She sits by the fire, sharpening spearpoints, and Raahosh rocks the baby. Hers is slightly younger than mine, and female, and sometimes I want to sit them side by side and just compare the differences. Liz's little Raashel is tiny compared to Rukhar, who has filled out and grown into his height. She's a dainty little thing and has zero tail, which I find fascinating. But that will all have to wait for some other day, because I have a mission today. "Knock knock," I say, approaching the entrance of the cave. "Can I come in or is this a bad time?"

"Of course you can come in," Liz says, putting aside her spear. "Your timing is good. We're about to head out for a quick jog down the trails, maybe hunt some game."

They are? I blink and realize that Raahosh is carrying the baby in a leather homemade carrier strapped to his chest, the tiny child tucked safely against his breastbone. I can't imagine going out hunting with a brand-new baby, but Liz doesn't like to sit by the fire and wait around. She's an active type, whereas I love nothing more than a warm fire and a project to tinker with. "Oh. Um, okay. I actually wanted to talk to Raahosh about Rukh. I think he's having more dreams about his dad, and it's affecting his mood."

Raahosh grunts. He strokes a big hand over Raashel's tiny head and looks over at his mate. "I can do nothing about his dreams."

"I know that," I say, fighting to keep my frustration back. "But, like, you're his family. You know what his father was like. Can you talk to him? Reassure him that no one here hates him or wants ill for him? We're just all trying to make it through each day the best we can. He snapped at Kemli this morning and

I just don't know what to do to help. I want to help him work through it, but maybe talking to you will help him put it into new perspective?"

"About our father?" Raahosh shakes his head. "Vaashan was a hard male. You do not want Rukh to be like him."

"No, I don't. I want Rukh to be Rukh." I give Liz a helpless look, as if she can somehow help me figure out how to get this through to her mate. "That's the thing. Rukh loves me, but I'm his mate so everything I say doesn't register because he feels like he has to be here at the cave for me. It's not what he wants. He thinks he's betraying his father by being here. But you're his brother and another hunter. He respects you. He wants to get to know you better. I think it would mean so much if you just talked to him a little."

Liz gets to her feet. "Babe, what Harlow is saying is she wants you to tell Rukh to get his head out of his ass."

The look Raahosh gives her is puzzled. "His head is not in his ass. I do not even think his head could reach his ass."

I'd laugh if I wasn't so frustrated.

Liz just waves a hand. "Figure of speech. It means he's being stubborn as hell for no reason and he's stressing out his mate. You know what your father was like. She needs you to tell Rukh that just because your father was crazy, it doesn't mean he has to be."

"I just want him to be happy," I blurt. "And I think he has it in his head that he can't be happy here. He can only be happy alone."

Raahosh sighs heavily, as if he's annoyed at all of this. He palms the baby's small head, stroking the downy hair atop her skull. "I will talk to him."

Rukh

I wade into the waters with my spear, the heat sending pleasant prickles through my body. Hunting here is not like hunting by the great salt lake, where the water was so very cold that it rustled with ice when the waves rolled in. The streams here are warm and smell bad, but they have beautiful fish in them, and those fish are very tasty. If I must be truthful with myself, I like fishing in the mountains far more than fishing by the salty waters.

My Har-loh wants one for her evening meal, and so I will get her one. My mate eats too little as it is. She is delicate, and I would love for her to be plump with health. I smile down at the water, thinking of my mate and kit, how Har-loh's face will crease with happiness when I show her a nice fat fish. After Rukhar eats his fill, I plan on dragging my mate back into our furs and touching her, making her emit those soft little sounds of pleasure I love to hear so very much. Distracted by the thought of Har-loh, I do not notice the iridescent fish near my legs until it swims away.

Ah well. There will be others.

Focusing, I pay attention to the surface of the water . . . or at least, I try to. A scent cuts through the pungent stink of the stream, and I lift my head. My brother—Raahosh—approaches. He must have followed my scent trail through the snows to find me. I raise a hand to him in greeting, and when the shiny fish flashes through the waters at my feet again, I stab with my spear.

And miss.

Growling, I clench my jaw and wait for the waters to clear again as Raahosh settles on the banks of the shore. There are no fang-face fish here in this stream, no menacing reeds blocking the view from the water's edge. I do not move, watching the waters, but I am aware of my brother's movements nearby. He settles on the shore, hunkering down, and watches me.

"Leezh taught me to fish with a stick and some sinew," he says, interrupting my concentration.

Eh? A stick and sinew? "You mock me."

"It is true." I glance over and he raises his hands in the air, as if this will make his words sensible. "She puts food on the sinew and ties it to the stick. You dangle it in the water, and the fish come to eat it. When they snap on the food, you yank them from the water and toss them onto the bank. It does not work every time, but it is easier than waiting with a spear."

It sounds strange to me. The waters at my legs are clear and I bite back a sigh. There will be no fish for my mate at this rate. "You came here to tell me this?"

Raahosh is quiet for a moment. "No. I came to speak with you because your mate is worried you are not happy."

Not happy with my mate? "Har-loh is perfect. I am happy."

"The problem is not with her, but with the tribe," Raahosh says. "I think she frets that you are miserable being around so many people. I imagine it is a lot to take in, but you have your mate at your side to make things better." He shrugs. "I told her I would speak with you. She suspects you think of our father and it makes you sad."

Har-loh is clever. She knows me far too well, and for a moment I am struck by how strange it is for another person to know everything about me. I am used to being secretive, to hiding in the shadows, to watching the others instead of living amongst them. I am used to being alone and keeping my secrets, and Har-loh knows me so well that she sends Raahosh out to speak with me? I feel a rush of affection for my mate. She desperately wants me to be "happy" with her. I am happy, but I do not think my happy looks like her happy, and this is what brings her fear.

I settle my spear and shift my feet, then turn my attention back on the water, waiting for another fish to swim by. "Father would not like the cave. He told me many times to avoid it."

Raahosh snorts. "Father did not like anything. If you lived your life by his rules, you would have no mate and no kit. You would be alone. Do not pick and choose which of Father's rules to follow. You must either be his son entirely or you must realize that he was wrong about a great many things."

Picking and choosing Father's rules? I turn my head slightly, glaring at my brother.

"You know I am right."

I do, and that is what angers me. Father's rules for me were absolute. I do not talk to the bad ones. I do not help the bad ones. I do not let them see me. I do not let them know I exist. I avoid them at all costs. If I followed Vaashan's rules, Har-loh would not be my mate. I would not know words to speak with her, or what it is like to have a mate put her arms around me and take me into her body. I would not have my son, who makes my heart ache when he laughs and coos and reaches for me. Rukhar makes me feel as if I would do anything for him. Anything. It is the same fierce devotion I have for my mate, but a different flavor.

Vaashan—my father—would want me to have neither. And even though he visits me in my dreams and tells me he does not approve, Raahosh is right. If I listen to him, I lose what is most precious to me.

And I cannot lose Har-loh and Rukhar. I already almost lost my mate once. I will not lose her again, simply because my father did not like the tribe he was born into.

"It is . . . difficult," I say after a moment. "Har-loh tells me one thing, and I think she right, but I hear Father's voice in my head, and . . ."

"I know." Raahosh's response is simple. "I remember him enough, and the tribe remembers him, too. He has told you lies and filled your head with the wrong ideas. It will take time to break free of those."

I turn to look at my brother, forgetting all about fishing. "What do I do? How do I make Father go away from dreams?"

"Talk to your mate," my brother says. "She is new to the tribe, too, but look at how they treat her. Look at how they treat your kit. Do those seem like the actions of a people that wish you harm?" When I am silent, pondering this, he continues. "Speak with Har-loh. If something feels wrong to you, talk to her about it. Do you think she would wish you to do something that would make you unhappy in your spirit?"

I consider this. "No."

"Then talk to her. Or talk to me."

I eye my brother. He wears the clothes of the tribe and smells like their soapberries. He wears his mane the way they wear theirs. He is good friends with the chief. "But you have been polluted—"

Raahosh throws up his hands. "Then talk to your mate and not to me. But talk to someone. No one wishes ill for you or Rukhar. They are not bad ones. They are just people that disagreed with Father."

"They are noisy," I admit after a moment.

"They are," Raahosh agrees, surprising me. "They are noisy and underfoot and sometimes it can be a pain. Farli and Sessah scare all the game from the trails near the caves. Kemli and Sevvah are always trying to feed me. Vaza will give you advice on how to pleasure your mate." He shakes a warning finger at me. "And do not listen to him. He is full of an elder's foolishness."

I blink in surprise at his vehemence.

"Sometimes it feels as if we are all crowded into a cave and breathing each other's air, this is true," Raahosh says. "But when I was a small kit with no father and no mother, they fed me and kept me clothed. Sevvah always makes sure I have the tea I like. Drayan and Drenol sharpen spears so I do not have to waste time on them. Hemalo and Kashrem keep the unmated hunters in leathers. The human females cook for each other when someone is too tired to make food. If Leezh wants time alone with me, there are many that are eager to watch our kit for us. It is many people, yes, but that does not make it bad always. Do you understand?"

My brother's words are passionate. It is strange, because Raahosh is scarred and surly, and walks as if all around him bother him. Yet he defends the tribe and speaks fondly of them. He speaks of a people that share chores to make life easier. That was one of the things that was so surprising—and so welcome—when I first met my Har-loh. That she would help me and not everything was on my shoulders alone.

I rub my face, thinking. "I will consider your words, brother."

"Good. See that you do." He gets to his feet and gestures. "Your fish is coming back."

I ready my spear above the water, grinning. Perhaps my mate will have her favorite food tonight after all.

Harlow

Rukh returns just as I've set Rukhar down for an afternoon nap. He brandishes an enormous iridescent fish with a satisfied smile, holding it up by the tail.

"Oh," I exclaim, startled to turn around and nearly collide with three feet of shiny-looking fish corpse. "Wow! That's a big one."

He nods. "I found biggest one for you."

Eek. I like fish, but I don't like second-day fish. This one is big enough that it could feed several in the tribe . . . and it's probably going to have to. "You're wonderful, Rukh," I tell him, beaming as I take the fish from him. I put a finger to my lips and point at the baby, but Rukhar's a heavy sleeper. I glance around the cramped cave and then move out toward the entrance, where I keep my "prep" station, because smells tend to linger in the smaller caves longer than the larger main cave. I hand the fish back to him briefly and then unroll my "countertop"—a heavily stained, thick slab of leather that I use for prepping food. Once it's in place, Rukh tosses the fish down and I contemplate how best to prep it.

I glance up at my mate. He seems like he's in a good mood. Is . . . this because Raahosh managed to talk to him? Or is it because he hasn't talked to Raahosh yet and his mood will sour once he does? Sometimes it's hard to tell what Rukh is thinking. "Great job, baby. Hand me my knife?"

Rukh frowns and then moves to kneel next to me. "You tired. I do this." He begins the messy work of gutting and cleaning, and I want to kiss him for it. I love the taste of fish, but cleaning them is not my favorite. Not in the slightest. Vegetarian me would shriek in horror at what I have to do to have a decent meal these days, but the practical side of me knows that meat and protein is the way to survive here.

"Thank you," I breathe, watching him work. "You're a good mate."

He grunts, cutting a slit up the belly and then pulling the organs out. He's quiet for a moment, and then looks over at me. "Is true? Your people catch fish with sticks?"

"With sticks?"

"Stick and sinew. Raahosh says so."

So Raahosh did have a chat with him? I'm bursting to know what it was about, but I'm stymied by the mental image of sticks and sinew. "We have nets, and . . . oh wait." I snap my fingers. "Fishing rods and line. Yes! That's one way of doing it."

"You show me?"

"Of course! I'd love to show you." I beam at my mate, loving that this is something I can contribute. Most of what I know— how to change the oil in a car, how to build a computer from scratch, how to repair a 1950s jukebox—is stuff I learned from my dad and not exactly useful here on the ice planet. But fishing? Fishing I can show.

My mate nods, working on the fish. He glances up at me out of the corner of his eye. "Raahosh said many things."

I lick my lips, trying not to worry. "Oh? What about?"

"That our father was wrong. That I cannot listen to his voice in my head. That I have good mate and son, and I should not create problems."

A small smile curves my mouth. "I don't think you're creating problems, love. I think you're just adjusting. It's hard for everyone, but harder for you because of where you came from. I hope you don't think I'm upset with you."

Rukh looks over at me, his eyes intense. "I think you are best thing ever happen to me. I think . . ." He gazes down at his hands and makes a face. "I think I wish to kiss you, but my hands are . . ." He shakes them off, and slimy stuff goes flying.

Wrinkling my nose, I gently guide his hands out of the way and then fling my arms around his neck. "I'll kiss *you* instead."

Rukh goes still as I lean in and press my lips to his. He kisses me back, his mouth gentle and sweet on mine. "My Har-loh," he murmurs, and then nips at my lip, sending shivers of pleasure through me. "Shall we go inside?"

"What about the fish?"

"It not leaving."

I chuckle at that. "What about the baby? I just put him down."

He gives me an intense look, his lips moving over mine again. "I can be quiet."

Hot, hungry need races through me. We just recently got the go-ahead to return to sex, and I've been incredibly needy ever since. The moment he suggests it, I'm dying to have his cock inside me. A quick, desperate round of sex is exactly what we both need. "Wash your hands," I whisper. "Quick. I'll go get undressed."

I race into the cave we share, checking on the baby first. He's asleep, his little fists level with his ears as he sleeps on his back, his lashes long and dark against his pale blue skin. I want to touch the round little head. His hair was pale at first, but it's been darkening steadily since the birth, and I think soon enough he'll be the image of his father. I can't wait to see that. Satisfied that Rukhar will sleep for a bit longer, I quickly strip out of my clothing, pulling off my boots and leggings. The cold air means us humans are constantly burying ourselves in layers, which makes it difficult to get undressed in a sexy manner, so I just skip that part entirely. As long as I'm naked and Rukh is naked, that's good enough. Once I'm nude, I wrap a fur around me to keep warm and wait by the firepit.

My mate enters the cave we share, pulling the screen behind him. I immediately press a hand to my mouth to stifle a giggle, because Rukh is completely soaked, his mane wet and his skin gleaming with droplets. His loincloth is soaked, too, and his boots are gone. I suspect if I went out, I'd find them abandoned next to the heated pool in the center of the main cave. He rakes a hand through his wet mane, approaching me with a hungry look in his eyes.

"You didn't have to take a bath," I whisper, moving toward him.

He raises his hands in the air, wiggling his fingers. "All clean." His voice is low and husky as he slinks toward me. As I watch with a riveted gaze, he tugs on the ties that keep his loincloth in place, and the wet material drops to the floor. "Now we mate."

Sounds good to me. I lift my arms, intending for him to bend down so we can kiss. Instead, he tears the fur off of me and grabs me by the hips. Before I know it, he has me lifted up against the cave wall and pressed against him. Oh. Okay, I *like* this. I bite back a gasp as he nuzzles at my throat, hitching my thighs around him. Normally we head straight for the furs, but I'm down with a bit of against-the-wall sex. My lips part as he moves, rubbing the head of his cock between my legs. I bite back a gasp, digging my nails into his shoulders as he shifts my weight, seeking out the entrance to my body. He's there a moment later, and it takes *everything* I have not to squeal at the hard thrust he gives me. I'm not as wet as I could be, but I love the stretch and burn of my body accommodating his.

Rukh adjusts my weight again, and then his spur hits right against the hood of my clit. My legs jerk in response, and I can feel the rumble of his laughter deep in his chest, as if my response amuses him. I suck in a breath, clinging to him as he rocks his hips. His gaze meets mine, and then Rukh thrusts into me, rubbing my clit as he pumps deep.

Oh God, it is *so* hard to be quiet at times like this.

He rocks into me, his hips jerking with frenzied, quick motions. I scrabble at his back, trying to find the perfect spot to hold on, to brace myself against the wild ride he's giving me. My back thumps against the wall as he uses me, and I give up trying to anchor myself and just cling to him, holding on. I'm not going to last long anyhow, not with the way his spur is dragging against the side of my clit like a big fat finger that knows just how to rub—

A hand clamps over my mouth just as a choked sound escapes me. Rukh watches me with heated eyes, hammering into my body as I clench around him, and then I come, and come, and come, and it's so good that I see spots dance behind my eyes. Oh God. *Oh God*.

Oh God, I love this man's body.

Dazed, I hang on to my mate as he pounds into me, his movements becoming erratic as he reaches toward his climax. His breath rasps, and his grip tightens on my hip. I squeeze my legs tighter around him, squeezing my pussy, too, and I lick the palm still over my mouth.

The breath explodes out of him as he comes, and he buries his face against my neck once more, trying to muffle the sound. I wrap my arms around him, straining my ears to hear the baby. Did we wake him? There's a little whimper that makes both of us stop, but when nothing follows it, I exhale in relief. He's drifted back to sleep.

Somehow, when I imagined myself as a parent, I never pictured furtive, silent sex between naps. I'm pretty sure that needs to be in the instruction manual . . . not that there is one. Even if there was, I'm pretty sure having an alien half-feral spouse and a half-alien baby wouldn't be covered by said manual. Just as well. I stroke Rukh's cheek, smiling up at his sated expression. "Feel better?"

He presses his forehead to mine. "My heart," he whispers. "You must speak if I make sad. If I am difficult."

"You're not. I promise you're not. I know it's hard sometimes." I trail my fingers through his mane, trying not to squirm because his spur is pressed rather insistently against a very sensitive part of my anatomy. "Everyone just wants the best for you and for Rukhar both. But I totally get that sometimes it can be too much. Maybe . . . maybe we make it a point to get out of the cave regularly? When the weather is nice, you and me and the baby can go out for the day. Get some fresh air and get away."

Rukh's expression brightens. "You do this for me?"

He sounds so surprised, and it breaks my heart. I think it still hasn't set in for him that we're a team. That we do this together. That everything we do in the future is for Harlow and Rukh, not just Rukh by himself, Rukh the loner. "Of course I would. I love spending time with you. Always." I rub my nose against his. "Maybe we could even go fishing together."

My mate gives me a flash of fangs, a reluctant smile spreading across his face. "I like." Rukh shifts his body and then leaves mine, setting me down on the floor. My feet have barely touched the ground before he finds a soft leather we use as a towel and he begins to clean between my thighs. "I try harder, too. I be nice to elders." He pauses and glances up at me. "Even if nosy."

I smile. "That's all I can ask, love."

Rukh

Har-loh feasts on the fish I brought her, and when Rukhar wakes, he cries and cries until she changes him, and then settles him against her teat for his meal. Her expression is weary, her smile gentle as she looks at me, and my heart feels heavy with pleasure at the sight of my mate feeding our kit.

"More fish?" I ask, feeling a need to contribute. I cannot feed Rukhar, but I can feed Har-loh at least.

She shakes her head. "I am fished out. It was delicious, but I'm not sure I want any more. Maybe offer the rest to the elders so it doesn't go bad? I'd hate for it to be wasted."

I nod agreement, moving the slab of flaking fish onto one of the bone platters. There is still a great deal of it remaining, more than I can eat alone if I decide to keep it, and I know Har-loh does not like meat when it sits for days. It must be freshly cooked or it must be smoked, or she gags on the taste. She told me once that at her home she did not eat meat, but I cannot imagine such a thing. I picture her gnawing on roots all day long and wonder if that is what made her so fragile.

A small part of me hates the thought of giving this food to the rest of the tribe. My father would be furious. He would say if they needed to be fed, they should hunt. That each person must take care of themselves. I think of the words I shared with Raahosh, though. I cannot follow Father's rules and expect to be happy with my mate.

I choose Har-loh. There is no question in my mind. I glance one more time at my sleepy mate. She is covered in my scent, a flushed spot on her neck from where I mouthed her too eagerly as we mated. Her expression is dreamy, her gaze locked upon Rukhar as he nurses. Again, my heart feels too small for all the joy it contains. If it means I must humor the elders to keep her safe, I will do so. I take the cooked fish on the platter and head out of our small cave into the main living area.

My first choice is to give it to my brother and his mate, but Raahosh caught a fish of his own for his female, and I do not think he would welcome mine. Reluctantly, I glance over at the central fire. A small crowd is near it. The eldest males of the tribe sit there, bowls in their hands as they eat stew. The nosy female with the gray braids is near the fire, her gaze moving over me. I bite back a sigh of irritation. Har-loh says she means well, and so I must believe it.

So I approach. As I do, a human female gets to her feet, her pregnant belly huge, and I wonder how my father's rules would apply to her. She giggles and puts a hand to the small of her back, moving to speak with another pregnant female. They both look at me, grinning, and I realize I have forgotten my loincloth. Humans and their strange ways, hiding the body all the time. I hesitate, not wishing to upset Har-loh by my actions. Will she be mad I did not wear clothes as she has asked?

"Pay them no mind," the gray-maned female says, moving to

my side. "They are heavy with kit and bored. Your body is a fine one." She waves a hand in their direction, and her expression is the same doting, amused look I have seen Har-loh give Rukhar when he makes a funny noise. It is the face of a mother amused at a kit.

She is giving me the same look as well, as if I am a kit of hers, too. I think of what Raahosh said, of how the tribe took care of the hunters when they had no one else. It makes me feel less annoyed, and I hold the platter of fish out. "Har-loh says for you."

The elderly female takes the platter and sniffs it. She tsks, but a smile is on her face. "You cooked it."

"My mate likes cooked food."

She rolls her eyes, but her expression is both doting and amused. "Humans and their strange tongues. Do you eat your food raw?" When I nod, she gives me a look of approval. "Smart. Do you want some tea, my son? I made extra. Come sit by the fire and hear the stories. Eklan is telling a good one this evening."

I am her *son*? I frown at that, my every instinct screaming that I should fling away the hand she puts on my shoulder as she tries to steer me forward. My father would hate this, hate her, hate that I am here . . . I squeeze my eyes shut, blotting out those thoughts. I think of my Har-loh and her bright eyes. She wants the others to have our fish. She wants the others to like me.

For Har-loh and Rukhar, I must try.

So I let the female pull me along toward the main fire. I never sit here with the others, and it feels strange to see all their faces brighten as I approach. They look pleased to see me. It is . . . odd. Someone stands up and moves across the fire, and the elder female at my side steers me toward the now-empty place. I thump down, and gaze at the faces around me. There are many elders, but there is a younger male, too, leather sewing in his hands. I have been told all their names, but I do not recall them, and I feel a moment of sheer panic. Everyone is silent. Are they waiting for me to speak? I have nothing to say.

"Back to your story, Eklan," the female says, moving back to my side. She flings a warm fur over my naked thighs and then offers me a plate of food. A moment later, a cup of warm tea is pushed into my hand.

Across the fire, a white-maned elder shakes his head. His face is heavily lined, his skin faded to a pale blue. "You have heard my stories time and time again, Kemli. I would hear what this one can tell us."

Kemli. I make a mental note to remember the female's name, but then a moment later, it registers what the elder is saying. He wishes me to speak? I stare. I have spoken to them before, have I not? What new words do they wish now? "Tell you . . . what?"

A young female with arms like twigs sits next to me, her expression eager. "Tell us about how you lived alone for so long!"

"Farli!" Kemli scolds. "If he wishes to speak of that, he will."

"Then tell us about the great salt water," young Farli continues, unruffled by the older female's irritation. She leans forward, all excitement. "I heard there are huge creatures in it! Bigger than dvisti!"

This, I am more comfortable talking about. Did those creatures not fascinate me as a young kit as well? "There are," I say slowly. "I have seen some, big as this cave." I move to stretch my hands out, but I have tea in my grip and take a sip of it instead. "Many tentacles."

Her eyes grow round with fascination. "Did you hunt one?"

"No," I say. "I like living."

A ripple of laughter cuts across the group. I am surprised, because only Har-loh laughs at my words. But hearing this group ripple with amusement makes me feel . . . good. My father's disapproving face rises into my thoughts, and I quickly shove it aside again. Har-loh thinks they will be good for us, and Har-loh is everything.

I trust in her, instead.

I talk in my halting language of the creatures that live on the shore. I talk of the strange ones I have glimpsed only from very far away, or the time that the skies filled with ash and the waters receded so far I could see fish flopping on the sands—only to have the waters surge back a moment later and crash me against the distant cliffs. That only happened once, and I nearly lost my life. I managed to survive by clinging to the dead body of a gigantic fish as it floated and bobbed atop the waters. I tell them of my father's final resting place near the shore, and of the metlaks that wander through the mountains and my run-ins with them. I talk and talk, and I keep waiting to run out of things to say, but they all listen with fascination. Kemli puts one cup of tea after another into my grip, and she keeps my plate full of tasty raw tidbits that I share with young Farli.

And when I am done talking, old Eklan picks up his story once more, telling of a hunt he and many of the males went on when they were young. My father is in the story as a young, brash hunter, and I listen intently. Eklan's memories of him are of a good male with a bad temper, and a relentless hunter. This matches my memories of him, and it fills me with a mellow ache. I miss my father . . . but at the same time, I am glad he is not here. He would not like this evening by the fire and I have enjoyed myself far too much.

When everyone scatters for the night, I help clean up and

bank the fire, as it does not seem right to leave those chores to another. Another elder, Vaza, is in charge of cleaning up, and he gives me a look of appreciation as I assist. We tidy things up in silence, and then I head off to find my mate. I feel a twinge of guilt at abandoning her for so long, but Har-loh could join us at any time. She knew where I was. Perhaps I should have stayed to help with the kit, though. As I duck into our cave, I see Rukhar is in his bed and Har-loh is curled up in our furs. She rouses the moment I slip in next to her, moving close to snuggle against me.

"Did you have fun talking to the others?" she whispers.

"It was odd," I admit. "Not unpleasant, but odd."

"Give it time. They're just people like anyone else. And they're good people." She tucks her cheek against my chest.

If she believes they are good, then they must be. My Har-loh would not lie to me. I feel as if I have accomplished something this night, even if I did nothing but sit around the fire.

My mate curls up in my arms and drifts off to sleep, and I do, as well.

For the first night in many, many nights, my father does not appear in my dreams.

ICE PLANET
HONEYMOON

RUKH & HARLOW

Harlow

One of the first mornings at the beach, I wake up to something scuttling over my foot.

It hasn't been the most comfortable night's sleep already. Sand is everywhere, and the cave we're bunking in is tiny and cold. Those things don't matter the moment I look up at the sunlight streaming in from outside and see one of the scorpion-things perched on my boot. I kick it off, sliding backward in the cave in horror. Everywhere I look, there's more of the damn things. They're on the furs, at the mouth of the cave, and I swear there's one on the wall. I make a noise of distress at the sight.

My mate, Rukh, is instantly awake at my terrified sound. He sits up, growling and ready to protect me, a question in his eyes. I point at one of the things. They're horrid, a cross between a crab and a scorpion with lots of legs and a segmented tail. Rukh plucks the nearest one off the wall and promptly bites the head off.

I squeal in horror again.

He holds the limp thing out to me, an offering. "Har-loh?"

"I'm not eating that," I cry. "Not on your life!" The defunct vegetarian in me is appalled at the thought. I've had to make a lot of changes since coming to this icy planet, not the least of them being a change in my dietary habits. And so far eating meat hasn't been too bad, even if I do randomly get cravings for a hamburger of all things. But seeing Rukh holding that awful-looking thing out to me to eat? Raw and dripping? I can't do it. My throat clenched tight, I shake my head.

He stares at it, and the look in his eyes is uneasy. "Har-loh . . . no?"

"No," I manage. "My seafood has to be cooked."

"Cookt?" he echoes, shaking the floppy thing at me. "Rukh cookt?"

Rukh doesn't know a lot of language—any at all—because he's been feral for so long. He's picking up some of my words, though, desperate to talk to me. And "cook" is one of them he knows.

I stare at the thing, trying to get over my initial disgust. It's food, I remind myself. It's food it's food it's food.

"Cook it, sure," I manage. "Thank you."

Rukh grunts, the sound full of pleasure, and tosses the dead thing down on the ground. Then he grabs another one of the things. He lifts it to his mouth, ready to bite the head off, and then glances over at me. As if recalling the horror on my face, he changes tactics at the last moment and snaps the head off instead. It makes an awful crunching sound, followed by a splat of liquid, and then he tosses it down onto the other. Within moments, we have a neat, tidy little pile. He doesn't care that they pinch at him with their stinger-pincher things, or that they scuttle away fast when they see his hand descending. Rukh is faster than them, and something tells me he's done this plenty of times before.

I can't begrudge the man for surviving, even if it is a little rough on my sensibilities.

I curl up in the back of the small cave and watch Rukh as he chases the smaller ones out of the cave with a flick of his hand and beheads the larger ones. It hasn't been very long at all since Rukh and I resonated. Not very long since he hit me over the head and stole me, and I'm still adjusting. It's a lot to take in all at once—leaving behind the sa-khui tribe that's welcomed me since I got to this planet to go out into the wild alone with Rukh, but he's made it clear that, to him, they're the enemy.

Since he's my person, I'm not leaving his side. We'll just have to figure out how to manage with just the two of us.

It's one reason we're at this beach, I think. From what I can tell from our (admittedly short and mostly inferred) conversations, the weather will be warmer here throughout the wintry brutal season, and we're much farther away from the tribe that he wants so desperately to avoid. His father's grave is here, too, and I suspect he just likes the beach. It's pretty, even if it's nothing like the beaches back home. It's cold and rocky and a little violent, but the tide still rolls in to hit the sands, and there's a comforting familiarity with that, even if the sands are greenish and the tide is slushy with ice.

Rukh piles up all the dead scorpion-crabs and then begins to make a fire near the entrance to the cave. It's a small one, and I inwardly wince when he tosses the dead things directly onto the flames. I have to remind myself that Rukh's used to eating his food cold and raw, and the fire's for me. I can't really complain that he's not skilled at grilling his food if he's never grilled before, can I?

He's trying to please me, and really, that's all a girl can ask for.

Once they're all on the fire, he looks over at me with expectation. I beam approval at him, and love that a slow smile curves his mouth. "Thank you," I say softly. "They're not as gross when cooked."

"Cook," Rukh says as he moves around the fire and back to my side. "Rukh cook Har-loh."

I giggle. I know what he means, but it just sounds a little funny to hear. "You're doing lovely, Rukh. I appreciate it."

He sits extremely close to me, pushing aside some of the loose furs I piled atop us when we slept. He's naked—he's pretty much always naked—and Rukh leans in close, touching my jaw. "Rukh kiss Har-loh," he murmurs. "Yes?"

He's definitely learned all the "important" words, my wild, ferocious mate. He's got "kiss" down pat, that's for sure. "Kiss," I whisper, and lean in to brush my lips over his. I won't think about him biting off the head of one of those scorpion-crab things, because I might think it's gross, but to him, it's just food. I don't want him to ever feel ashamed around me. There's nothing wrong with him; it's me that has to adjust to life here.

So I touch his face gently and kiss him. Kissing Rukh is never a chore. If anything, it feels a bit like Christmas every time, which is an odd way to think about it, but it fits. He acts as if every time I kiss him, it's a gift. And I feel like every time that I kiss him, I'm being given something special as well. So . . . Christmas. It makes me happy to touch him, to kiss his firm mouth, to give him pleasure. I think about all the years he grew up in the wild without anyone to talk to, much less anyone to kiss, and I'm happy that resonance paired us together. It doesn't matter that he scared me in the beginning. I saw the lonely, aching man beneath all the dirt and fell in love.

Rukh groans softly against my mouth, tugging me to the furs. He's ravenous for attention, my mate. Doesn't matter how insignificant the touch is, he wants more. I keep that in mind as I kiss him, making sure to touch him all over, brushing my fingers over his skin and down his neck. I murmur his name between little presses of our lips, letting him know how pleased I am with him and how happy I am to be here with him. He can't understand my words yet, so I'll give it to him in actions.

"Har-loh," he rumbles, his khui purring despite the fact that we've already resonated. Just being around one another is enough to make our khuis respond, and I place my hand over his heart, where his khui "sings" to me.

Rukh brushes his nose against mine, then nips at my lower lip. His hand slides to the loose waist of my leggings and slips inside. He's ravenous, my mate, and it's an eagerness that I share. I thought things were supposed to slow down with resonance, but it's been a few days now and I still feel as insanely hungry for him as ever. I still wake up with him touching me in the middle of the night, and it excites me.

It's not a chore to be touched by him. Not in the slightest. I'm still getting used to this planet, to resonance, and to the thought that we've made a baby. But adjusting to him? No hardship at all. "Touch me," I whisper. "I don't mind."

"Touch," he rumbles, and his hand steals between my thighs. He's a quick learner, and all it took was for me to show him once what I liked and now he's determined to do it right every damn time. I moan, clinging to his shoulders as he rubs lightly at my clit. "Har-loh mine." His voice is so possessive as he leans in and nips at my ear, repeating the words. "Har-loh mine."

Fuck, when did he learn "mine" and do I even care? I rock against his hand as he works my pussy, his finger lightly dancing over my clit. I bury my hands in his hair and clench my body against him as he nibbles on my ear and seems determined to give me a hard and fast orgasm even before breakfast. Need ratchets up in my body, and before I can even process things, I'm coming hard and fast, my pussy flooding with my release. I let out a little cry as I come, dazed at how he can make me get off so darn quickly.

He kisses me again, his movements gentle and tender. "Har-loh."

"Rukh mine," I tell him softly. I smile up at him, all dopey-eyed pleasure, and run my hand along his chest.

This makes him happy, too. He gives me a fierce look, as if he likes the idea of me calling him mine. In that moment, though, the sand-scorpions start to pop and sizzle on the fire. Reluctantly, he pulls away and moves to the food. "Rukh food Har-loh," he says instead.

"If we must," I say, fighting back a little disappointment. I wouldn't mind rolling around in the furs for a while, but I guess that's not how you survive out here. It's a lot of work, and I need to start thinking like my barbarian does. "Food, and then we start to make a home, right? Right."

Rukh only grunts an answer.

Rukh

I will never grow tired of watching my female eat the food I have brought for her. I know she does not like the look of the crawlers, but she enjoys the flavor when they are sizzled atop the fire. I must remember to do that every time. Har-loh likes all her food warm. Har-loh likes everything warm, I realize, as she piles a few of the furs over her body before coming to join me by the fire. She does not walk about in nothing but her speckled skin. Instead, she piles the skins of others atop her and shivers when she does not have enough of them.

This is another thing I must learn when it comes to my mate. Har-loh is fragile and weak compared to me. I must take care of her. I must handle all the things that are too difficult or that she does not like to do, because I am her mate. I hand her one of the hard-shelled things and she immediately drops it into the sand, hissing and licking her fingers. "S'tewhawt," she fusses, sucking on her thumb. "Gimmemowment."

I touch the hard-shelled creature, but it does not seem too warm to me. She has gotten sand on hers, though, so I crack mine open, revealing all the tasty white flesh inside, and set it down on a corner of the animal skin in front of her.

Har-loh's expression grows soft. "Dankyewbehbeh," she tells me, and my cock surges in response to her soft words. I love hearing her speak.

I nod and take the one she dropped, brushing off the grains of sand before cracking it open and eating it. I watch as she picks at hers with dainty fingertips, nibbling on the tiny bits of flesh she pulls free. She is so . . . soft. And pink. I worry that I will not be a good mate to her. That I will not be able to take care of her like I should. I am fine with sleeping in the sand. I am fine when the weather turns brisk and the clouds come and do not leave for days and days. But these things will be hard on my little mate, and the thought of that makes my gut clench with fear.

I cannot lose Har-loh like I lost my father. I cannot go back to having no one at all. Har-loh is everything to me. She showed me how to kiss, and how to put a kit inside her. She showed me how to wash. She smiles at me and she is teaching me words. I have never been so happy as I am now, with Har-loh at my side. It scares me, a little. I know of too many nights when I woke up and there was no one to talk to, no one to give me food when I was hungry. Too many times I was sad and alone, missing my father.

I will not let my Har-loh be sad and alone. With that thought racing through my mind, I pick up another crawler, crack the hard shell open, and offer it to my mate. "Eat."

After we eat our fill, Har-loh makes noises that she wishes to leave the cave. It is safest for her inside, but if she wishes to see the great salt water, I will not deny her. It is a fascinating thing to look at, and I find the constant roar of the waves soothing. I watch as my mate puts on all the furs, covering her speckled skin, and then smiles at me. "Reddytewgoh."

I grunt and wait for her to leave the cave. I plan on staying at her side for as long as possible. Har-loh is clever about a great many things, but she is not as hardy as she should be. She is delicate and fragile, and I will not have her hurt.

When she emerges from the cave, she reaches for my hand. I wait, wondering if she has something to show me, but all she does is hold my hand. At my baffled look, she just chuckles and reaches up to touch my face with her other hand. "Snew to yew-issit?" But she gives my hand a squeeze and does not let go, then tugs me along, indicating I should follow her.

I do. I would follow her anywhere.

Har-loh talks in her happy voice as we walk on the beach, but I do not know the things she says. I am content to listen to her babble and to walk at her side, drinking in her scent and watching her movements. Her bright mane tangles in the breeze and she pushes it behind her small ears constantly, but she never stops talking. She does not let go of me, either, and I decide I like the warm press of her hand clutching at mine. Does she hold on to me so I will not leave her side?

As if I would ever leave her behind.

My mate crouches and picks up something from the sand. It is a hard shell, one that comes from a creature with many legs. "Takedis wif us," she says to me, holding it out.

She wants me to look at it? I lift it to my nose and sniff it, but the creature inside is long gone. I examine it for a moment, and then toss it back to the ground.

"No!" Har-loh cries, letting go of my hand. She picks the thing up, and the look on her face is sad when she picks up the two broken pieces of it. "Rukh, no."

"No?" I do not understand. I make the gesture for food, confused. Is she hungry? "Eat? Har-loh eat?"

"No," she says again, a little more calmly. There is frustration on her face as she pushes the two pieces together again. "Couldabeen playt." She looks up at me. "Needta mayk a home."

I stare at her, trying to understand. I hate that I do not have the mouth sounds like she does. I want to tell her how lovely she is. How looking at her makes me happier than a full belly. How when I wake up in the morning and she is at my side, there is such joy in my heart that it makes me ache all over. That I love the speckles on her face as much as I love the little sounds she makes when I am putting my cock inside her. I want to say so many things to her.

But the words I have are very small. "Har-loh . . . repeat?"

The look on her face turns soft, and she moves forward, pressing her teats to my chest. She tilts her head back and lifts her face to mine like she does when she wants to push her mouth against mine in a "kiss." I lean down and give her one, and she smiles up at me. "Home," she tells me. "Har-loh Rukh mayk home."

"Home," I echo, then point at the broken shell. "Home?"

She chuckles and shakes her head, tugging on my hand again. "Home," she repeats, leading me away from the water's edge. She pulls me along after her, returning to the cave we slept in last night. Then she turns and gestures at me. "Rukh Har-loh home."

She's . . . tired? I try to grasp what she is saying. Does she wish to sleep? I motion to go inside, but she shakes her head again. Frustration flashes through her gaze and she gestures at the entirety of the small cave. "Home . . . sew wekkan haf home fur behbeh." She pats her flat stomach. "Kit."

I touch her stomach, trying to understand. Is her kit coming now?

Har-loh shakes her head again. She purses her lips, thinking. "Rukh, Har-loh, kit." She pauses and gestures at the firepit. "Fire. Furs. Cave." She makes a big circling gesture with her hand and looks at me again. "Home."

I frown, trying to follow. All these things are this word? Both of us, our kit, the furs, the shell she wished to keep . . . and then realization strikes me. I have seen animals make a nest for their young. Does Har-loh wish to make a nest? I put a hand to her belly. "Home . . . Har-loh Rukh kit home?"

She nods excitedly. "Dinkyew gottit, behbeh."

"Home," I repeat to myself. A nest. A safe place for my mate and I to have our kit. It should be comfortable, and safe. I think of the distressed sounds she made this morning when the crawlers were on her boots. I look at the small cave, tinier than the one I left behind in the mountains and not nearly as comfortable. This will not do.

My Har-loh and my kit deserve a better nest than this.

I take my mate's hand. "Home," I say again, and tug her along with me. This beach is full of small caves of varying sizes. We will find a better one for our nest and then Har-loh will be happy. I will make a home for my family, and we will be together, always.

Harlow

We need so many things.

As we go up and down the beach, I gather everything that might be useful. Shells big enough to work as utensils or plates, reeds that can be dried and woven into baskets, stones that work well for cooking—everything can be repurposed. It doesn't take long to fill my bag, and as we drop off our findings, I realize just how much we need. We need stones to surround the firepit. We need utensils and cooking tools. We need furs for clothing and boots and warm blankets.

We need a bigger cave.

I chew on my lip, trying not to fret over everything. I'm a worrier, it's just who I am. I'm sure being diagnosed with cancer influenced that. My cancer's in remission now, though, thanks to my khui. I can afford to look on the bright side of things.

And I've got Rukh at my side. Whatever it is I need, he'll help me get it because he adores me as much as I adore him.

So I eye our small cave and then turn to my mate. "We need a bigger place."

He frowns. "Repeat, Har-loh?"

"Small," I say, gesturing at the cave. "It's too small." I tap on the low ceiling, which he has to crouch under. "Small. We want big." I spread my hands. "Big cave."

Recognition dawns across his face. He takes my hand, gesturing farther down the beach.

I get excited. "Is there another cave? You know of one?" I shouldn't be surprised. The mountains here are positively honey-combed with caves and fissures everywhere. I'm no scientist, but I can't help but think it has something to do with all the hot springs everywhere. Whatever the reason, I'm glad for it. We can make the tiny cave work, but I'd much rather have someplace where we can stretch out and enjoy ourselves if this is going to be our new home.

We hike across the beach, Rukh holding my hand tightly even when it's inconvenient. It's like he doesn't want to let me go. I don't mind. I'm happy to be held on to. We scramble across rocks and move to the far end of the cove. We're a short distance from the tall cliffs, but not so far that it'll be an all-day hike to get into the snowy hills, where the animals with fur tend to hang out. I haven't seen anything furry wander across the beach. I don't know if we're scaring them off or if they just don't come down here. There are a few big, fearsome-looking birds—ostriches with anger issues, I like to think of them—that we avoid. Mostly, though, it's just crabs and things like that.

Feels weird to be on a beach and not hear the constant cries of seagulls.

Just when I'm ready to take a break because it feels as if we've crossed the entire beach, Rukh heads toward a rocky out-crop. Farther back, I can see a few blind canyons framed by rock, but he doesn't head toward them. He heads to the outcrop and it takes a moment, but then I see the entrance to the cave.

It's a large one, all right. Even from here, I can tell that the ceiling is tall enough for Rukh to stand fully, without his horns scraping against the ceiling. I glance around. We're in the most protected part of the cove here, with the waves a short distance away, but not so close that we have to worry about tides. The interior isn't extremely deep, but it's spacious, with a shallow front chamber studded with stalactites and then a deeper inner chamber that's large and roomy. It's a little messy—there's a layer of grit all over the floor and what look like dead crab shells along the walls, but cleaning is easy enough.

Best of all, there's a trickle of water gliding into a tiny pool near the front. It looks like it's coming straight from the stone, which means it's fresh water, not salt water. I catch a few drops on my fingers and taste it. Yup. Fresh and cold.

I turn to look at Rukh. He's watching me with a guarded expression, as if he's worried I won't like the place. I suspect that if I told him it was terrible, he'd keep on searching until he found me something better, even if it took years. That's just who he is. He wants the best for me, even if it means far more work.

I move to him and take his hands. "It's perfect." I beam at him. "This is a very good cave. We can make our family here."

"Yes?" he asks.

"Yes," I agree, squeezing his hands. "A very big yes!"

Rukh

My mate never stops working, even in the new cave. We bring our small pile of possessions over to our new spot, and Har-loh works on sweeping out all of the dead things and the sand on the floor. It is not an easy task, but when everything is finally clean and all the debris gone, we gather rocks and make a firepit near the entrance, so the smoke has a place to leave. Har-loh makes a nest with the furs she wears, but I notice that she shivers when she peels them off.

We need more furs, I realize. Some for wearing, and some for sleeping. We will have to hunt together, and that worries me. Har-loh is a soft creature, and hunting is hard work. The mountains are not too far of a walk, but I would rather her be safe and comfortable here in the cave. Perhaps I can go out and hunt while she stays here.

I do not like the idea, but I also do not like the idea of taking my mate with me on a dangerous hunt. Many of the animals in the snows have long claws and sharp fangs, and Har-loh's spotted flesh would tear easily. It will gut me to be apart from her for a day, but it will be necessary.

Har-loh must be kept warm, and this beach does not have fur.

It is a worry for another day, though. Har-loh looks tired, her pale face drawn as we sit near the fire. I tug her closer to me and she leans on my shoulder. I like this, my mate pressed against my side. She wraps her arms around me, shivering, and I worry she is too cold. I am a bad mate, letting my female shiver inside a cave when we could be wearing furs.

Tomorrow, then, I decide. In the morning, when the sun is up, I will go hunting for furs. I finger one of the ones she wears and nudge her. "Har-loh, repeat?"

"Mmm?" She sits up, giving me a curious look, and when I say the words again, she understands. "Fur?"

"Fffhuuurr," I echo, trying to memorize the word. "Har-loh fur. Yes?"

"Harlow's fur?" She says the words, a question on her face.

"Har-loh, fur." I wish I had the words to tell her I will hunt her many animals tomorrow. That I will not rest until she has warm skins to drape her body in. She is mine to protect, and I will not have her shivering.

"Fur?" my mate repeats again, and then takes my hand in hers. She guides it between her thighs, over the patch of fur she has on her mound. "Yes?"

There is a sultry note in her voice that I missed hearing before. She thinks I am asking to touch her, that I want to claim her. My frustration at not being able to communicate fades, because I do want to touch her. Touching my mate and making her feel good is still new and exciting. I lean toward her, brushing my mouth over hers in a kiss, because I know she likes those.

Har-loh sighs and nudges her mouth against mine, even as her thighs slide apart.

I groan low in my throat. How did I get so lucky as to have this mate? After so many seasons alone, it is astonishing to me that I have a mate to touch and to care for. That we will have a kit of our own. That we will be a family.

That she is mine and I am not alone.

"Har-loh," I breathe against her soft lips, even as I seek out the nub nestled in the folds of her cunt. She has shown me how she likes to be touched, and every time, I get a little better at such things. I am learning what pleases her most, what caresses make her body tighten and which ones make her cry out. Our mouths meet, my tongue lightly flicking against hers as I slide my fingers up and down her wet channel. I push one deep inside her, into the hot well of her cunt, and use my thumb to make circles around the little bud of flesh called a "clit."

She whimpers and clings to me, her thighs tightening around my hand. "Rukh," she pants, and her cunt squeezes me tight. "Feelsoguhd."

I stroke into her, using my fingers like I would my cock, driving into the softness of her body even as I work her clit. I love watching the pleasure build through her. She gasps, rocking against me, and then her movements become more frantic. Hurried. Her cunt grows wetter with every stroke of my fingers inside her, and she presses her forehead to mine, straddling me as I work her soft body with my hand. I need to watch her come. There is no sight I like better than when she climaxes, the tension on her face giving way to such languid pleasure. I love the way she hums afterward when her body relaxes. I am fascinated by everything, and if I could, I would be mounted atop her all day long, watching the pleasure come over her face.

She kisses me hungrily, making soft noises in her throat as she pumps her hips, determined to come. I hold her against me, pulling her in, and when one of her teats bounces enticingly near my mouth, I duck my head and lick the tip.

Har-loh cries out, her hands on my horns. I feel her press her cheek against one as she grips them tight, her movements faster and faster.

My cock aches with need, the tip leaking fluid down my shaft, and I want nothing more than to rub it against her. Or inside her. I want her to come first, though. I like the sight of her release even more than I like my own. I tease the tip of her nipple with my tongue, licking it and then sucking on the small bud. Sometimes she likes my teeth, so I add them, too, but gently, gently.

Her tight cunt squeezes my fingers. Har-loh's body trembles against me, and then she's panting, a small whine in her throat. She stiffens, and then moisture floods my hand and her release quakes through her.

I hold her against me, running my mouth over her soft, speckled skin as she comes down from her climax. She hums softly when she relaxes, and then begins to press kisses along my jaw and my neck. "Ur tuhrn behbeh." Her words are nonsense, but her tone is clear. I made her feel good. I rumble with satisfaction, rubbing her flanks. She slides a leg over my hips and straddles my cock, then presses another kiss to my mouth. "Gunnaride yew."

"Repeat," I rasp, desperately wanting to understand what my mate is telling me.

But she only gives me a sly smile and rubs her wet cunt up and down my shaft. When I groan, she leans in to lightly kiss my mouth, and then settles back. Her fingers stroke my cock and then she holds me steady . . .

And slowly seats herself upon my length.

I do not dare move.

Never have I imagined such a thing. Mating is still new to me. My Har-loh had to show me how to put my cock inside her. I had the desire, but I did not have the knowledge. Ever since then, we have been ravenous for one another, and Har-loh constantly shows me new ways to pleasure her. I have taken her while she is on her back, and I have taken her from behind, like the animals do. Her straddling me and feeding my cock into her body . . . is new.

And I like it.

I groan with pleasure as she wriggles atop me, her body taking my entire length. She pants, her gaze locked on me, her hands tight on my arms. "Rukh." She breathes my name as if it brings her joy just to say it. Then, as we watch each other, she raises her hips slowly and then seats herself upon me again.

Nothing has ever felt better.

My seed threatens to spill forth quickly, but I want this moment to last. I am fascinated by the sight of her riding me, of my cock disappearing into her body. I grip her hips and guide her up and down, faster and faster until she's whimpering once more, my name a breath on her lips. I grit my teeth, determined to last until she clenches over me again. I have learned that if I do things just right, Har-loh will climax twice, and it is my new goal to do this every time.

She cries out, throwing her head back, and her nails dig into my arms as she rides me faster and harder. Despite my intentions of taking my time, I cannot. This is too good, my mate too beautiful, her cunt too tight and wet and perfect. The moment I feel her clench tight around me and she makes a gaspy sound in her throat, I come. My release explodes out of me and I clutch her tightly against my chest as my seed spills into her heat and her body quakes over mine.

Nothing feels better than this. Nothing.

Moments pass. Har-loh hums in her throat, smoothing my mane back from my face. The strands of my mane are sticking to her skin as well as mine, and she makes noises in her throat, talking. I cannot follow her words, but I like her happy sounds. I hold her against me, stroking her soft skin.

I have never been so happy. Having Har-loh is . . . I do not know the words. I only know my heart is so full that sometimes it hurts in my chest.

She murmurs something, and then pulls a fur over both of us. I arrange it, making sure to cover my mate, because she is the one that is always chilled. Har-loh smiles at me and then tucks herself against my chest, talking softly. Her cunt still clasps my cock deep inside her, and I can feel every quiver of her body. I like this.

The fur is a reminder of what I must do tomorrow, though. I must go out and hunt. I have trapped and fished since we arrived here on the beach, because I did not wish to leave my mate's side. Har-loh is fragile and there are many, many things she does not understand about taking care of herself. She does not know how to set traps or to make a spear. It is lucky she has me, because I can do these things for her. But hunting is dangerous. I cannot take Har-loh with me. I do not know what I would do if a herd of dvisti turned the wrong way and trampled her. I do not know what I would do if a snow-cat attacked her.

Har-loh must stay safe in the cave, with the fire. I will hunt.

Harlow

When I wake up in the morning, Rukh is gone.

Huh.

Normally we wake up tangled together in the furs for some predawn snuggling and a before-breakfast quickie, but this morning, he's nowhere to be seen. I rub my eyes and peer out of the cave, but no Rukh. Probably fishing, then. Maybe he woke up with a burning need to get some fish in or something. We're still not great at communicating yet, and a lot of what goes between us is guesswork. With a yawn, I wrap the few furs we have tightly around my body and stoke the fire. The coals have gone down while I slept, and I poke them until they get hot once more, then I work on setting up the makeshift tripod we have for heating water.

I wish we had more things. I've taken for granted just how many supplies there are back at the main cave, and how hard everyone has worked to make those supplies. When I think of how much time I have to put in just to make a cooking pouch, I have a whole new appreciation for those giving, thoughtful sa-khui people who took a bunch of humans into their homes, no questions asked, and fed and clothed us.

Rukh thinks of them as the enemy, but they were always kind to me. I've made my choices, though. I'm with Rukh now, and that means starting over in all ways.

I pad to the entrance of the cave, my toes curling on the icy rocks, and peer out, looking for my mate's broad shoulders and long, wild hair. I don't see him on the beach, either, but it doesn't mean that he's not around. He's probably gathering food. I wet a soft scrap of leather, take a quickie bath with the melted water, and then add a bit more from the trickle in the cave. Once my pouch is full, I add the last few leaves for hot tea and get dressed. Maybe while Rukh is fishing, I can find some of the plants that the sa-khui always used for tea. I can start our supplies there, I decide. Leaves are easy. It's everything else that's daunting.

One thing at a time, Harlow, I remind myself.

I head out to the cliffs, noticing that Rukh's spear is gone from inside the cave. Definitely hunting. The sight of it missing actually makes me feel a little better, and I concentrate on picking leaves for tea. I'm proud of myself for actually recognizing several of the plants that cling to the cliffs here. It's weird, because for an ice-covered planet, there's a surprising amount of greenery to be found if you know where to look. There are the not-potato trees that grow incredibly tall stalks, but there aren't any near the beach that I can see. There are all kinds of vines crisscrossing the rocks and growing into the crevices. And I know that if I go up into the mountains, I can dig under the snow and find plenty of strange, wiry plants that somehow grow despite the cold and the gray, weak sunshine.

I gather leaves until my little pouch won't hold any more and my hands are full. I look around for Rukh again, but there's still no sign of him. I can't let that worry me. He knows what he's doing. Next time, I'll tell him that if he heads out, he needs to take me with him. I need to get better at hunting, too.

No sense in being angry about it, though. And I'm not, really. I'm just frustrated that our communication is falling down again. It's one thing I wish we were both quicker at. There are so many things I want to say to him, and I can tell he wishes he could speak freely. We're getting there, but we're both impatient for more. Thinking about Rukh and words I can teach him distracts me, and I'm back at the cave and spreading out leaves to dry before I know it. Near the entrance of the cave, I see the piles of seaweed I scavenged from the beach, and I lay them out to dry, as well. When they dry up, they harden into thick reeds that can be braided and woven into baskets, and the thought of making my own is exciting.

Storage. Who'd have thought I'd be so damn thrilled for storage? Blows my mind.

There's a lot to get done, though, and I can't sit around. With that thought in mind, I get to work.

By the time I gather my last handfuls of leaves and have them spread out on a fur near my tiny fire, I realize it's almost dark.

No, scratch that, it *is* dark. The skies are just bright because the stars are shining overhead. It's completely dark out and the moons are up. And there's still no sign of my mate. I kept busy all day, because sitting by the fire and worrying doesn't do me any good, but he's never been gone for so long. I can't help but panic a little.

Okay, a lot.

I go to the entrance of the cave, hugging my fur wraps to my body, and scan the dark beach. No Rukh. What do I do? Should I grab my makeshift spear and head into the hills after him? It's dark, and all kinds of weird creatures come out at night, so I don't know if that's such a smart idea. But if he's out there, hurt, I can't just leave him and keep my happy ass warm by the fire.

I don't know what to do. Sit and wait? Go after him?

I consider my options for a few moments, and then bank the fire. I wrap up in furs, grab my spear, and head out after him. I make my way to the cliffs, stumbling over icy rocks in the darkness. There's a small natural path that leads up through the cliffs to the rolling, wintry hills above that become mountains. I go up a few steps and then pause, listening. There's a noise of something walking on the sands, the crunch of footsteps.

Rukh?

I head back down the path toward it. "Is that you, Rukh?"

The sound gets louder, and then I pause. There's a dark shape on the sand that is not Rukh. Not in the slightest. In fact, it looks like a crustacean of some kind, but it's the size of an Earth crocodile . . . or bigger. It's got two tentacles with eyes on the end, and they swivel toward me.

I let out a horrified squeal and stumble backward, clutching my spear. The thing scuttles away, as if it's just as scared of me as I am of it.

I stare after the creature, heart pounding. My hands are slippery on my spear, and the wind picks up, blowing my hair in my face. A helpless feeling overtakes me. I don't know enough about this world to handle my shit alone at night. What if that crab wasn't the biggest thing on this beach at night? What if the next one doesn't run?

And I don't know where Rukh is. What if I head into the mountains and I never find him?

Beyond frustrated, I retreat back to the safety of my cave and build up the fire. Our supplies of the dung chips are going to disappear quickly, too. That's another thing we need to hunt.

None of that matters if Rukh doesn't come back, though. I can't do this on my own. I can't live on this beach alone. I need my mate. Hot tears leak from my eyes as I lie next to the fire and wait for my mate to return.

When I wake up again, it's morning.

No Rukh.

The fire's completely out, and no amount of poking the coals makes it revive, which is just frustrating. It means I have to build one from scratch, and part of me wonders why I even bother. Rukh hasn't returned. He's left me. I'm sure it's not on purpose—he wouldn't do that—which means only one thing. Something bad has happened to him and he can't return on his own.

I have to go find him, then.

I braid my hair and put on my leathers. I wrap extra leather around my boots, reinforcing them, since the mountains are colder and rocky, and the snow can hide all kinds of dangers. I double-check the point of my spear to make sure it's sharp and grab my waterskin and the last of our dried rations. I'm not coming back until I find Rukh. "I'm coming, baby."

The moment I step outside the cave, though, I stop.

Two dead dvisti are neatly laid out a short distance away.

I approach them, puzzled, but they are definitely dead. There's ice crusting on their fur, and the throats have been slashed as well as wounds in the belly from hunting. I kneel next to one, and it's been bled so the meat will stay good. Rukh must have done this, and the thought fills me with relief. Dvisti don't come down on the beach. In the few days since we've been here, I've seen the occasional one up on the ridge, but they don't come below. I guess it's too hard on their feet.

Glancing up, I scan the beach, but there's no sign of my mate. "Rukh?"

My voice echoes on the cliffs. There's nothing but silence.

I get to my feet and follow the tracks of footprints in the sand, but they lead back to the cliffs and disappear. He went back out? Without waking me? Without talking to me? I don't understand.

Why wouldn't he come and wake up his mate? Kiss me hello before running off again? I totally understand if there's a lot to be done and he feels the pressure to provide. Maybe he senses a storm is coming and wants to get a lot of meat preserved. He's used to being on his own. He knows what has to be done to make it in this harsh environment.

Even so . . . I feel a little abandoned.

This is all new for me, and I'm lonely. Yesterday, I was so terrified something had happened to him that I couldn't think straight. I had to throw myself into chores or else I'd lose my mind with worry.

Instead, he's just out hunting . . . and I guess he doesn't want to be disturbed by his mate.

I chew on my lip, worried. Am I too clingy? Is that why he's run off into the hills? Does he need a break from me? The thought cuts like a knife, and yet . . . it makes sense. Rukh is used to being alone. Of course he'd find my constant presence a bit annoying. He's probably going off on his own to get a breather, and I need to just accept it.

We're in this together. He's my mate, and we just need to get used to how the other operates. When he comes home, I'll try to be less clingy and needy and more independent. I don't want him to feel smothered.

I'm still hurt, though. Oh sure, some of it's hormones, but I guess when I envisioned us living on the beach together, I had an idea in my head that we'd be . . . together. But maybe his idea was different.

Frustrated, I grab the first dvisti by the leg and start dragging it back to the cave. There's no time to mope. I've got to process this meat and get the skin off of it, and there's no one to do it but me. Hurt feelings won't give us food to eat in the brutal season, so I'd better hop to it.

Rukh

When I return to the cave that night, I have another dvisti and, this time, two dead snow-cats. I am also scratched, bloodied, tired, and want nothing more than to hold my mate. But this is not enough fur to keep her warm, and the colder weather will be upon us soon. I will not have my mate shivering when I can hunt meat and take the furs from animals, so I must keep going out.

I drop my kills a safe distance away from the cave and arrange them so Har-loh will know it is me. Even though I know this is necessary work, I hate being apart from her. I wish I could slide under the furs with her and drink in her scent, touch her until she wakes up and reaches for me. I wish I could go to sleep with my arms around her. I wish for a great many things, but wishes will not keep my Har-loh warm. With a frustrated sigh, I turn and head back to the hills again.

Harlow

Rukh's been here again.

I want to scream with frustration when I see the new kills lined up a short distance from the cave. I can't believe my mate came back—again—and didn't say shit to me. He didn't even bother to come into the cave. I laid out a fine covering of sand across the entrance to check for such a thing. If he came in—even just to look at me—it'd show a footprint or two. Sure enough, it wasn't touched.

I'm moving quickly beyond hurt into anger. I realize he's used to being on his own, but what the fuck? Did I say something to make him angry? Or is this just him needing even more space? How long will this go on for?

I have no answers. I can't even write him a note in the sands. We can barely talk to each other, much less communicate in other ways. I have no choice but to wait this out. I can't even go and find him now, because the meat he's bringing in has to be processed. I have to chop it up, remove all the usable bits, cut it into strips, smoke or dry the meat, and clean the usable organs.

The hides are sitting rolled up, and I need to scrape those, too. There aren't enough hours in the day, and I worked until I fell asleep by the fire last night.

And now I get to do it all over again.

I stare, exhausted, at the kills. The sa-khui have caches in the deep snows where they keep their meat. I can't drag these things into the mountains, though, and a pit here on the beach would just get eaten up by crabs. It wouldn't stay cold enough, either. It all has to be cooked and processed and . . . I just want to cry.

With a weary sigh, I drag them toward the cave.

Another problem crops up, of course. I run out of fuel for my fire. The dung chips that are so plentiful in the mountains are nonexistent here, and there's nothing for me to burn. All of the meat is going to go to waste unless I figure out something. I gaze at the charnel house of my cave around me, looking for something to burn. There's bloody meat everywhere in varying stages of drying. There are long chains of intestines hung, and the stripped animal heads glare at me from nearby, waiting for their brains to be used to work the skins. Six months ago, the sight of this would have made me run away screaming at the horror. Survivor me knows it's all useful, though. Messy, but useful.

I'm fucked if I have no fire, though.

I drum my fingers on my filthy hip, trying to think. Okay, if I don't have fire, how else can I handle this? How did they preserve meat?

Salt. Salted meat.

"Bingo," I say to no one, and head down to the shore. I can wet one of the furs in the ocean water and lay it out to dry, I think, and scrape the salt off of it as it dries up. Not the fastest method, but maybe there'll be a salt deposit of some kind on the beach that I'll be able to use.

There isn't, of course. But there is a gigantic, half-rotted log.

I stare at it in wonder as it lies at the edge of the tideline. The trees here are all flimsy, ridiculous little things that can't be used for regular wood. The only real firewood grows high, high in the mountains, I'm told, and it's so remote that going there for wood isn't even an option. But this hunk of wood looks like a chunk of tree you might find back on Earth. It's thick . . . and with luck, it'll burn.

Ignoring the sand-scorpions scuttling nearby, I move to the tree trunk. It's still a little wet, but with luck and some quick thinking, maybe I can make it burn. It's too heavy to lift, though, so I spend most of the afternoon rolling it, little by little, toward the cave. When it's close enough, I dig a firepit, use my precious dried-out seaweed reeds as tinder, and start a slow, smoky fire on the beach and drape meat nearby to dry.

I'm exhausted, but I'll have to stay up and watch so predators don't come steal the food. Maybe I'll even catch a glimpse of my mate.

Rukh

Two more dvisti are mine by the time I decide to head back to the beach, where my pretty mate is safe. There is a large herd of the fat creatures tantalizingly close, but I can only handle so much as I am alone. I haul the two carcasses back with me—one over my shoulders and another in my arms.

I am tired and I have not slept in days, but every kill I bring in is more meat for my Har-loh, more furs to warm her. So I must keep working. Two more, I think. No, four. Better to be safe and have extra furs in case the weather is exceedingly cold.

As I approach the beach, however, I see an orange, flickering light. A fire. It is outside the cave instead of inside, and my heart pounds with worry. Why is the beach on fire? I move closer, rushing, and it is only by sheer stubbornness that I do not fling down my kills and race toward my mate. I know if I put them down, some scavenger will come along and snatch them. It is a firepit, I realize as I jog toward the light. A firepit with someone sitting in front of it.

It is not until I am directly upon the fire that I realize it is my Har-loh.

She has fallen asleep sitting up, a stick in her hand as if she drowsed while poking the fire. Strips of meat are spread atop the surfaces of many rocks and hung carefully from the shaft of her spear high above the flames. There is a great deal of meat, and all of it smells good. A short distance from the fire, however, I see crabs and crawlers and all kinds of things waiting to snatch a bite. That must be why she has stayed out here.

Her eyes do not open when I approach, nor when I set my two kills down. Her face is drawn, with dark circles smudging her face. She is dirty, too. Dried blood crusts her clothing and there are rings of grime underneath her nails and smears of blood on her face. This is not like my Har-loh. She loves to be clean. It was one of the first things she taught me, and she is always quick to bathe.

Why has she not bathed now? Is she injured?

Worried, I drop to my knees at her side and study her face. Her speckles are as bright as ever. That is a good sign, I think. But she is thin, and I do not like how she has not roused even though I am in camp, making noise. "Har-loh," I murmur, brushing my fingers over her cheek to wake her. "Har-loh."

She jerks awake with a funny little snort, her eyes unfocused. Her gaze settles on me, and her mouth parts in surprise. "Rukh. Yerbak." Then, she bursts into noisy tears. "Wydijooleaf me?"

"Har-loh?" I caress her cheek, worried. She weeps at the sight of me? Is she tired of having me for a mate because I cannot provide enough for her? The thought is like a blow to the chest, and I suck in a miserable breath. I wish I had the words to ask what is wrong, but all I can offer is a simple one. "No?"

"Wutdoes datmeen?" She sobs. But she reaches forward and runs her hands along my face, as if touching me with the same concern that I touched her. "Har yew okay? Hurt?"

We can do word noises tomorrow, I decide. I do not like how tired she looks. Too sleepy, and she could fall into the fire. I get to my feet, gathering her against me. "Har-loh cave?"

"Oh." She shakes her head, even though she is wobbly with exhaustion. "No. Wehafta stayen protek dameet." She prods me to release her, and when I do, she gestures at the strips covering all the surfaces. "Food."

Aah. I understand now . . . and she is right. It will require a lot of effort to pull everything inside so the predators do not snatch it from us. She is smart to sit out here with the food, but she is cold and tired. At least I can help with that. I sit down by the fire again and indicate she should sit next to me. To my relief, she comes to me immediately, pressing herself against my side and snuggling in. I wrap her cape around both of our shoulders and hug my mate close.

She sighs happily and slides her cold fingers against my stomach. "Weel tokabuddit inda mornin."

I think she tells me I am wise and clever for deciding to guard the food. Pleased at her praise, I press a kiss to her bright mane and stare into the fire. Her hands clutch me tightly, one curling around my tail as if she wishes to anchor me against her. It makes my cock uncomfortably hard, but I do not wake her for matings. Har-loh needs sleep. I hold her and watch the fire, and even though I am tired, I do not drift off. I can stay awake for a very, very long time if I need to, and right now Har-loh needs sleep more than me.

I watch over my mate until the darkness turns to a pale gray, and the skies lighten. The twin suns will be up soon. If I am to find that dvisti herd again, I should leave before long. It is difficult, when all I want to do is hold Har-loh and watch her sleep, knowing that she is safe and comfortable and rested.

But holding my mate does not feed her, and so I quietly tug her hands off of me. I slip out of her grasp and get to my feet. I am sore, I realize, and there are a few scratches from one of the fiercer snow-cats along my shoulder that ache this morning. I rotate one shoulder, testing my stiff muscles.

A hand goes around my tail, grabbing it and holding it still.

I look down and my sleepy-eyed mate is gazing up at me. "Where dyew tink yergoin?"

She is beautiful, and even though I am tired, my cock stirs at the sight of her. I tap her cheek with gentle fingers, and then gesture at the hills. Her brows furrow together, and I think she does not understand, so I point at my spear.

Har-loh gets to her feet and moves to my spear. She grabs it . . . and then flings it away from us. It skids into the sand a short distance away and I look at my mate in confusion. Why did she do that?

She points at me. "Yewnmee needta tok."

"Har-loh." I move to go pick up my spear, but she makes an outraged noise and steps in front of it before I can. "Har-loh meat." I point at the kills I brought in last night, because I remember the word for food. "Meat, yes. Fur, yes. Har-loh, yes."

Her gaze goes to my catches, and then she shakes her head. "Staaaah," she says softly. She gestures at the ground, and it takes me a moment to realize that she does not wish for me to go. She wants me to remain here with her.

"Meat," I say again, but I worry she does not understand. "Yes meat." I point at the animals. "Yes. Yes. Yes." I make a gesture for an enormous amount of meat. "Har-loh meat." I pat my stomach, indicating I want her to have a full belly. "Mmmm."

Her hand goes to her mouth, and her lips twitch. I would much rather she smile and laugh than weep, and I smile back at her.

"Rukh," she says softly, taking my hand. She pauses for a moment, studying our surroundings. "Iyam tieherrrd." She pauses and makes a great big yawn. "Tired." She points at the meat, and with each strip, she says her name again. She points at the fire and says her name. She points into the cave, and then gives me another weary look, then yawns again. "Har-loh tired." She moves toward me and brushes her fingers over my face. "Rukh tired."

I make a noise of frustration. How do I make her understand that it is my responsibility to make sure that she is fed and warm? That I am a poor mate if I cannot keep her comfortable? I indicate the hides on the animals. "Fur. Har-loh fur. No brrrr." I mock-shiver. "Rukh mate, Har-loh fur." I nod, as if this answers everything.

She shakes her head again. "Stay," she says in the soft voice again. "Tired. Rukh tired. Har-loh tired. Fur later." She moves toward me and wraps her arms around my torso, pressing her cheek against my chest. She is warm and soft, and I am a weak, weak male. Stay at her side? I would like nothing more.

I pet her mane, loving the nearness of her, of the press of her skin to mine. "Lay-turr?" I echo. I do not know this word, but I suspect it means tomorrow. That we rest today, and tomorrow I hunt again.

"Later," she agrees.

Very well. A day of rest, then.

Rukh

It is not a day of rest after all. The moment Har-loh and I eat a bite and wash it down with water, my mate gets to work. I thought that by leaving her behind, she would relax and sleep by the fire, waiting comfortably for me to return. This is not the truth, though. When I go into the cave we have claimed for ourselves, I see dried meat on every surface, the hides rolled up and the heads rotting in the corner of the cave. When I return to Har-loh's side, she is already hard at work, butchering the dvisti. She uses her small stone knife to hack it apart and to peel the skin away. She slices open the gut and pulls out the organs, then takes them to the water's edge to clean them out and hangs them to dry, too.

I cannot have my mate doing all this work, so I pitch in and help, and she tosses me a grateful look.

By the end of the day, I understand why my Har-loh is so tired. I understand now why she did not wish for me to run off into the mountains with the easy task of hunting. Preparing the meat and the fur is time consuming, and messy, and exhausting.

We work until the suns fall beyond the edge of the sky again and it grows dark. At the end of it, the skins are rolled up and bundled, and Har-loh makes motions that she will scrape them tomorrow. I think of all the skins waiting inside the cave, too. Of all the meat. Of the strips of reeds she dries so she can make something with them. Of the organs she carefully saves and gestures that she will make something with them.

It is very different from when I have hunted on my own. If I was hungry, I would kill something and eat it until there was no more meat. If I did not finish all of it, I would shove it into a snowbank and gnaw on the frozen meat the next day. I did not think about the future. But with Har-loh, we must think of many turns of the moon from now.

We must think of when our kit arrives. We must have everything ready.

Harlow

Rukh stays after dark, and I'm so incredibly glad that he does.

I think his leaving before without saying a word was a misunderstanding. I don't think he hates me. I don't think he's tired of me. I think he's unused to having to discuss his actions with anyone else, so he didn't think anything of up and leaving. To him, it was no big deal. He doesn't realize how it looked to me. It just boils down to communication. We need to learn to talk to each other, and that starts with language. No matter how difficult it is, I've got to get more words into him and I need to learn how he thinks. We can figure this out.

Once the meat is cooked enough that it won't rot, we hang it in the cave to dry. There's an endless list of things to accomplish, and when the meat is all done, I work on getting the brains out of the skulls to use for the skins tomorrow. By the time I'm finished, I'm so weary I want to fall over, and I barely have the strength to wash my hands before I collapse into the furs, exhausted. Rukh joins me and I curl up next to him and sleep like the dead.

When I wake up, the inside of the cave is cold and empty. I'm terrified that he's left again. "Rukh?"

"Har-loh," he calls back from outside.

Relief crashes over me and I fight back the sob that rises in my throat. I compose myself, shove my feet into my boots, and trot out to meet him. To my relief, my mate's there by the make-shift fire. He's got it going again, burning the rest of the massive log that didn't completely catch last night. I see he's spread a few more strips to dry, and there's a pouch for breakfast tea hanging over the fire.

On the sand, Rukh has one of the skins unrolled and he's busy scraping the underside.

He's here. He's here and he's helping me. He's not going any-where. I'm so relieved I sink to my knees and choke up again.

"Har-loh?" Rukh gets up from his spot by the skin and moves to my side. I watch through my tears as he studies his gross, blood-covered hands, as if he wants to hug me but can't. He drops to a squat next to me instead, tilting his head so he can see my face. "Yes?"

It's the wrong word, but I know what he's asking. I manage a smile and wipe my eyes. "I'm fine. Just emotional. Probably the pregnancy." Or that there's just been a lot going on for the last while, but I can't really tell him that now. "Thank you for staying."

He watches me, then moves in and kisses the top of my head. "Tea?"

"Oh." I get all sentimental and blubbery again, but I hide it better this time. He knows the word for tea. "Tea would be great, thank you." With just that small gesture, everything seems right in the world again.

Having Rukh's help makes everything seem not quite so daunting. Before I know it, all the meat is smoked, all the furs are scraped and the brains rubbed into the underside of the skin. It's not the best job I've ever done on skins. I know there are more steps to be taken to ensure the skin is the softest it can be—lots of stretching and drying, stretching and drying. But our priority is quantity rather than quality—quality can come later.

When I finish with my last hide and look around, I don't see anything urgent that has to be done. For the first time in days, there's nothing so pressing that it can't wait until tomorrow.

I want to collapse with relief. Instead, I just wipe my sweaty brow and give a hearty sigh. "I think we're done for now, baby."

Rukh frowns at me, and wipes at my brow with his thumbs. Oh. I must have smeared something. I glance down at my hands . . . and grimace. I am utterly disgusting. My fingernails are ringed with dirt, my skin is covered with dried bits of unnameable things, and I'm sweaty and nasty. I glance over at Rukh and it's the same for him. He's dirty, too, and his long hair is sticking to his skin.

Now that the worst of the work is done, there's nothing I want more than a hot bath. "Let's wash up, shall we?" I make a scrubbing motion at my mate, indicating cleaning. "Wash."

He nods. "Wash."

As we've worked side by side today, I've gone over basic words with him. Hide. Meat. Scrape. Rock. Wave. Sea. Anything I could point at or easily do, I gave words to, and Rukh repeated them. I'm not sure if he'll be able to recall everything that we went over, but I'm hoping that day by day, we'll fall into an easier understanding of one another.

I poke the fire, stoking it, while Rukh fills up both of our pouches with water to warm over the flames. There are a few smaller rocks that I keep warming near the fire that I slip into the heated water to warm things faster as Rukh disappears into the cave again. To my delight, he returns with my soapberries. "Wash," he says again, and gestures at the small, dried fruits. "Repeat?"

He's asking for the word for them. "Soapberry," I say, and add a few to the water. They've withered because I've had them for so long but I'm hoping that heating them in the water will squeeze a bit of the cleansing juice out. If nothing else, we'll smell nice and fruity.

As the water warms, Rukh moves toward me. I smile at him, tired. I'm half-expecting another word question, but instead, he tugs at the laces on my tunic. "Wash," he murmurs. "Wash Har-loh."

"I am pretty dirty." I smile up at him, standing still so he can pull at the ties. "Days and days of dirt. It'll feel good to get clean."

He narrows his eyes at me, and I can tell he's trying to follow along with my words.

I put my hand on a smear on his rock-hard abdomen and brush at it. "Dirty," I tell him. I rub at another stripe of dirt on his arm. "Dirty."

Rukh grunts. He peels open the front of my tunic, revealing my breasts. My nipples prick at the cold, and his gaze goes there. A hungry ache starts low in my belly, and I wonder if this is going to turn sexy. But Rukh just pulls the tunic off of me and then eyes my lower arms and the grime there. "Dirty."

Yeah, I am pretty gross. I suppose it's a good thing that we're not getting sexy . . . though to be honest, I'm less and less concerned with how I look around Rukh. I know he likes me no matter what. My hair could be a disgusting mop and he'd still think I was beautiful. It's a rather freeing feeling. I rub my fingers over his chest, because I'm tired and sore and filthy but I'm also getting turned on. It's been days and days since I've had sex with my mate, and I miss it. I miss him.

Plus, the way he says "dirty" in that caressing way is pretty damn hot.

He's completely naked—like usual—and I want to run my hands all over him. I want to take his cock and rub those ridges until he's so hard that he's leaking, and then he'll lose control and fling me down onto the sand and we'll have hot, filthy sex.

Except the sand is pretty nasty, and my skin is, too. I sigh at the thought, because I'm sticky and a bit itchy. "Dirty, dirty Harlow."

Rukh chuckles. He leans over and puts a soft leather rag into the water, swishing it like I do when I'm bathing. Then he pulls it out and presses it to my skin, a look of intense concentration on his face as he washes me. A girl could get used to this. I sigh happily, holding my hair up off my neck as he mops me with the lukewarm water. I try not to look at the trickles of water creeping down my skin, because I'm sure they're discolored and gross and I just want to focus on getting warm. "You wash me first and then I'll wash you," I tell my mate as he bathes my arm. "Sound good?"

"Rukh wash Har-loh," he says in a low voice, sliding that bit of damp leather over my skin. "Good, good."

He's definitely a fast learner. My nipples are tight and hard with need, and when Rukh turns to washing my front, I don't complain. It's not dirty—my tunic protected me from the worst of the grossness—but I desperately need his touch over my sensitive breasts. He grazes one tip and I suck in a breath, hot arousal flooding through me.

But all Rukh says is "Dirty" and keeps washing me.

When I'm clean, I feel better. Much better. I'll wash my hair tomorrow, maybe, but for now it's enough to just be clean and sweet-smelling. I sigh happily as he tugs my filthy leggings off and then gets to work on the rest of me as I wash my hands and scrub at my nails. By the time he's happy with how clean I am, I'm shivering and wearing nothing but my boots, body chilled as the breeze dries my skin. It's Rukh's turn now, though. I take the small rag from him and soak it, then gesture that he should turn around. "Now I'll do you."

He doesn't even hesitate. Rukh presents me with his spine, his tail flicking back and forth languidly, and when I touch him with the warm cloth, he makes a sound of pleasure in his throat. My body responds, my pussy growing wet as I wipe down his strong limbs. God, he's pretty. I'm so lucky to have him. Even our "issues" aren't big ones. We can't communicate all that well, and we're out here on our own, but they seem like small things in the wake of having this big, gorgeous man at my side. I can forgive everything in this moment, which means I am super, super hard up for some sex.

The thought's an amusing one and I make sure to scrub at Rukh's skin as quickly as I can. The moment he's clean of gore and grime, I'm absolutely going to jump his bones. Part of me wants to turn this into a sexy sponge bath, but there's too much blue skin that needs to be cleaned and it's too chilly to loiter.

Unsexy sponge bath first, I decide, and then into the cave. Then we can be as sexy as we like.

I'm having a hard time sticking to my own plan, though. Rukh was naked as he helped me, which means he's dirty everywhere. It's hard to tell myself to wait and be patient when I have to towel off his perfect, hard buns. Or when I run the washcloth down each strong leg. As I make my way to his front, I notice he's not unaffected, either. His cock has stiffened and is standing proud and erect as I wash up his thighs.

Well, I just have to make sure he's clean there, too, don't I? It's my duty as a loving mate.

So I wet the rag again and take great care washing his sac and every ridge of that big, thick cock. I wash his spur, and then give a little sigh of disappointment when I work my way up to his chest. I'd rather stay between his thighs, but that won't get the rest of him clean. By the time I straighten to do his shoulders, he's watching me with a glittering, intense stare that takes my breath away.

"I think I'm done," I manage, tossing the rag into the last of the water in the pouch. "All good. Now—"

He shakes his head, trapping my arm before I can leave. "Har-loh dirty."

"Still?" I glance down at my body, holding my boobs to look at everything underneath. I'm not as sparkling clean as I would be in a hot shower, but I thought we'd done pretty well. I feel refreshed and good. I feel more than ready to have my mate touch me, which I couldn't say an hour ago. "Where?"

Rukh makes a noise in his throat and then leans over the firepit, pulling out the towel again. He gives me a scorching look. "Rukh wash."

And then he drops to his knees in front of me.

I . . . Oh. My breath comes faster, and I think about how much I enjoyed cleaning his cock, even though I didn't have to. Perhaps I spent a bit too much loving time on it and he got ideas in his head. Or maybe he just misses my touch as much as I miss his. Whatever it is, I'm not about to complain. "Rukh," I breathe, brushing strands of hair back from his face. "Where are you going to wash me, baby?"

He gives me a sly look that takes my breath away, and then presses the warm rag right between my thighs.

I squirm at the feel of it against my folds. It feels good, warm and wet, but it's not what I want there. "Are you telling me I'm a dirty girl?"

"Clean Har-loh," he says softly, rubbing the cloth back and forth. The friction just gets me wetter, and I can't stay still. Not when he's that close to my pussy and when he's talking in that low, hungry voice. He's going to make me absolutely crazy with need. Rukh considers for a moment, then tosses aside the rag. He wraps an arm around my hips and pulls me close, until his face brushes against my stomach.

Then he growls and lifts one of my legs over his arm, spreading my thighs.

I squeak in surprise, reaching forward and grabbing his horns for balance. He doesn't stop, though, just hauls me forward until my leg is over one shoulder and my pussy practically in his face. "Rukh," I whimper. My pulse feels as if it's beating between my thighs, heat coursing through my body . . . and yet he's still not touching me. It's all still a big tease. "Am I clean enough for you? Or do you need a closer inspection?"

He looks at my pussy thoughtfully, and then reaches up a finger to trace over my folds. "Kiss Har-loh," he murmurs, glancing up at me. "Yes?"

He wants to kiss my pussy? Put his mouth there? Uh, as if I even have to think twice. "Yes," I say, encouragingly. "Yes, yes. All the kisses."

My mate makes a hungry sound low in his throat. Clenching

my hips, he pushes his face between my thighs and licks my folds. I moan, holding tight to his horns as he groans with pleasure and moves in for another taste. He's still so tall when he's seated like this that I have to stand on tiptoe to angle his mouth just right. When he shifts his weight, I threaten to topple into the fire. "Rukh," I pant. "Wait, wait."

Rukh looks up at me, his eyes dark blue with arousal, his mouth wet with my juices. Even as I gaze down at him, he licks his lips.

"Let's go into the cave." I point at our home a short distance away and mime a shiver. "Cold out here. There's nowhere to lie down."

He gazes at our surroundings, blinking, and it's as if it takes him a moment to realize where we're at. I can see why. If he threw me down into the sand to fuck me, I doubt I'd care once he put his mouth on me again. But he pulls me close for a quick kiss to the tuft between my thighs, then sets my leg down. He gets to his feet, and that's the only warning I get before he grabs me and hauls me over his shoulder.

Then, ass in the air, he carries me back to our cave.

I laugh. "So impatient you won't even let me walk, huh? I see how it is."

"Rukh kiss," he tells me, patting my ass and then caressing it. Funny how he doesn't have a big vocabulary, but with those two words, he's able to make me wetter than heck. I squirm with anticipation on his hard shoulder, and he rubs my butt cheek again. He must like having me under his hand, because he rumbles with pleasure, his khui purring loudly, and then delves his fingers into my cleft.

Oh God. The unexpected touch makes me squeal in surprise, and when his rough finger pads brush over the entrance to my core, I moan. I probably sound ridiculous, making all these noises, but there's no one here to hear us.

"Mmm, Rukh kiss," he says again, his fingers dipping deeper into my wet heat.

"Does that mean you're going to kiss me there?" I ask, panting. "Because if so, I am down with that."

He carries me into the cave, the world bobbing around me, and I hold on to him as best I can. It's difficult to concentrate, especially when he's got his fingers deep inside me. It's the most erotic, confusing feeling, but I kind of love it.

He pauses and then his fingers leave my body, and I could just cry with how much I need them back. I whimper a protest, and he sets me upright, his gaze locked on me. As I stare up at my mate, Rukh puts his wet fingers to his mouth and licks them.

"Oh," I breathe. Heat flutters through my belly. My khui is purring back at his. After our initial resonance, it hums gently when I'm extremely turned on or when I feel strongly. It's humming right now, pleasure pulsing through me. Is there anything more erotic than watching my mate lick my taste off his fingers?

Rukh bends down and kisses me. Slowly. Gently. I close my eyes, entranced by the sheer delicacy of the kiss. Of his touch. Considering that just a short time ago this was a wild man who'd been on his own for almost all of his life, he's incredibly careful with me. I never feel uneasy or threatened. I always feel safe and cherished and so damn loved in his arms. His tongue flicks against mine, and I reach for him, wanting to wrap my arms around his neck and lose myself in his mouth for a while. But my mate grabs my hands in his and won't let me twine myself about him. Instead, he drops to his knees on our sleeping furs—cold with disuse—and pulls me down with him.

Well, I don't need much convincing. The moment I sit down,

he gently pushes me onto my back and slides between my thighs. It's obvious that he wants to continue the "kissing" he started outside by the fire. I brush his thick, messy hair back from his face. I'm so full of love (and lust) for this man. "And here I thought you were tired of me," I whisper. "I can be a real idiot sometimes, can't I?"

He presses his mouth to the inside of my thigh, rubbing his lips against my skin. "Rukh kiss Har-loh."

"Please do." I spread my legs for him, encouraging him with my actions. "Kiss me all you want. Har-loh loves your kisses. And your mouth." I slide my fingers over his lips. "Mouth. This is your mouth."

He nips at my fingertips. "Kiss."

I chuckle. "Right. Sorry. No distractions from the kissing right now. No word games, just kissing." I wiggle against him, and when he drags my thigh back over his shoulder, I can't help the little whimper of anticipation that sneaks out of me. Do I want him? Do I want more kisses over the most sensitive part of my body? Do I want his tongue delving between every little fold and caressing my clit? Oh fuck yes, I absolutely do. I make a needy sound in my throat as I tangle my hands in his hair. "Kiss, please. Kiss."

Rukh growls in a way that is absolutely a possessive claim and my toes curl in response. God, I love it when he gets possessive of my pussy. He leans in and nuzzles at my mound, his lips drifting over my folds before he parts them and spreads me wide for his "kissing." His tongue slicks over my pussy, and then he's licking me with fierce, hungry intensity in such a way that the breath escapes my lungs. I'm stunned by his need—and by mine. He's ravenous, my mate, his mouth and lips ferocious on my sensitive parts. I gasp with each lick and caress, hunger escalating quickly.

I need him inside me, and soon. "Please," I whimper. "Oh please, Rukh. I'm so close."

"Kiss," is all my handsome mate says when he lifts his mouth, only to immediately dive back for another taste. He tries a variety of things, light and sweet, then firm and commanding. He teases my clit and then moves to the entrance to my core, and I know he's gauging my responses. When I moan over something he does, I get more of it. If I'm silent, he moves on to something else.

We may not have the words, but he's listening.

Rukh licks around the hood of my clit, and then closes his mouth over the entire area and begins to suck.

Oh my God. I cry out, my hands flying to his horns and I practically come off the blankets. He growls with pleasure, holding me in place and continuing his ministrations now that he knows he's found the magic spot. I cling to him as he worships my clit with that intense suction, my orgasm building hard and fast. It's over even before I can think about it, my body climaxing and shuddering as my release sweeps over me. Everything clenches tight in the most blissful way and I ride the waves even as Rukh continues to work me over.

By the time the climax ebbs, I'm oversensitive. I push at Rukh's head, indicating I want him to stop. He gives me one last possessive lick and then lifts his head. Our eyes meet and his are ferocious with need, his mouth wet from my juices. God, he's sexy. I reach for him, dazed, because I want to feel his weight over me. There's nothing I like more than Rukh's body over mine, pressing me into the furs. It's been far too long since I felt it, and I need it just as much as I needed that hard, fierce orgasm.

Rukh moves over me, and I lift my knees, sliding my legs around his hips. I sigh as he braces himself over me, because I love this next part. The feel of him pushing into me is sheer bliss, and I close my eyes as his cock nudges at my entrance.

"Har-loh," he murmurs. His hair, loose and wild, tickles at my skin as it falls over me.

"I'm yours," I tell him. "Har-loh's all yours."

He sinks deep in one swift stroke and I suck in a breath. Oh God, I love the feel of my body stretching around him, adjusting to his length. That first press is the best, and when he shifts his weight, his spur rubs against my oversensitive clit. I moan, wrapping my arms around him as he begins to work his hips. Rukh's still new to sex and his stamina is not what it could be, but I don't mind. He always makes me come at least once before he finishes, and that's good enough for me. I love the touching and being wrapped around each other. I love the connection.

I love being owned by him.

Rukh

I come far too quickly. I always want to last longer, to make every moment seated deep inside Har-loh's body last forever, but it never does. Hot pleasure rushes through me as I fill her with my seed, and she holds me close as I collapse atop her. My mate strokes my mane and murmurs sounds at me, her voice sweet and gentle.

"Rukh," she says, and taps my chest. Then she taps hers. "Har-loh." She gestures at the two of us. "Together."

Her meaning is clear. We are a pair, meant to be one. "To-geddur," I agree, and am rewarded with a happy smile. Har-loh is mine, and I am Har-loh's. We are togeddur. In this moment, and in everything.

I wake up with my mate's warm body wrapped around me. Har-loh clings to me in her sleep, and it makes me happy. It is as if she misses me, even when her eyes are closed. I like that. I hold her tight, stroking her soft skin as she dozes, content to watch her. I could lie here in the furs with her all day long, breathing in her sweet scent and pushing my cock into her wet cunt. It would be a good day.

But it does not feed my mate, and there is much to be done. We must have food, and we must be ready for our kit when it comes. I touch her belly, careful not to wake her. She is still flat here, but if it is like the animals in nature, she will swell up when our kit is coming. I cannot wait to see that.

For the first time in my life, I look forward to more than just the next meal, the next sleep. I look forward to a life with Har-loh, warm and snug in our cave, our kit bundled into the furs with us.

I ease out of our nest, making sure that Har-loh is covered with the thick furs, and head outside. The beach is quiet, the only sound the constant roll of the tide and the occasional screech of a distant bird. The skies are gray but it does not look like snow. It is a good day to go hunting, and we still need more things. We need more meat, more furs. We need fuel for the fire—I noticed we were out. There are plants to gather and berries to find. There are—

"Rukh?"

I turn and look at my mate. She stands in the entrance to the cave, furs clutched to her bare skin. There is a sad look on her speckled face.

"Yewgoin huntin?" she asks. "Hunt?"

I know the word "hunt." I know what she asks . . . and I hate to see the disappointment on her face. I will be gone all day again and she will have to do all the hard work on her own. It is not easy for her when I bring the meat back to the beach. I realize that now. It creates more work for her and to do it alone is . . . a lot.

And suddenly, I do not want to leave my mate behind. Har-loh is smart. If she cannot hunt, she can stay back at a distance and help me carry things. She can gather plants and fuel for the fire. When we return, we can work on the meat and the hides together. All of it can be done by one, but it goes faster with help. I am still thinking like I am alone, and I should not be. Har-loh wants to be at my side, and I want to be at hers.

So I nod. "Rukh hunt." I hold my hand out to her. "Har-loh hunt? Togeddur?"

A brilliant smile blooms across her face, and it is the most beautiful thing I have ever seen.

"Togeddur," she agrees.

I am pleased. Everything is better together.

AUTHOR'S NOTE

Hello there!

For the first three books of the Ice Planet Barbarians series, I knew exactly who I wanted the heroes and heroines to be. I wasn't sure if I'd ever get to write past book three, so I wanted to hit the main triad first. When book four started becoming a real possibility, I realized I needed to think about who I wanted the hero and heroine to be in that one. I'd matched up so many people at first sight that I felt like I had a limited pool of characters left to draw from (in retrospect, hahahaha), so I chose Harlow. I liked Harlow. She was plucky and determined, happy to have a khui, and willing to dig into life on the planet. After Kira and her more downbeat mentality, I liked the idea of someone peppier. Mentally, I tried matching Harlow up with all the "bachelors" I had available, and while there were a few decent matches, I wasn't in love with any of the pairings.

Then I had An Incredible Idea.

Well, sort of. As I've mentioned in previous notes, a lot of my ideas don't come as a single lightning bolt out of the skies, with complete clarity and a fully formed plot (though, man, I'd love that). Rather, small ideas roll around in my head and they end up sticking to other ideas and the whole "idea ball" keeps growing until it forms a plot. Somewhere in that "idea ball," I'd had the concept of having a *really* barbarian hero. Not just a male with hunter-gatherer, Paleolithic culture. Someone with *no* culture. Someone who had been abandoned. In essence, Tarzan without all the gross, uncomfortable colonialism aspects.

This seemed like such a fun idea that I ran with it. I dropped hints in Kira's book that there was someone else out there, and poor Harlow got clubbed over the head like a baby seal and disappeared. I got a lot of worried emails about Harlow, but I am first and foremost a romance writer, so *of course* she was going to be okay.

I still gave her a host of problems, though, like the brain tumor, along with being the possession of an absolutely feral hero who had no concept of mating or language.

At this point I'd written several books where the hero is the instigator of the sexual relationship, driven by the khui (or in Aehako's case, driven by love first, khui later). I realized that Harlow was going to have to be the sexual instigator with Rukh. He was getting bombarded with all the feelings from the khui, but he had no idea how to move forward and act on those feelings. He only knew that he wanted her with him. I'm sure it goes without saying that it was so much damn fun to write that I wished I'd made all my heroes feral like Rukh. Sure, it'd stretch the boundaries of reality a little (okay, a lot) but, man, what fun to write.

Of course, a sa-khui male can't appear out of thin air. He'd have family. A history. It made sense to tie him in with Raahosh and his angry, determined father, who'd taken Raahosh away from the tribe and returned him only after he was injured. I liked the aspect of both of these surly loners having a family bond that they didn't know what to do with.

In short, I had far too much fun with this book. It also allowed me to set up future plotlines, a lot of them stemming from that pesky "computer" in the elders' cave. If it's so smart and useful, why isn't everyone using it constantly, right? But in my head, that computer has been running for a really long time without any maintenance. What if this computer is corrupted and giving them bad information? What if the aliens haven't been here just two hundred–odd years? What if that's just what the computer's assuming? Anyone who's had to reset a clock after a storm knows that these things are extremely fallible. I liked the idea of the computer just giving them all kinds of false information and I'm filled with so many ideas of how I can work with that concept.

In short, I love chaos.

A lot of readers wrote me asking for more about Rukh and Harlow when they were alone on the beach together, so their honeymoon story is a step backward in the timeline, whereas their "bonus story" follows the end of the actual book itself. I hope that's not terribly confusing. If it seems odd to you, shove the honeymoon story right before the one-year jump and read in that order, and hopefully it'll make sense.

Also, I'd like to take this moment to give a shout-out to the Berkley team. I'm in love with the covers and so in awe of how hard everyone has worked on these books. Thank you to Cindy Hwang, Angela Kim, Michelle Kasper, the marketing and publicity departments (Jessica Brock, Jessica Mangicaro, and Yazmine Hassan), and the fantastic cover artist, Kelly Wagner, who never flinched for a moment at the prospect of drawing big blue alien himbos. Big thanks to my agent, Holly Root, who also never flinched back when I told her what I was writing. You embrace my weirdness, Holly, and I appreciate that!

LOVE TO ALL,
RUBY

THE PEOPLE OF
BARBARIAN MINE

The Main Cave

THE CHIEF AND HIS MATE

VEKTAL (Vehk-tall)—Chief of the sa-khui tribe. Son of Hektar, the prior chief, who died of khui-sickness. He is a dedicated hunter and leader, and carries a sword and a bola for weapons. He is the one who finds Georgie, and resonance between them is so strong that he resonates prior to her receiving her khui.

GEORGIE—Unofficial leader of the human women. Originally from Orlando, Florida, she has long golden-brown curls and a determined attitude. Newly pregnant after resonating to Vektal.

FAMILIES

RAAHOSH (Rah-hosh)—A quiet but surly hunter. One of his horns is broken off and his face scarred. Older son of Vaashan and Daya (both deceased). Vektal's close friend. Impatient and rash, he steals Liz the moment she receives her khui. They resonate, and he is exiled for stealing her. Brother to Rukh.

LIZ—A loudmouth huntress from Oklahoma who loves Star Wars and giving her opinion. Raahosh kidnaps her the moment she receives her lifesaving khui. She was a champion archer as a teenager. Resonates to Raahosh and voluntarily chooses exile with him.

RAASHEL—Their newborn daughter.

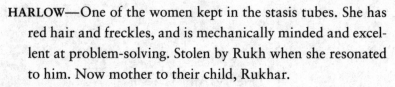

HARLOW—One of the women kept in the stasis tubes. She has red hair and freckles, and is mechanically minded and excellent at problem-solving. Stolen by Rukh when she resonated to him. Now mother to their child, Rukhar.

RUKH—The long-lost son of Vaashan and Daya; brother to Raahosh. His full name is Maarukh. He grew up alone and wild, convinced by his father that the tribe was full of "bad ones," and has recently been brought back by Harlow.

RUKHAR—Their newborn kit.

ARIANA—One of the women kept in the stasis tubes. Hails from New Jersey and was an anthropology student. She tended to cry a lot when first rescued. Has a delicate frame and dark brown hair. Resonates to Zolaya. Still cries a lot.

ZOLAYA (Zoh-lay-uh)—A skilled hunter. Steady and patient, he resonates to Ariana and seems to be the only one not bothered by her weepiness.

MARLENE (Mar-lenn)—One of the women kept in the stasis tubes. French speaking. Quiet and confident, and exudes sexuality. Resonates to Zennek.

ZENNEK (Zehn-eck)—A quiet and shy hunter. Brother to Pashov, Salukh, and Farli. He is the son of Borran and Kemli. Resonates to Marlene.

NORA—One of the women kept in the stasis tubes. A nurturing sort who was rather angry she was dumped on an ice planet. Quickly resonates to Dagesh. No longer quite so angry.

DAGESH (Dah-zzhesh; the *g* sound is swallowed)—A calm, hard-working, and responsible hunter. Resonates to Nora.

STACY—One of the women kept in the stasis tubes. She was weepy when she first awakened. Loves to cook and worked in a bakery prior to abduction. Resonates to Pashov and seems quite happy.

PASHOV (Pah-showv)—The son of Kemli and Borran; brother to Farli, Salukh, and Zennek. A hunter described as "quiet." Resonates to Stacy.

MAYLAK (May-lack)—One of the few female sa-khui. She is the tribe healer and Vektal's former pleasure mate. She resonated to Kashrem, ending her relationship with Vektal. Sister to Bek.

KASHREM (Cash-rehm)—A gentle tribal tanner. Mated to Maylak.

ESHA (Esh-uh)—Their young female kit.

SEVVAH (Sev-uh)—A tribe elder and one of the few sa-khui females. She is mother to Aehako, Rokan, and Sessah, and acts like a mom to the others in the cave. Her entire family was spared when khui-sickness hit fifteen years ago.

OSHEN (Aw-shen)—A tribe elder and Sevvah's mate. Brewer.

SESSAH (Ses-uh)—Their youngest child, a juvenile male.

MEGAN—Megan was early in a pregnancy when she was captured, but the aliens terminated it. She tends toward a sunny disposition when not abducted by aliens. Resonates to Cashol.

CASHOL (Cash-awl)—A distractible and slightly goofy-natured hunter. Cousin to Vektal. Resonates to Megan.

THE UNMATED HUNTERS

EREVEN (Air-uh-ven)—A quiet, easygoing hunter.

ROKAN (Row-can)—The son of Sevvah and Oshen; brother to Aehako and young Sessah. A hunter known for his strange predictions that come true all too often.

WARREK (War-eck)—The son of Elder Eklan. He is a very quiet and mild hunter, with long, sleek black hair. Warrek teaches the young kits how to hunt.

ELDERS

ELDER EKLAN—A calm, kind elder. Father to Warrek, he also helped raise Harrec.

THE SOUTH CAVE

FAMILIES

AEHAKO (Eye-ha-koh)—A laughing, flirty hunter. The son of Sevvah and Oshen; brother to Rokan and young Sessah. He seems to be in a permanent good mood. Close friends with Haeden. Has recently resonated to Kira and is acting leader of the South Cave.

KIRA—The first of the human women to be kidnapped, Kira had a large metallic translator attached to her ear by the aliens. She is quiet and serious, with somber eyes. Her translator has been newly removed, and she has resonated to Aehako despite believing herself to be infertile.

KEMLI (Kemm-lee)—An elder female, mother to Salukh, Pashov, Zennek, and Farli. The tribe's expert on plants.

BORRAN (Bore-awn)—Kemli's much younger mate and an elder.

FARLI (Far-lee)—A preteen female sa-khui. Her brothers are Salukh, Pashov, and Zennek.

ASHA (Ah-shuh)—A mated female sa-khui. She is mated to Hemalo but has not been seen in his furs for some time. Their kit died shortly after birth.

HEMALO (Hee-mah-lo)—A tanner and a quiet sort. He is mated (unhappily) to Asha.

THE UNMATED HUMAN FEMALES

CLAIRE—A quiet, slender blonde with a pixie cut. She finds her new world extremely frightening.

JOSIE—One of the original kidnapped women, she broke her leg in the ship crash. Short and adorable, Josie is an excessive talker, a gossip, and a bit of a dreamer. Likes to sing.

TIFFANY—A "farm girl" back on Earth, she suffered greatly while waiting for Georgie to return. She has been traumatized by her alien abduction. She is a perfectionist and a hard worker.

THE UNMATED HUNTERS

BEK (Behk)—A hunter generally thought of as short-tempered and unpleasant. Brother to Maylak.

HAEDEN (Hi-den)—A grim and unsmiling hunter with "dead" eyes, Haeden formerly resonated but his female died of khui-sickness before they could mate. His current khui is new. He is very private.

HARREC (Hair-ek)—A hunter who has no family and finds his place in the tribe by constantly joking and teasing. A bit accident-prone.

HASSEN (Hass-en)—A passionate and brave hunter, Hassen is impulsive and tends to act before he thinks.

SALUKH (Sah-luke)—The brawny son of Kemli and Borran; brother to Farli, Pashov, and Zennek. Very strong and intense.

TAUSHEN (Tow—rhymes with "cow"—shen)—A teenage hunter, newly into adulthood. Eager to prove himself.

ELDERS

ELDER DRAYAN—A smiling elder who uses a cane to help him walk.

ELDER DRENOL—A grumpy, antisocial elder.

ELDER VADREN (Vaw-dren)—An elder.

ELDER VAZA (Vaw-zhuh)—A lonely widower and hunter. He tries to be as helpful as possible. He is very interested in the new females.

THE DEAD

DOMINIQUE—A redheaded human female. Her mind was broken when she was abused by the aliens on the ship. When she arrived on Not-Hoth, she ran out into the snow and deliberately froze.

KRISSY—A human female, dead in the crash.

PEG—A human female, dead in the crash.

ABOUT THE AUTHOR

RUBY DIXON is an author of all things science fiction romance. She is a Sagittarius and a Reylo shipper, and loves farming sims (but not actual housework). She lives in the South with her husband and a couple of geriatric cats, and can't think of anything else to put in her biography. Truly, she is boring.

VISIT RUBY DIXON ONLINE

RubyDixon.com
 RubyDixonBooks
 Author.Ruby.Dixon

Ready to find
your next great read?

Let us help.

Visit prh.com/nextread

Penguin
Random
House